English Governess in Paris

a Victorian romance saga

HOPE DAWSON

First published worldwide
on Amazon Kindle,
in August 2023.

This paperback edition first published
in Great Britain in 2023.

ISBN: 9798858223726

This novel is a work of fiction. The characters, names, places, events and incidents in it are entirely the work of the author's imagination or used in a fictitious manner. Any resemblance or similarity to actual persons, living or dead, events or places is entirely coincidental.

www.hopedawson.com

This story is part of

The Victorian Orphans Trilogy

Book 1

The Courtesan's Maid

Book 2

The Ragged Slum Princess

Book 3

An English Governess in Paris

Chapter One

Jane's heart fluttered like a caged bird as the carriage rolled to a stop outside the quaint village church. Smoothing down her white gown and adjusting the lace veil covering her gently curled hair, Jane stepped out of the carriage while her heart raced with jittery anticipation.

Smiling at the sight of the charming scenery before her, she took a deep breath and savoured the fragrant smell of the summer air.

Birds sang their sweet serenade of love in nearby trees, while a colourful sea of flowers in the grounds surrounding the church spread their heavenly scent on a gentle breeze. And as she stared up at the pretty little church, she noticed how its stone walls and stained glass windows seemed to glimmer in the morning sun.

Everything about this momentous day was just perfect.

This is it, Jane thought with a tickling of butterflies in her stomach. *I'm going to become Georgie's wife.* Her hands trembled, so she clutched her bouquet tightly to steady them.

Her elder sister Abbie appeared by her side and gave her a reassuring smile. "Let's go," she said, offering Jane a hand. "Your groom awaits."

"Abbie, I'm so nervous," Jane whispered. "My legs feel like they're made of jelly. I'm not even sure I can manage to walk up the path to the church doors."

"Of course you can," Abbie chuckled. "Remember what a nervous wreck I was when I married Joe? You just put one foot in front of the other. And think of that wonderful young man who's waiting for you by the altar."

Jane nodded and summoned all the strength she possessed. She still felt a little weak at the knees, but in her mind's eye, she pictured Georgie's lovely face smiling proudly at her.

Just as the two sisters entered the church, golden rays of sunshine came piercing through the stained glass windows, cascading rainbow hues of light onto the centuries-old flagstone floor.

Gracefully moving down the aisle, Jane could feel the admiring gaze of the wedding guests. Everywhere she looked, friends and acquaintances were gathered, their faces beaming with joy.

Jane and Abbie didn't have any surviving relatives, but Jane thought she could sense the loving presence of their parents somehow.

Mama and Papa, I know you'll be praying for our happiness, she told them gratefully.

When she caught sight of Georgie, a surge of pure joy leapt up in her heart. His handsome face radiated with affection, and his eyes shone with delight as he watched her march slowly down the aisle.

For a brief moment, their eyes locked. The happy cheers and excited murmurs of the guests seemed to dissolve into the background. And it felt as if she and Georgie were the only two people there, cocooned in a world of their own – a world of love and devotion.

Next to Georgie, looking almost just as pleased as the groom, stood Jane's brother-in-law and Abbie's husband, Joe Thompson.

As a little boy, Georgie had never known his real parents. And since Joe had taken him under his wing from an early age, it was only natural that he should now act as Georgie's surrogate father.

When Jane and Abbie reached them, Georgie smiled that dazzling smile of his – the one that had made her heart skip a beat so many times before.

He lifted up her veil, and in a passionate whisper, he said, "You look breathtaking, my love."

His tender words sent a pleasant shiver down Jane's spine and all the nerves she'd felt just moments before seemed to melt away. Gazing deeply into his eyes, she found herself burning to know what their very first embrace as husband and wife would be like.

She yearned for that moment when his lips would finally meet hers. With every heartbeat, her desire seemed to grow stronger, until she thought the longing might overwhelm her. She wanted nothing more than to feel the warmth of his tender touch and to luxuriate in the sensation of his lips against hers.

Soon, she sighed inwardly. Soon she would be his. And then he would caress her cheek with his hand, lean in closer – slowly – and give her the kiss she had been aching for since so many moons. If she closed her eyes now, she could already taste his lips.

So sweet, so soft, so–

“Did you like it, Jane?” a girl’s voice asked. “Was it any good?”

Snapping out of her daydream, Jane blinked her eyes rapidly a few times and glanced around the room, more than a little startled. “Sorry, what?”

“The music,” Rosie Parker said. “Did you like how I played it?” The girl was sitting by the piano, looking like a sweet angel with her hands folded neatly in her lap as she eyed her governess expectantly.

"I'm sorry, Rosie," Jane blushed. "This piece is so romantic and you played it so well that my mind drifted off into..." She cleared her throat before continuing. "Well, a whole other realm."

Rosie covered her mouth and giggled. "Were you daydreaming about Georgie again?"

"Possibly," Jane replied. She tried to keep a straight face, but the two of them couldn't help themselves and burst out laughing.

"Hush now," she said when their glee had subsided a bit. "We're supposed to be playing the piano, remember? What would your mother think if she were to walk in and find us in hysterics like this?"

Rosie shrugged. "You know her almost as well as I do, Jane. Mama would simply smile and want to know what all the fun was about – just so she could join in as well."

Jane smiled, knowing that Rosie was probably right. Mrs Parker wasn't like most other women. Her warmth and kindness were well known. And in the past, both Jane and her sister Abbie had benefited greatly from Mrs Parker's generosity of character.

"You must miss him something awful," Rosie said, bringing the topic of conversation back to Georgie while her hands returned to the piano and started playing a light and easy tune.

"I do," Jane sighed. "It's only for a year or so, but it's already beginning to feel like an eternity.

And Paris is so dreadfully far away from London."

"I know how you feel. I miss Philip too, ever since he's gone off to boarding school." Pausing her piano piece, she turned to Jane with a raised eyebrow. "And he's just my annoying little brother."

They laughed, after which Rosie continued to play. "But you have to remind yourself it's all for a good cause."

"Yes, I suppose so. Georgie is intent on becoming the best possible pastry chef. And there's no better place to learn the trade than Paris."

"Just think how spoiled you'll be after he marries you," Rosie chuckled. "You'll be eating cakes and croissants for breakfast every single day."

"His crêpes Suzette are to die for," Jane said, thinking back fondly to the delicious pancake dessert he had made for her and Abbie the evening they had first met him.

"You're a lucky girl, Jane."

"I know. And I know I should just be patient. When that year is over, Georgie is going to come back to England. And once he's set up his own pastry shop, he'll propose to me and then we'll all live happily ever after."

She let out a drawn-out, lovesick sigh. The dream was very much alive in her heart, but she would still have to wait so long before it could become a reality.

Finishing her improvisation at the piano, Rosie turned to Jane with a happy face. "And let's not forget: in the meantime, you get to make yourself useful by being my governess."

Jane returned the girl's smile and took Rosie's hands in hers. "But what a terrible governess I am, to be laughing and chatting with you like we're a pair of silly ninnies. You'll never become a proper lady that way, Miss Parker."

"Don't say that, Jane. You're the best governess I've ever had!"

Jane laughed. "I'm the *only* governess you've ever had – so far."

"And I'm sure I'll never have one as good as you. Whatever we do or talk about – whether it's French, literature, the piano, etiquette, or anything really – you never fail to make it interesting and just plain *fun*."

"Stop," Jane quipped. "Before you make me blush. You're sweet, but you're giving me too much credit, I think."

"No, I'm not. Are you still planning on going to Paris?"

Jane nodded and smiled mysteriously. "Yes, I've hatched a little plan. With some luck, I could be packing my bags and heading for France soon."

"I'll be sorry to see you leave. But I know how much you and Georgie love each other. So I hope this plan of yours will work."

"Fingers crossed. You have to promise me one thing however, young lady."

"Which is?"

"Promise me that whoever your new governess is, you won't make her life miserable."

"I promise," Rosie said, sounding overly sweet and innocent. "On one condition: that you'll come rushing straight back if Mama hires some nasty old crone."

"Agreed."

Rising from her seat, Rosie gave Jane a hug. "I'll miss you," the girl said, her voice thick with emotion.

Tears welled up in Jane's eyes as she hugged Rosie back. "I'll miss you, too."

And I'll count myself very lucky if my new charges will be half as nice as you are, she thought.

But even if they turned out to be disagreeable little pests, the aggravation would still be worth it to her. Being closer to Georgie was all that mattered.

Chapter Two

On a balmy Sunday afternoon, Jane rushed to the lavish home of her brother-in-law Joe Thompson and her sister Abbie. Earlier that week, she had received a telegram from Joe saying, 'Come see me at your earliest convenience. Good news.'

She had needed to restrain herself from dashing over the moment she got the message. Mrs Parker would undoubtedly have given her a few hours off if Jane had asked for it. But she didn't want to take advantage of the woman's kindheartedness. And so she had waited until Sunday came round, when she had the afternoon to herself.

Patience was a virtue, after all.

But now her heart was racing with anticipation and she was more than eager to learn what Joe had to tell her. Good news could only mean one thing: he must have found her a position as a governess in Paris.

Back when she had first brought up the subject – of how badly she missed Georgie and how sorry she was that she couldn't follow him to Paris – Joe had been the one to suggest a solution.

Being a successful businessman, he had an extensive network of friends, associates and acquaintances. His web of connections stretched far and wide these days, often reaching into the highest and wealthiest circles.

Joe had offered to ask around if anyone currently residing in Paris was looking for a governess, or perhaps a companion to a rich elderly widow. Certainly not a simple domestic – Jane and Abbie had both had their fill of that line of work in their tragic past.

Jane had written a few letters of introduction, for him to send to any potential families. And after that, she hadn't heard much from him for a while.

But then his telegram arrived. And now here she was, standing on his doorstep and knocking on his door with a hand that trembled with nervous excitement.

"Good day, Miss Lee," the housekeeper greeted her politely when she opened the door.

"Hello, Mrs Harrison. Lovely to see you."

Stepping aside to let Jane in, the housekeeper said, "Mrs Thompson is in the drawing room, Miss."

"Thank you, Mrs Harrison. But I have some business with Mr Thompson first."

"You'll find him in his study, Miss. Shall I go and tell him you're here?"

"No need for stuffy formalities," Jane chuckled as she headed towards Joe's work room. "My dear brother-in-law should be used by now to me barging into his home unannounced."

A faint smile of amusement briefly appeared on Mrs Harrison's face. She had been Joe's housekeeper from well before he had married Jane's sister. But she had learned to adapt to the fresh and dynamic whirlwind that Abbie had brought to the Thompson residence.

"What's this good news you have for me?" Jane asked impatiently as she burst into the study. "Am I going to Paris?"

Joe laughed and put down the sheets of paper he was studying. "Hello, my dearest sister-in-law. How wonderful to see you again. It's been so long. I hope you're keeping well?"

Jane rolled her eyes. "Oh, don't tell me you're going to insist on performing these trivial social niceties. Not with me you are."

Grinning, he came over to her and gave her a quick embrace. "I wouldn't dream of putting you through such an arduous ordeal."

"I got your telegram."

"And I'm surprised you've managed to wait until today."

"I admit I was very tempted to come sooner. But that wouldn't have been fair on Rosie."

"How is my darling little Rose?"

"Not so little any more. She's showing every promise of becoming a fine young lady." Jane was simply itching to hear the news Joe had promised her. But she knew he was the Parkers' best friend and that Rosie called him Uncle, despite there not being any family bond between them. So Jane was willing to humour him and grant him this brief chat.

"Right then," he finally said, eyeing her fidgeting hands with a grin. "Enough of this torment. We've found you a suitable position."

Jane jumped for joy. "Is it in Paris?"

"Naturally. Lord and Lady Crawford need a governess for their two children."

"A Lord no less?"

"An extremely wealthy one, too. A proper aristocrat. He's on some kind of unofficial diplomatic mission, apparently. Hobnobbing with the French and using the glamour of his title and wealth to defend the interests of Britain overseas. That sort of thing."

"Sounds impressive." In her mind, a vision emerged of a grand old continental palace; the kind of home where kings once roamed – before the French rabble chopped off their royal heads.

"Some even claim he's a secret government spy," Joe continued. "But that's probably just a baseless rumour."

"When do I leave?" His lordship could be the Queen's personal assassin for all Jane cared. As long as being the governess to his children meant she would be in the same city as Georgie, she would be happy.

"You're just like your sister," Joe laughed. "Always eager to jump into the unknown."

"You ought to be grateful," she teased him back. "Without that adventurous streak of ours, you might never even have met Abbie."

"Very true," he conceded gracefully. "I'll make arrangements for your passage as soon as I can. In the meantime–"

"Here you are," Abbie said as she entered the study. "I thought I had heard your voice." She came over to Jane and grinned, "Is your big sister so unimportant to you now that you don't want to come and see her first?"

Jane laughed and wrapped her arms around Abbie for a hug. "Of course not, silly. But I just couldn't wait to hear the latest from Joe. Has he told you?"

"He has. And I'm very happy for you."

"Are you, Abbie? Are you really?" Jane tilted her head slightly as she regarded her sister. She would have thought that Abbie's feelings about this were somewhat mixed.

"As I said, I'm very happy *for you*."

"But *you* don't like it very much."

"You know me too well, don't you?" Abbie laughed. "I won't lie to you, Jane: I'm not looking forward to the prospect of you moving abroad."

"It won't be forever. Just for a year, or however long Georgie decides to stay in Paris."

"It's just that we've been through a lot together, you and I. And now you'll be so far away from me."

Abbie paused and looked at Jane with a serious expression on her face. "You know you don't have to do this, don't you? There's no need for you to work. You're more than welcome to stay with us for as long as you like. Isn't she, Joe?"

"Absolutely," Abbie's husband replied. "Our home is your home."

"I know," Jane smiled. "And I'm truly grateful for your generosity. But I think I'd go mad from boredom if I had to sit around and wait for Georgie to propose to me."

Joe chuckled. "Now who does that impatience remind me of?"

Going over to him, Abbie gave him a playful slap on the chest before the happy couple linked arms in a sideways embrace.

"In all seriousness, Jane," Abbie said, "I understand why you want to go. But remember, whatever you decide, our door will always be open to you."

"Thank you, Abbie. I don't know what I would do without you."

"Oh, I think you'd manage just fine." Her sister smiled, but Jane could tell she was fighting back tears. They looked at each other and then Abbie let go of her husband so she could hug Jane.

"I'll miss you when you leave."

"I'll miss you, too," Jane replied while tears filled her eyes as well. "But I'm not gone yet. We'll say our proper goodbyes some other time."

When Abbie released her, Jane saw tears spilling down her sister's cheeks. Abbie quickly wiped them away with the back of her hand, sniffling a bit before she spoke again. "Promise me you'll write to me."

"Of course I will. I might even send you a little souvenir from time to time."

"Don't go spending your money on frivolous trinkets. A governess doesn't earn much. Even if she happens to work for a wealthy Lord."

"Yes, Mother," Jane teased, making her sister laugh.

She realised it would be difficult to leave behind her familiar life in England. But somehow the knowledge that Abbie loved her gave her strength for the journey ahead.

No matter what happened, no matter how far apart they were, Jane knew that they would always be connected by an unbreakable bond.

A polite knock at the door interrupted their emotional exchange. "Enter," Joe said.

"Pardon me, sir," the butler spoke. "Tea is ready. Would you like for it to be served here?"

"No, thank you, Mr Jenkins. We'll have it in the drawing room as planned. Ladies, shall we continue this conversation in more comfortable surroundings?"

They moved to the plush interior of the drawing room, where a maid soon brought in a tray with tea and sumptuous cake for the three of them. Jane was thankful, not just for the cake, but also for the fact that the conversation had switched to lighter topics than her upcoming grand adventure.

Because despite her impatience and her eagerness to be closer to her beloved Georgie, she had to admit that part of her was daunted by the whole undertaking. London was all she had ever known. Paris was a completely different city in a foreign country. She could speak French, that wasn't the issue. But would it be enough?

I suppose I'll find out soon enough, she mused as she helped herself to another slice of cake.

Chapter Three

A flock of seagulls circled and swooped overhead, their cries echoing in the air. Standing on the deck of the steamboat taking her to France, Jane stared at the white cliffs in the distance behind them. Funny how they appeared to be growing smaller, she thought, while the boat chugged along slowly on the dark and murky waves.

When she turned her head the other way, she was met with a sight considerably less cheerful than she had been feeling earlier that morning. As far as she could see, the grey skies blended into even greyer waters. A few times, the sun peeked out from behind the clouds before vanishing again just as quickly.

Not quite how she had imagined it would be. And certainly not like those romantic tales she had heard about life at sea.

But then again, this wasn't exactly the ocean. They were merely crossing the relatively short expanse of water separating Britain from France. The journey would only take a few hours, she had been told, and it would be boringly uneventful – especially when the weather was fair.

Before their departure, one of the stewards had assured her the sea wasn't too choppy today. Nevertheless, being unfamiliar with the gentle rolling of the boat on the waves, Jane's stomach began to protest shortly after they had left the port.

Fervently praying that she wouldn't be sick, she closed her eyes and placed a soothing hand over her churning tummy.

"I see you are not used to the sea, Mademoiselle," a friendly voice came from behind her.

Opening her eyes and turning around, she saw a tall, handsome gentleman. From his clothes and his accent, she gathered he was French.

"No, I'm afraid not," she replied.

He smiled and greeted her with a polite bow of the head. "Pierre Dubois at your service, Mademoiselle. I happen to travel between France and England quite frequently. May I offer you some advice on how to ease your *mal de mer*?"

Recognising the French word for seasickness, Jane nodded gratefully. "Any help would be most appreciated, Monsieur."

"First of all, keep your eyes fixed on the horizon as much as possible. This gives your mind a point of reference and as a result, it will be less disoriented by the movements of the ship – which is why you are feeling queasy."

"That makes sense, I suppose," she said, directing her gaze at the greyness in the distance.

"Fresh air will help as well," Mr Dubois continued. "So try to spend plenty of time on deck. It's healthier, too."

Calmly filling her lungs, Jane felt the salty breeze tickling her face. After a few deep breaths, her stomach did seem to settle down a bit.

"I think it's actually working, Monsieur Dubois. I'm most indebted to you."

"*Pas du tout*," he smiled with another polite nod. "Think nothing of it, Mademoiselle–?"

"Lee," she replied, extending her hand to shake his. "Jane Lee."

"Enchanté, Mademoiselle Lee."

"Enchantée, Monsieur."

When a sudden gust of wind sent up a fine spray of chilly seawater over the side of the ship, she shivered and pulled her shawl a bit tighter around her shoulders.

"I think that perhaps this is enough fresh air for now," Mr Dubois quipped. "May I invite you inside for some light refreshment, Mademoiselle? Both the ginger ale or the peppermint tea are excellent remedies against the *mal de mer*."

"Given the veracity of your previous piece of advice, I will gladly trust you on this one as well."

"You are too kind," he said as he invited her to accompany him to the catering deck.

They stepped into the warm, brightly lit room and Mr Dubois pointed at a table by one of the windows. "So you may keep your eye on the horizon from time to time," he grinned.

Just like a true gentleman, he pulled out a chair for her and after he had taken his own seat, he waved over one of the waiters to take their order. Ginger ale for him and peppermint tea for her.

"As a Frenchman, I usually prefer wine of course. But I've found that it's better to avoid alcohol while travelling at sea."

When the waiter had brought their drinks, Jane took her cup of tea and inhaled the hot swirls of vapour rising up from it. The refreshing aroma of the peppermint did the trick, just like Mr Dubois had said it would.

"Tell me, Monsieur Dubois. Are you always in the habit of saving damsels in distress at sea?"

He chuckled at her joke. "I wouldn't call it a habit of mine, no. But I do like to help people whenever I can."

"And I believe you mentioned that you make this crossing frequently. Business related, I assume?"

"You assume correctly, Mademoiselle," he smiled before taking a sip of his ginger ale.

"Are you a merchant then, trading goods between our two countries?" Jane realised it wasn't her business to ask a foreign stranger how he made a living. But she was grateful to have someone to talk to and chase away the boredom of the journey.

"Not exactly. I'm in a different sort of money-making business. I shall spare you the details, but let's just say that my profession is to give affluent people the opportunity to do more with their money."

"Ah, investments you mean?"

Acknowledging her reply with a nod, he said, "You appear to be more knowledgeable than most young women of your age, Mademoiselle."

"Some of us have interests that extend beyond the latest fashion and juicy gossip, Monsieur," she laughed. "It sounds like you might be in the same line of business as my brother-in-law. Perhaps you have heard of him: Mr Joseph Thompson?"

"Alas, I regret not to have had that pleasure yet. And what about you, Mademoiselle Lee? If I may hazard a guess, I would say that you are on your way to a position with an employer in France, possibly even Paris."

Jane tilted her head to one side in surprise. "Am I that obvious?"

"Not in the slightest," he smiled. "But it's just that over the years I have seen many young women like you on these crossings. And invariably, they are maids or domestics travelling to some wealthy family on the Continent."

"You're a keen observer, Monsieur Dubois." She folded her hands in front of her and rested her chin on them. "So what do you make of me then?"

"You seem too sophisticated to be a mere servant. I would think that someone has hired you either as a governess for their children or as a companion to a female member of the family."

Jane smiled, amazed at his perception. "You're quite a detective, Monsieur. You are correct in your assessment of my situation. I'm on my way to Paris to work as a governess for Lord and Lady Crawford."

His eyebrows shot up at the mention of that name. "Crawford, you say? Then your references and your talents must be even better than I had thought. Lord Crawford is a well-known and respected figure in Parisian society."

"It's my first time away from home," Jane sighed. "And I must admit that I'm feeling both excited and apprehensive about the prospect." She paused for a few seconds, leaning back in her chair with a faraway look in her eyes.

"Oh, but you will love Paris, believe me. It's a place *magnifique* for a young woman with your interests, Mademoiselle Lee. I should know – I have lived there almost my entire life."

"Is Paris as wonderful as they say it is?"

"More so," he exclaimed in delight. "The stories don't do it justice. You will find the City of Lights even more beautiful and more enchanting than its reputation suggests."

"Really?"

"The architecture is fabulous and the art galleries are unparalleled in their grandeur. You will be able to attend some of the most spectacular ballets and operas. And you can take leisurely strolls along the banks of the River Seine."

His voice trailed off as he took in Jane's captivated expression before continuing with a chuckle, "I could go on, but I wouldn't want you to think you were sitting next to a tour guide."

"Not at all," she was quick to assure him. "You make it all sound so lovely and inviting. I can hardly wait to get there."

He smiled in response and reached into his pocket to pull out a business card. "This is the hotel where I shall be staying," he said as he handed her the card. "Please feel free to contact me there if you ever need any help or advice. Paris is *fantastique*, but it is a very different city than London."

"Most generous of you, Monsieur," Jane said, gratefully accepting his card and putting it away safely in her purse. "But I wouldn't want to impose on you. I'm sure you're a very busy man."

"Ah, but Mademoiselle," he grinned with a glint in his eye. "You see, this is one of the many areas in which the French differ from the British: we have what we call *joie de vivre*. Are you familiar with that term?"

"It means 'the joy of living', does it not?"

"Yes, but it comprises so much more than those few simple words. It is a whole philosophy, Mademoiselle – an art form even."

"Then perhaps you will be able to instruct me in it sometime, Monsieur Dubois," she chuckled, amused by his evident Gallic passion.

"It would be both a privilege and an honour, Mademoiselle Lee," he replied most earnestly. "Please tell me, I take it you are travelling to Paris by train once we disembark?"

"Yes, I am. It's more expensive than a coach trip, but much faster and more comfortable."

"Then perhaps you will allow me to accompany you on this last part of your journey? Unless, of course, you grow tired of my presence and my stories already."

"I would be delighted to enjoy the pleasure of your company a little while longer, Monsieur," she replied without blushing.

In England, it would have been unheard of for a young lady to be talking to a stranger like this. But these Europeans were so much more open-minded, Jane thought.

And besides, I'm not a lady, she told herself, suppressing the urge to giggle. *Not in the proper sense anyway.*

Chapter Four

On the train journey to Paris, many miles of French countryside passed by their window while Jane and Mr Dubois chatted. The friendly businessman told her fascinating stories of what life was like in the capital, and he gave her plenty of tips for short trips and visits – more, in fact, than she could hope to get round to within that one single year she was planning to live and work in Paris.

"You will simply have to prolong your stay, Mademoiselle," he joked. "Or who knows, perhaps you will fall in love with the city and decide to make it your home."

Eventually, their train arrived at its final destination, slowly rolling into the station and coming to a halt in a cloud of steam and chimney smoke.

As she rose from her seat, Jane peered through the window to see if she could spot Georgie already. In his last letter, he had promised to be waiting for her. But of course, the train platform was much too crowded and busy to make out any individual faces.

All she could see was a swirling sea of activity and bustling people. Streams of passengers were coming and going with their luggage, while porters scurried about in their uniforms as they lugged heavy goods around on the various platforms.

"Please allow me to carry your valise, Mademoiselle," Mr Dubois offered kindly. "I wouldn't want your first impression of Paris to be an unfavourable one."

"*Merci, Monsieur.* If every Parisian is as friendly as you have been, then I'm certain I shall like the city even more."

He chuckled. "I wouldn't count on that too much. You are aware that we French have a reputation for being arrogant, no doubt? I'm afraid Paris does its best to live up to that reputation."

After they disembarked, Mr Dubois led the way, effortlessly guiding her through the crowds – his own carpet bag in one hand and Jane's large valise in the other.

"I take it you will be going to the Crawford residence?" he said. "Shall I direct you to the hired coaches outside?"

"No, that won't be necessary," she replied, still searching the throng of people for Georgie's face. "At least, I hope not. A friend of mine should be waiting for me here, somewhere."

"Is she a governess as well? Or is it someone from the Crawford household?"

"Neither. It's my fiancé," she said, blushing a little. "Well, strictly speaking, he isn't my fiancé yet. But that's mostly just a matter of time."

"Aha," he smiled. "Then hopefully, this enchanting city of ours will inspire your young man to do the right thing unto you soon."

Jane felt her cheeks heat up even more. She too fostered the modest hope that something beautiful might happen while she and Georgie were here.

She was about to reply to Mr Dubois when she heard a familiar voice calling out her name in the buzzing crowd around them. Turning her head, it was like the parting of the clouds in a storm when she spotted him standing there, waving at her.

"Georgie," she nearly squealed in her excitement. Without another thought, she dashed over to him, Mr Dubois following in her wake with their luggage.

She reached him in a few heartbeats – out of breath and barely able to contain her joy at seeing him again after their long separation.

Georgie swept her up in his arms and spun her around. Jane laughed and giggled with delight, feeling like she was flying. Back in England, such a public display of affection would have been frowned upon most severely. Here in Paris however, a few passers-by smiled knowingly while the rest simply carried on with their business, ignoring what they believed to be two young lovers.

"I thought I might never find you here in this chaos," Georgie said after he had put Jane down again. "But here you are. Safe and sound at last."

She gazed up at him dreamily, drinking in every little feature of his face. Not many people would have described Georgie as handsome. Not in the classical sense anyway. But he had the sweetest heart and, in that intense moment of their reunion, he was better-looking to her than any other man in the world.

"Well?" he laughed. "Don't tell me you've lost your tongue on your way over here."

She giggled. "Of course not, you silly. I've missed you so much."

"I've missed you, too. And we'll have–" Suddenly, he paused when someone behind her caught his eye. "Anything I can do to help, Monsieur?"

Jane glanced over her shoulder. She had forgotten all about Mr Dubois! The poor man was standing there with their luggage, sporting a charming, friendly smile on his face as always.

"Georgie, this is Monsieur Dubois. I met him on the boat to France and he kindly offered to accompany me on the train. Monsieur Dubois, this is my soon-to-be fiancé, Georges Thompson."

"A pleasure to meet you," Georgie said politely, shaking the other man's hand somewhat stiffly.

"Likewise," Mr Dubois replied with a nod of his head. "It is an honour to meet the lucky man who has won Mademoiselle's heart."

Jane thought she detected an awkward tension in the air as the two men seemed to size each other up, their cool gazes locked in a wordless contest of strength.

But then Mr Dubois ended the brief standoff by clearing his throat. "Now that you are reunited, I think it is time for me to bid you adieu." He bowed his head, first at Jane and then at Georgie.

"It has truly been a privilege meeting you," he continued. "And if you ever find yourself in need of any help or advice, Mademoiselle has my card."

"Thank you, Monsieur Dubois," Jane said warmly. "You have been most kind on this journey."

"Yes," Georgie added. "Thank you for keeping Jane safe, Monsieur."

"My pleasure. I wish you a wonderful time in Paris. It is a city of romance and beauty – the best place to be for two such deserving young people as yourselves."

After one final smile at Jane, he handed her suitcase over to Georgie. Then he picked up his own bag and walked away calmly, vanishing into the thick crowd.

"Such a nice gentleman," Jane said as she stared after him with a fond smile.

"Quite the charmer, I'm sure," Georgie replied, sounding slightly irritated.

Surprised at his tone, she looked at him and grinned. "Why, Georgie. If I didn't know any better, I would have said you were jealous."

"Me? Never."

"Liar," she teased.

"Just be careful with these Frenchmen, my love. They can be quite devious, you know. Always up to something."

"Your concern for my safety is adorable. Mr Dubois however has conducted himself in a perfectly decent and chivalrous manner."

Georgie muttered something under his breath.

"But enough about him," she said. "How about we get going? I'm sure you have lots of plans for us." She beamed at him and grabbed his arm affectionately.

"I have got plans, yes. But not for today." Carrying her suitcase, he started leading her towards the exit of the station. "I'm afraid I haven't got much time. Maître Leblanc only agreed to let me have a few hours off on the condition that I'd work longer tonight."

"He's the baker you're apprenticed with, isn't he?"

"*Maître pâtissier*, he is: a master pastry chef. Don't let him ever hear you call him a mere baker."

They emerged onto the street outside, and Georgie quickly looked around for a carriage.

"He sounds like a charming man," Jane said sarcastically.

Georgie spotted a waiting carriage and waved at the driver to get his attention. Taking Jane by the arm and holding her suitcase in his other hand, he hurried over before someone else could take their ride.

"Maître Leblanc isn't too bad, really," Georgie said as he helped her to climb into the carriage. "He tends to get a bit temperamental at times, but he's an artist when it comes to cakes and pastries. I'm learning loads."

"Where to?" the driver asked in French.

To Jane's surprise and disappointment, Georgie gave the man the address of the Crawford residence.

"We're not even going for a quick stroll?" she asked as the carriage set off. "Or a cup of French coffee in one of those romantic little cafés?"

"I haven't got the time, my darling. We can talk on our way over to the Crawfords, but then I really must dash back to the patisserie. Maître

Leblanc isn't the sort of man you want to keep waiting for too long."

Jane pouted. "I was hoping we could do something fun together. We haven't seen each other in ages."

"I know, my love. But we'll have more time on Sunday. I'll take you out for a walk then and show you some of the sights. I promise."

Smiling at her apologetically, he took her hand in his and gave it a gentle squeeze. Looking at him more closely, Jane noticed only now how tired he seemed.

"I thought you would have been happy to see me," she said sadly.

"But I am. Very happy in fact. It's just that–" He trailed off, not knowing how to continue.

"It's all right," she sighed. "I understand. Thank you for meeting me at the station. And for accompanying me as far as the Crawfords."

He smiled at her and softly caressed the side of her face with gentle fingers. But they spent most of the carriage ride in silence – Georgie staring out in front of him, while she gazed at the streets and the people they drove past.

Despite her disappointment, she was still grateful to be here. For the moment however, Paris seemed only half as gay and colourful to her as before.

Chapter Five

Jane watched as the carriage pulled away, taking her beloved Georgie with it. She was standing on the pavement in front of the Crawford residence – alone, with her suitcase next to her.

Georgie stuck his head out of the open side window to wave at her. Forcing a smile onto her face, she waved back. But as soon as the carriage rounded the corner, her smile faded and tears began to prickle behind her eyes. She had come all this way, only to be parted from Georgie again so soon.

I mustn't cry, she told herself. It wouldn't do to show up at the Crawfords with a tear-stained face. She was tired from the long journey, that was all.

And Georgie was tired, too. This French pastry chef clearly made him work hard. So wasn't it rather selfish of her to expect Georgie to simply drop everything and spend an entire afternoon with her in the middle of the week? Coming Sunday, they would be together again, he had promised her. Then they would have more time.

Besides, she reminded herself, she was here for at least a whole year. There would be plenty of opportunities for sightseeing and exploring.

And yet...

She sighed. No matter how much she tried to cheer herself up, the feeling of gloomy sadness lingered. And there was no more trace of the excitement she had experienced when she stepped off the train. Instead, she felt very lonely all of a sudden, in this unfamiliar city.

I'd better get inside now, she decided. Before anyone in the household came outside to ask why she was loitering about on the pavement.

Straightening her back, she picked up her suitcase and searched for the servants' entrance, casting an admiring glance at the magnificent façade of the house.

The place seemed more like a small palace than a home to her. But of course, the residence of a Lord and his Lady was meant to be so much more than a simple roof over one's head. It had to make a powerful impression, and convince its visitors of the importance of the people who resided here.

Jane smiled ruefully. Hard to imagine two young children living somewhere within those walls. She wondered what they would be like, the Crawford children.

Hopefully not too arrogant and spoiled.

She had only ever been a governess to Rosie Parker, who was always an absolute sweetheart, making Jane's work fairly easy.

Having located the servants' entrance, she took a deep breath and knocked. Moments later, a young maid answered the door. She probably worked in the kitchen, Jane gathered from the girl's simple apron and uniform.

"*Oui, Mademoiselle?*" the maid asked, eyeing Jane with the usual mixture of curiosity and suspicion reserved for anyone who came calling at the door unannounced.

"*Bonjour,* I am Miss Jane Lee, the new governess," Jane replied in French, assuming that the common servants didn't speak much English. The more senior staff would be British, naturally, but kitchen maids and the likes were probably recruited locally.

The maid nodded and stepped aside to let her in.

"*Suivez-moi, s'il vous plaît,*" the girl said after closing the door behind Jane. "Follow me, please. I will take you to Madame 'ill."

"Is she the housekeeper?"

"*Oui.*"

Passing by the busy kitchen and through a sombre service corridor, they arrived at the open door of a small office. A middle-aged woman wearing a dark and modest dress sat at a wooden desk. The ledger she was writing in seemed far too large for her tiny desk.

"Madame 'ill?" the maid said demurely. "A visitor to see you."

The housekeeper looked up from her work, peering at Jane over the edge of her reading glasses.

"Good afternoon, Mrs Hill," Jane said. "I'm Jane Lee. Lord and Lady Crawford hired me as the new governess?"

"Ah, yes. Her ladyship mentioned that you would be arriving today." Turning to the maid, she said, "Thank you, Marie. You can go back to the kitchen now."

Marie bobbed a quick curtsy and left, stealing a last inquisitive glance at Jane. *The whole household will know about me well before I've had a chance to unpack my bags,* Jane chuckled inwardly.

"Please sit down, Miss Lee," the housekeeper said, gesturing at the only other chair that had been squeezed into the cramped office.

Placing her suitcase by her feet, Jane took a seat and smiled politely at Mrs Hill. She tried to gauge what sort of person the housekeeper might be. But Mrs Hill was hard to read.

"I trust you had a safe journey?"

"It was long, but mercifully uneventful."

"Have you been to Paris before?"

"No, this is my first time. My first time abroad as well."

"You'll find the French to be an odd bunch. And these Parisians even more so. Not like us Englishmen and women at all. But you'll get used to them soon enough."

"I'm sure I will."

"And at any rate, you won't have to deal with them very often. You'll be spending most of your time with the children." Mrs Hill took off her reading glasses. "You are aware of course that, as their governess, you will be sharing your meals with them in the nursery?"

Jane nodded. "That is indeed the general custom, yes." She knew a governess' position was a bit of a special one. Not necessarily one to be envious of, but certainly different. She was more than a maid or a nanny, but not as senior as the butler or the housekeeper. As a governess, you didn't really rank anywhere in the hierarchy of the household.

"You will have Sunday afternoons off," Mrs Hill continued. "But you don't have to venture outside if you don't want to. You're welcome to stay in the house and read for instance. Personally, I'm rather partial to doing a bit of knitting whenever I have the time."

Jane blinked and tried not to stare at the housekeeper in disbelief. The poor woman must really hate Paris, she thought. Or maybe she had been here for so long that the city had lost its charm.

"Lady Crawford will instruct you on the finer details of your responsibilities. She has insisted on doing so herself – a mother's duty and all that."

"Of course," Jane said graciously.

"At the moment, her ladyship is occupied with other matters. But she shouldn't be long. You can go to the kitchen in the meantime and ask one of the girls to serve you a cup of tea and some light refreshments."

Their brief interview over, Jane got up and thanked Mrs Hill, before retracing her steps back to the kitchen.

So far, things seemed to be going well, she thought. Apart from her apparent dislike of the French, Mrs Hill hadn't been too disagreeable.

Jane was looking forward to meeting Lady Crawford next. In her imagination, she pictured an aristocratic woman elegantly descending the grand staircase dressed in an exquisite gown and sporting a string of outrageously expensive pearls around her graceful neck. Only when having arrived at the bottom of the stairs, she would acknowledge Jane's presence and greet her with one of those cool and detached smiles that the nobility did so well.

It'll be marvellous, Jane smiled to herself.

After that, she would be introduced to the children. And then her work – and her life here in Paris – would begin in earnest.

Chapter Six

With her mind full of happy thoughts and nervous excitement, Jane entered the kitchen. She spotted Marie, who was whipping up cream in a large bowl, while another maid stood kneading dough for bread.

Elsewhere in the buzzing kitchen, two more maids were preparing ingredients for tonight's dinner. A man was supervising them closely and making comments while they worked. A cook's apron was bound tightly around his impressive belly.

"Anything I can do to help, Miss?" he asked in French when he saw Jane entering his kitchen.

"Bonjour, Monsieur. I'm Jane Lee, the new governess."

"So Marie tells us," he said with a nod in the direction of the maid who had escorted Jane to the housekeeper. "What do you want?"

His tone sounded a bit gruff, but Jane wasn't daunted by that. She gathered it was just the normal French way of being direct, with none of the British polite formality she was accustomed to.

"Mrs Hill told me to come down here while I wait for Lady Crawford, Monsieur–?"

"Alphonse," he replied. "I'm the chef in this crazy household." He gestured broadly at the kitchen around them, the domain over which he ruled supreme.

"*Enchantée,* Monsieur Alphonse," she said pleasantly, hoping a friendly smile might help to charm him somewhat. "Mrs Hill said that perhaps you would like to offer me some tea and a quick bite to eat?"

He shrugged. "We still have some cake left over if you like?"

"I love cake, Monsieur! Did you bake it yourself?"

"*Mais évidemment,*" he replied proudly. "Obviously! Everything you eat in this house is made in my kitchen."

"Then I am certain that I will love your cake even better, Monsieur Alphonse."

Duly mollified, he inclined his head to her and pointed to an open door on the other side of the kitchen. "Through there, if you please, Mademoiselle. That's the staff dining room. I'll send one of the girls over with a little something for you."

After thanking him profusely, Jane went into the empty dining room and sat down at a corner of the large wooden table with her suitcase by her feet.

A few moments later, Marie entered with the 'little something' as the chef had called it.

Jane smiled eagerly when the maid placed the tray before her on the table. Because not only was Mr Alphonse giving her a pot of steaming tea and a large helping of cake – he had also included a plate full of sandwiches cut into small triangles.

All of it neatly presented, as if she was a visitor above stairs and not some simple member of staff.

"Thank you, Marie."

The maid nodded and grinned before disappearing back to the kitchen. Settling in for her wait, Jane slowly sipped her tea and savoured every morsel of the food. The cake turned out to be just as delicious as it looked.

She was alone in the dining room at this time of day. But through the open door, she could keep an eye on what was going on in the kitchen while she ate.

Jane watched as the girls chopped vegetables, stirred pots of sauces and tended to bubbling cauldrons over open flames – all under Monsieur Alphonse's watchful eye. Every now and then, he would taste this or that and make a grumbling comment when things weren't perfectly to his liking.

But at the same time as Jane was observing the people and proceedings in the kitchen, the maids also cast glances at her, whispering and giggling among themselves.

Probably discussing what sort of person I am, Jane guessed. The sniggering and grinning told her that their first impression of her might not be a favourable one.

She had finished off the food when a handful of young boys came rushing into the dining room through the kitchen. Ranging in age from about seven to eleven or twelve from the looks of it, they seemed like typical boys: noisy, rowdy and playful.

They were surprised to find her sitting there, but then their hungry bellies got the better of them and they quickly slid onto the benches at the other side of the table.

Jane assumed they worked as boot boys, stable hands and garden helpers: the usual assortment of cheap labour in the large household of a wealthy family.

She heard them whispering as they stared and gawked at her. "*C'est la nouvelle Anglaise,*" one of them said. "That's the new English girl."

"Hush, she'll hear you!"

"So what?" the first boy shrugged. "Probably doesn't speak a word of French anyway." Jane suppressed the urge to grin at their silly exchange.

A loud cheer went up when Marie brought in a tray with a cup of milk and an apple for each of them. Leaving the boys to sort it out among themselves, she placed the tray on the table and left the room again.

But not before a mocking grin appeared on her face when she passed by Jane.

That one dislikes me already, Jane frowned.

Meanwhile, an argument had broken out among the boys over who would get the biggest apples. Naturally, the eldest boys were laying claim to those.

"Hey, Petit Jean," one of the big louts said to the smallest boy in the group. "You want to give your apple to me, don't you?"

"No, I don't," the little boy laughed.

"It's too big for you. Give it to me."

"No," he said firmly, pressing the apple close to his chest.

But the older bully slapped Petit Jean over the head and then snatched the apple out of the poor boy's hands.

"That's mine," Petit Jean shouted, angrily lunging at the apple thief, who was much stronger. An unfair scuffle broke out between the two. And Petit Jean ended up on the floor in no time at all.

"Enough," Jane shouted in French. "Stop fighting. Now!"

The boys were stunned into silence and stared at her as if she had just grown a second head.

"You speak French?" the bully asked.

"Of course I speak French, you little idiot. Now give back that apple to your friend."

"He's not my friend," he grumbled.

"Give it back anyway," Jane insisted.

"What's all this racket then?" Monsieur Alphonse barked, standing in the open doorway. "Do I need to come in and knock some sense into those foolish empty heads of yours, boys?"

Rolling his eyes at Jane, he mumbled "Boys, tsk" and went back to his kitchen.

Under Jane's stern gaze, the bully reluctantly handed the apple back to Petit Jean, who was already up on his feet again. The little boy smiled gratefully at her and took a bite out of his apple.

"Are you all right?" she asked him.

"Yes, Miss. Thank you."

Just then Marie came in with a tray of freshly baked fruit tarts, much to the audible delight of the boys. But this time, there were no arguments or fights. Politely and calmly, they each took a tart – like sweet little angels.

"I think you'd better grab yours too," Jane smiled at Petit Jean. He nodded and joined the others at the table, while she returned to her own seat.

Marie may not like me very much, she thought as she sat down. *But it seems I've made another friend here today.*

She grinned and poured some more tea into her cup.

Chapter Seven

Long after the boys had returned to their chores, Jane was still waiting in the deserted staff room. Having drunk the last of her tea, she sat and drummed her fingers on the weathered wooden surface of the long dining table.

This is becoming ridiculous, she grumbled silently. Why hadn't they shown her to her room first? She could have unpacked her suitcase and freshened up a little by now, instead of sitting here and doing nothing.

Just when she was thinking of getting up to ask someone if maybe they had forgotten about her, Mrs Hill appeared in the doorway.

"Miss Lee? Lady Crawford is ready to see you now," the housekeeper said. "Follow me, please."

Relieved that her enforced idleness had finally come to an end, Jane stood up and took her valise. She followed Mrs Hill through a disorienting number of corridors and staircases until they reached a double door.

The housekeeper knocked and opened the door to what appeared to be a spacious drawing room. "Miss Lee for you, milady," she announced formally.

"Show her in," Lady Crawford replied without looking up from the sheets of fashion drawings she held in her hands. The lady of the house was sitting on a chaise longue, surrounded by an array of silk and satin fabrics.

Leaving her suitcase by the door, Jane stepped inside and did a quick curtsy, while she lowered her eyes respectfully. She had no idea if you were supposed to do that type of thing, but she thought it wouldn't hurt.

Behind her, the housekeeper discreetly left the room and closed the door.

Lady Crawford made a deliberate show of not addressing Jane just yet. First, she glanced a short while longer at the sheets in her hand. Then, she sighed and threw the fashion drawings on the floor with a bored and tired gesture.

"I'm simply exhausted," she lamented melodramatically. When she placed a hand on her forehead, it was impossible not to notice the sparkling diamonds in the ring on her finger.

"The French are such dastardly difficult people to work with, don't you know?" she said to Jane with her eyes closed.

"I'm afraid I can't say I've had many dealings with them yet, ma'am."

"Well, you may take it from me then. As you can undoubtedly tell from all this dreadful mess around me, I've just had a very long meeting with my *modiste*."

With a theatrical flick of the wrist, she tossed one of the fabric samples off the chaise lounge.

"The woman is a talented artist, and she knows all about the latest fashion. But good heavens, it's so hard to make these people understand *anything*."

Lady Crawford rose to her feet and went over to the drinks cabinet, where she poured herself a small glass of an amber-coloured liquid from one of the crystal decanters.

"Sherry?" she offered to Jane, who politely declined.

"Anyway, Madame de Villeneuve ended up taking up so much more of my precious time than anticipated. I hope you haven't been waiting too long?"

"Not at all, ma'am," Jane lied.

"Good, good," Lady Crawford said, dismissing the matter with a casual wave of the hand. An apology was far beneath her, obviously.

She sat down on the chaise longue again, took a sip of her sherry and stared directly at Jane, who was still standing up.

"Let's get straight down to business, Miss Lee," Lady Crawford said. "My children are in dire need of a governess. They've gone through five in the past year alone. Each and every one of your predecessors was, quite honestly, wholly unsuitable."

Jane kept a straight face, but she found that statement hard to believe. Perhaps her ladyship was simply too demanding?

"I need someone who can instil discipline and respect in young and undeveloped minds," Lady Crawford continued. "Someone who knows how to handle difficult children."

Jane felt a knot forming in her stomach. Difficult children? Visions of two spoiled brats making her life hell on earth floated through the back of her head.

"I must warn you, Miss Lee: I set a very high standard. Simply because I must. What with Lord Crawford having such an important and rather sensitive position. I'm not allowed to say much about it of course, but I'm sure you've heard all the rumours."

"I'm not in the habit of lending credence to gossip and hearsay, ma'am."

"Splendid. That is precisely the kind of attitude I appreciate in my staff. And it's so rare these days. Now, let me explain your duties and responsibilities."

She took another sip of sherry, before continuing, "You will teach them the usual topics: French, literature, piano and etiquette, as well as proper manners and deportment. Alistair will be going to boarding school sometime next year of course. But as the offspring of a Lord, he and his sister must be trained to live up to the standards expected of their elevated social standing."

To emphasise her point, Lady Crawford downed the rest of her sherry and then got up again to pour herself another glass.

"Once a week, you will report back directly to me – in writing – about the children's progress." She cast a radiant smile at Jane. "As a mother, I do love to be kept apprised of how well my darling little cherubs are doing."

Jane nodded and smiled politely. She had a feeling her reports would need to be positively glowing. Or else.

"For the rest, you are allowed to take the children outside – on walks and excursions for instance. But only after you've obtained permission from me through Mrs Hill. And she will then arrange for a footman to accompany you at all times. You can't be too careful with these foreigners around."

Lady Crawford drank a sizeable gulp of her sherry and asked, "Any questions?"

"No, ma'am. Everything is perfectly clear."

"Wonderful," Lady Crawford beamed. "As you can see, Miss Lee, I don't ask for much. Should you fail to meet my expectations however, you'll be out on the street before you know it."

How delightful, Jane thought sarcastically. But she knew this was the way of things in the world.

"Now then," Lady Crawford said as she downed her sherry in one. "Let me introduce you to the children. I believe I left them in the library while I had my meeting with Madame de Villeneuve."

She placed the empty glass on a small side table and strode to the door, without swaying.

Her ladyship can hold her drink, that's for sure, Jane sniggered inwardly as she followed her to the library.

"They're so incredibly bright, you know," Lady Crawford boasted. "We'll probably find them lost in a whole stack of books when we come in."

She smiled proudly and pushed open the double doors to the library. But her smile vanished instantly upon seeing the scene before them.

Dozens and dozens of thick, leather-bound volumes were piled high as a makeshift wall, with countless more tomes lying scattered across the floor. A young girl stood on one side of the improvised wall, while on the other side a boy who seemed younger than her was brandishing a fireplace poker above his head.

"*Sacré bleu,*" Lady Crawford gasped. "Alistair! Penelope!"

Alistair let the poker drop to the floor with a loud clatter. Brother and sister both turned pale and stared at their feet, speechless.

"Well?" their mother bristled. "Have you lost your tongue as well as your senses? What is the meaning of this?"

The children exchanged shy and guilty glances with each other. Being the eldest, Penelope decided to go first. "We were bored," she said.

"Bored? You have all these books to read and you got bored?"

"We did read at first, Mama," Alistair said. "Just like you told us to. But then you stayed away for so awfully long."

"Don't you dare blame me for this," their mother replied sternly. "I told you to behave and wait. What in heaven's name possessed you to ransack the place?"

The children stared at each other again, as if they were trying to remember how they had ended up in the present mess.

"Alistair was looking at the history books," Penelope said.

"I love history," he explained, turning to Jane with a broad smile. "It's my favourite subject."

"Yes, and then you found that book on pirates," his sister continued. "And you started telling me all about them."

"I love pirates even more," the young boy declared with so much glee that Jane had to bite the inside of her cheek to stop herself from laughing.

"One thing led to the other," Penelope said. "And then we decided to build a castle out of books, so we could play pirates."

"What?!" Lady Crawford shrieked.

"I'm the pirate captain," Alistair explained most helpfully. "I'm coming in from the high seas to raid Penny's castle on the cliffs." He sounded just as excited as he had been while playing his role.

"But why?" their mother demanded to know.

"We've already told you, Mama. Because you kept us waiting for so long."

Lady Crawford turned to Jane. "You see what I am up against, Miss Lee. Savages have better manners than these two." Gesturing at the complete mess in the library, she let out an exasperated huff.

Meanwhile, her children seemed to be holding their breaths, waiting for a reaction from their new governess.

"I've seen worse, ma'am," Jane said mildly as she surveyed the damage. Apart from the countless books strewn around like discarded litter, she spotted a vase and a small statue that had been knocked over. And some of the furniture was in disarray.

"Granted, this library isn't exactly conducive to learning and quiet reflection at the moment," she admitted. "But we'll soon fix that."

She clapped her hands. *"Allez, mes enfants!* Come, children. We are going to put all of these books back where they belong. And then you are going to apologise to your mother."

"Yes, Miss," Alistair and Penelope replied meekly in unison. Relieved to be spared any further punishments, they quickly set to work, picking up books and carrying them back to their shelves.

Jane kept an eye on them, checking if they were putting the books in the right place – for as far as she could tell.

After a few minutes, Lady Crawford grew tired of watching them and left the room.

As soon as she heard the door close, Jane couldn't help but smile. "I've never seen a castle made out of books before," she whispered to the children. "If it wasn't for the fact that you have both been very naughty, I would admire your ingenuity."

Penelope and Alistair briefly stopped what they were doing, exchanged startled looks... and then burst out giggling.

I think the three of us are going to get along just fine, Jane grinned silently.

Chapter Eight

On Sunday, Jane woke up with happy butterflies fluttering about in her belly. Today was her first half day off! She only needed to attend morning service at the church with the children, and then she had the rest of the day all to herself.

Georgie had promised he would show her some of his favourite sights. Finally, she would have a chance to explore the city. And with Georgie as her guide, she was sure she would find out why people said there was something magical about Paris.

Excitement surged through her veins as she made her way to the nearby park where they had arranged to meet. And when she saw him waiting for her, she had to stop herself from leaping into his arms. Because that sort of behaviour would have been frowned upon by the other members of the public. Even in Paris.

"Good morning, Jane," he greeted her with a wide smile. "You look wonderful today."

"Thank you," she replied, blushing at the compliment. "And you look handsome as ever."

Georgie chuckled. "Flattery will get you everywhere, my dear. Are you ready to be dazzled by the wonders of Paris?"

"Absolutely! I can't wait."

Giddily slipping her hands around his arm, they set off on what was sure to be a grand adventure. She felt like a child, wide-eyed and curious, as they passed by street performers and vendors selling their wares.

Georgie led her through small winding streets and across broad boulevards, pointing out landmarks and interesting sights as they went. Jane listened intently, and every time she gazed up at him, a blissful little sigh escaped her lips.

They took a short stroll along the river Seine as well, admiring the beautiful bridges and watching the barges that floated lazily up and down the slow-moving stream.

The boats were nothing special: plain and ordinary steam-powered crafts, really. But to Jane's eyes, they spoke of a simple and romantic existence.

She could easily picture herself and Georgie living on one of them. Sailing between Paris and other cities and towns along the river. During the day, they would ship a variety of goods to wherever they were wanted. And when evening came and the light began to fade, he would steer their humble boat towards the safety of the reed-covered shore and throw out the anchor.

She would bring up the simple yet delicious meal she had prepared for the two of them. And they would enjoy it out in the open air on the deck, after he had uncorked a nice bottle of wine.

Then, with their bellies full and their minds at peace, they would sit and watch the sunset... until it was time to retire to their small, cosy bed below deck.

There, he would draw her closer to him. And she would yearn to feel the warm touch of his hands on her skin – while she waited, with bated breath, for their lips to meet.

"Wait here," the real Georgie said, snapping her out of her reveries. They stopped and she saw that they were standing in front of a flower stall. Georgie walked up to the elderly woman running the stall and bought Jane a bunch of fragrant lavender.

"Thank you," she smiled, pressing the purple blossoms to her chest and inhaling their sweet, delicate scent. "They're lovely."

"Not half as lovely as you are though," he said softly. "I've missed you, Jane."

She looked up at him, bewitched by the tenderness she saw in his eyes. "I've missed you too, Georgie."

They gazed longingly into each other's eyes for a moment – a moment that could have lasted forever for all she cared. Then they smiled and continued their peaceful stroll.

"I'm sorry for rushing off the other day," he said. "I was just so busy with work."

"It's all right. I understand. Besides, today more than makes up for it."

"I'm glad you think so. And there's one more surprise I have for you."

"What is it?" Jane asked, her curiosity piqued.

"You'll see," he grinned.

He first took her to a small bakery tucked away in an alley, where the smell of fresh bread and pastries filled the air. As they stepped inside, Jane's eyes widened at the sight of the mouthwatering displays of baked goods and treats.

They chose a long, baton-shaped loaf of French bread and afterwards Georgie also purchased some cheese and a bottle of wine at a nearby market.

"You aren't expecting us to eat that out here on the street, are you?" she asked.

"Not out here, no," he replied, smiling somewhat mysteriously. "I know a far better place. Follow me."

Carrying their food, he led her to an open green space with several lawns, lots of trees and a big fountain in the middle of the grounds. The park had been constructed on a sloping hill and when they reached the top they were rewarded with a great view.

"Georgie, this is magnificent," Jane exclaimed, looking out over the river and the city.

"Isn't it just?" he smiled. "It's one of my favourite places in Paris. I thought we might have a picnic here. Let's go and sit underneath those trees over there."

She followed him across the grass and then they sat down in a quiet spot that offered plenty of shade. The rays of the sun sparkled through the trees, and a gentle breeze caressed her skin as if it were nature's playful way of welcoming her.

Under different circumstances, their meal of bread and cheese would have been fairly unremarkable. But here, sitting on the grass with a gorgeous view over Paris and with her beloved Georgie by her side, it tasted like a banquet fit for royalty. They ate in blissful silence, enjoying the food after their walk and savouring each other's company.

Once he had finished off the last of the cheese and nearly half the bottle of wine, Georgie stretched out on the grass, with his hands behind his head and a contented smile on his face.

"You haven't told me about your first week yet," he said. "What's it like to be a governess for a wealthy family like the Crawfords?"

"I haven't met Lord Crawford yet. But his wife is – how shall I say this – every bit the aristocrat I was afraid she would be: arrogant, haughty and quite demanding."

Georgie let out a short, scornful huff.

"Fortunately, the children are lovely," Jane continued. "Not at all like their mother. They're sweet, and very eager to learn new things."

She giggled when she remembered the disorderly scene in the library. "You should have been there when Lady Crawford first introduced me to them. The children had built this castle out of books, and they were playing pirates. Her ladyship was absolutely mortified with embarrassment."

Jane laughed at the memory and turned to Georgie. But instead of a chuckle, all she got from him was a soft snoring sound. He had fallen asleep while she was talking.

"Well, I'll be," she half grumbled. But then she saw his serene face, and she smiled. He looked so peaceful lying on the grass beside her, while his chest rose and fell in a slow and steady rhythm. Admiring his handsome features, she carefully reached out and brushed a strand of hair away from his forehead.

Suddenly, her lips curled up in a playful grin as an idea came to her. She picked one of the stems out of the bunch of lavender he had bought for her, and started tickling his cheek with it.

Gradually, he stirred from his slumber. His eyes lit up when he saw her smiling face hovering above him.

"Oh, hello," he said, still somewhat drowsy.

"How very dare you, good sir," she teased. "To fall asleep while your lady friend was talking. Most uncivilised of you."

He yawned and stretched his arms, before sitting up. "Sorry. It's been a rough week. Maître Leblanc makes us work very hard at the patisserie."

"You poor darling. Then perhaps it would be best if we called it a day and slowly started heading back home?" She'd hoped for more time together, but these few hours had been heavenly nonetheless.

"And at any rate," she said chirpily as they rose to their feet, "we'll see each other again next Sunday. Where are you planning to take me then? Could we go and visit the Louvre? Please?"

Georgie grimaced uncomfortably. Rubbing the back of his neck, he said, "Next Sunday... right. Listen, Jane, I ought to have told you this earlier, but–"

"But what?" She noticed that he wasn't meeting her eyes. And the hesitant tone in his voice filled her heart with dread. "What's wrong? Tell me."

"We can't meet each other next week. I have to work."

"On a Sunday?"

He nodded, but he kept staring at his feet. "It's awfully busy at the patisserie, I'm afraid. We have a wedding and two banquets to prepare for."

"I see."

She understood he didn't have much of a say in the matter. Georgie was an apprentice, and if this Maître Leblanc said he needed to work on a Sunday, well, then that was the end of it. But she felt bitterly disappointed nonetheless.

"I'm really sorry, my love," he said.

"I'm sorry too, Georgie. You didn't have time for me when I arrived in Paris. You fell asleep today. And now you're telling me we won't be able to see each other next week?"

"I know, my precious angel. And believe me, I don't like it any more than you do. But I'll make it up to you, I promise."

"You promise? Oh, well. That's all right then, I suppose," she bristled. "I moved to Paris so we'd be closer to each other again. But now I'm beginning to doubt whether you want me around at all."

"Jane, that's not fair. You haven't even been here for a full week. We'll have plenty of opportunities to be together."

"Will we though, Georgie? Or will you be running off to your precious Maître Leblanc each time he snaps his fingers at you?"

Without waiting for his reply, she turned on her heel and walked away. She heard him calling after her a few times, but he didn't follow her. Close to tears, she made her way back to the Crawford residence.

Everywhere around her, she saw people having fun and enjoying their Sunday afternoon in one of the most wonderful cities of the world. Yet here she was, all alone. Deserted by the love of her life.

Her first week in Paris hadn't got off to the brilliant start she had been hoping for. And as she approached the servants' entrance of her new temporary home, her brooding mind wondered what the second week would bring.

Chapter Nine

A day later, Jane's feelings were still bruised and battered from her hurtful spat with Georgie. And when she received word in the afternoon that Lady Crawford wanted to see her in the drawing room, Jane's heart sank.

The French chambermaid who came round to the nursery to deliver this summoning said that Madame wanted to discuss Jane's first weekly report about the children.

Discuss it? Jane questioned silently. *Or criticise and berate me for every little detail that isn't to her liking?*

She knew her employer was a difficult woman. Virtually impossible to please and more unpredictable than the English weather.

"Children," she said to her two loveable charges. "I need to go and see your Mama. Please pick a book and do some reading while I'm gone. No building castles this time, mind you. I shan't be long."

Like a pair of obedient angels, Alistair and Penelope rushed to the bookcase. Once they had both settled down with their book of choice, Jane made them promise to behave and then she left the room.

She had prepared her report carefully, Jane reminded herself. And she was confident that it was accurate, balanced and thorough. But Lady Crawford was certain to find fault with it anyway.

Her stomach churned and twisted into a hard knot as she descended the staircase. In the large hallway, sinister shadows seemed to loom in every corner. Like ghosts – lying in wait and ready to reach out to her with their cold spidery hands.

With every step, her apprehension grew. When she finally reached the polished wooden doors to the drawing room, she took a deep breath and knocked softly.

"Enter," Lady Crawford's voice sounded from within.

Jane went inside, feeling every bit like a schoolgirl being called into the office of the stern headmistress.

"You asked to see me, milady?"

Mrs Hill was present as well, and Jane wondered if the housekeeper would be involved in the conversation, too. In which case the situation was even worse than she feared.

"Ah, Miss Lee," Lady Crawford said coldly. "Just a moment. Mrs Hill and I are nearly done."

Jane breathed an invisible sigh of relief, while Lady Crawford turned back to her housekeeper.

"You may go now, Mrs Hill. But please heed my words. You must ensure that the maids perform their duties with greater care and diligence. I realise they are simple-minded creatures, as one has come to expect from the lower classes. But we cannot let that be an excuse for negligence."

"Understood, milady," the housekeeper acknowledged with a polite nod.

"Very well," Lady Crawford said. "That will be all."

"Thank you, milady," Mrs Hill said before leaving the room and closing the door behind her without a sound.

Jane watched her go, grateful that the housekeeper wouldn't be there to hear Lady Crawford's criticism of Jane's report firsthand.

But her relief was short-lived when Lady Crawford fixed Jane with a disapproving look on her face.

"I have read your report, Miss Lee. And I must say that I am deeply worried by it."

"Worried, milady? In what way, if I may ask?" Jane knew Lady Crawford was playing a game with her – a cruel and vicious game that Jane was certain to lose. But she had no other choice than to go along.

"It is my impression that you are being too soft on the children," Lady Crawford declared drily. "They need rigour and discipline if they are to learn how to behave properly."

When they are with me, they always behave, Jane wanted to say. But it wasn't hard to guess how Lady Crawford would react to a reply like that. She'd blow up and accuse Jane of being insolent.

"Furthermore," her ladyship continued, "I've received oral reports about sounds of laughter coming from the nursery – while *you* were with the children."

Jane resisted the urge to roll her eyes. *Heaven forbid a young child should laugh and giggle every now and then,* she thought sarcastically.

"So you see, Miss Lee. I have grave concerns about your relationship with the children." Lady Crawford sighed. "I trust you understand that your role as a governess is to educate and discipline them, not to become their playmate?"

"I do understand, Lady Crawford," Jane replied, trying to keep her voice steady. "But I believe that building a rapport with the children is an important part of my role as their governess. It allows me to understand their personalities, so I can tailor my lessons to their individual needs."

Lady Crawford scoffed. "And do you think playing games and telling stories is the best way to achieve that goal?"

Jane opened her mouth, but then closed it again. This discussion was going nowhere. And it was better for her to remain silent, before she said something that she would end up regretting.

"I'm willing to believe that your intentions are good, Miss Lee. For now anyway. But you must keep a more professional distance."

Knowing that it was useless to argue, Jane simply nodded and acted demurely. "I shall strive to do better in the future, milady."

"Please do, Miss Lee." Lady Crawford picked up a sheaf of papers from a side table and pretended to start reading through them. "Dismissed," she said without looking up.

Jane slipped out of the drawing room and paused for a moment to steady herself in the deserted corridor. Pressing her back against the wall, she inhaled deeply before releasing a long and slow breath.

Anger and frustration boiled in her veins. Her fists clenched when she thought of Lady Crawford's criticism. Unfair, it had been. Unfair and harsh. It wasn't Jane's fault that Alistair and Penelope seemed to genuinely like her. Or was she now expected to make the lives of those two darling children miserable?

A deep frown creased Jane's brow when she thought of something else Lady Crawford had mentioned: the 'oral reports' she claimed to have received about laughter in the nursery.

That meant someone was spying on her!

Some of the staff – heaven knows who or how many of them – were keeping a close watch on her. And then eagerly reporting back to their wicked mistress. Like a pack of sneaky informants.

The injustice of it all stung.

Could it be the housekeeper, Mrs Hill? Or perhaps one of the maids? Jane knew that Marie and the other French girls down at the kitchen certainly had taken a dislike to her.

A chill ran through her body as the realisation sunk in. If this was true, then Jane had no friends or allies in this house. Not a single soul to turn to. No one she could trust. A deep wave of sadness consumed her and she felt more alone than ever before.

Fighting back her tears, Jane willed herself to take a deep breath. She was not ready to give up yet.

No matter what Lady Crawford said or thought about her, she was determined to be the best governess for Alistair and Penelope that she could possibly be. She wasn't going to let those two angels suffer just because of their mother's unpleasant character.

And she vowed not to be frightened off by the backhanded machinations of others, who liked to ingratiate themselves with the manipulative lady of the house.

Taking one step at a time, Jane straightened her shoulders and went back to the nursery where she knew joy and laughter would await her.

A smile tugged at the corners of her mouth as she imagined the two children running around, their happy faces glowing with delight. For a moment, all the sadness lifted from her heart as if it had never been there in the first place.

"Miss Lee, you're back," Penelope beamed gleefully the moment Jane entered the nursery.

"We got so bored," Alistair said, rolling his eyes.

"I trust you were reading like I asked you to?" Jane said, her eyes quickly scanning the room for any signs of mischief.

"Of course we did," he replied. "We promised you that we would, didn't we?"

Jane smiled and stroked his hair. "You're a good boy, Alistair."

"What did Mama want to see you about, Miss Lee?" Penelope asked. "Anything we did wrong?"

"No," Jane said, trying to put more reassurance in her voice than she was feeling. "Nothing for you to be concerned about."

Her heart ached for them. *So sad,* she sighed inwardly. That two adorable children like this wonderful pair should have such a nasty, cold-hearted mother. And she prayed that, despite their loveless home, they might somehow find a way to develop into kind and caring adults.

"What are we going to do next, Miss Lee? Will you read us another story, please?"

"I have a better idea," Jane replied. "Why don't we go outside to the garden for a little while? I think the two of you could probably do with a breath of fresh air."

I know I certainly do, she added silently.

The children leapt up and hurried to the door, giggling and tugging at each other in their excitement.

"But remember," Jane warned them. "No running or shouting as we go outside. We can't have the son and daughter of a distinguished Lord bounding down the stairs like a couple of savages, can we?"

She tried to make light of it. But after what Lady Crawford had told her, she wanted the children to be on their best behaviour.

Thankfully, Alistair and Penelope left the room in an orderly fashion, walking peacefully side by side. Nevertheless, Jane felt a slight unease in her stomach as they proceeded down the hallway and onto the grand staircase. She could not shake off the feeling that somebody was keeping an eye on their every move.

Not wanting to alarm the children, she did her best to keep her composure and to pretend she didn't have a care in the world.

Her nerves were as tight as the strings on a violin however. And when they arrived in the garden, she let out a relieved sigh. They had made it.

Outside, all was peace and quiet. The sun shone brightly overhead, birds chirped happily from treetops and flowers scented the air with a delicate perfume.

An old gardener was tending to some of the shrubs with the help of one of his young assistants. The latter smiled and waved at Jane when he saw her coming into the garden. It was Petit Jean, the little boy she had stood up for in the kitchen on her first day.

Jane nodded at him, but she didn't want to acknowledge him any further. After all, someone might report her to Lady Crawford for fraternising with a lowly servant boy.

Alistair and Penelope ran across the path, spinning circles around each other and giggling with joy as they raced to see who could reach one of the trees first.

Jane watched them fondly, drinking in this rare moment of untroubled calmness before it would be gone again. After sitting down on a stone bench, her eyes wandered around the garden, taking in its well-manicured beauty.

But then her gaze drifted off towards the house. And immediately her mental anguish returned. She studied every single window, wondering whether it was just her anxious imagination getting the better of her. Or if someone really was peering out at them from the shadows within.

"Miss Lee?" Penelope asked suddenly, startling Jane out of her jittery fears.

"Yes, Penelope?" She let out a slow breath, trying to ease her pounding heart. "What is it, my dear?"

"Are you sure everything is all right?" The girl eyed her with a concerned frown on her rosy face. "You seem distracted."

"I'm absolutely fine," Jane lied. "I was merely thinking about... certain things."

"If it's because of your meeting with Mama, then I wouldn't worry too much if I were you. She's just jealous. Because she thinks we like you more than her."

Jane was speechless. This young girl seemed wise beyond her years. But that did little to put Jane's mind to rest.

"Run along now," she smiled weakly. "Before your brother gets up to any trouble."

Alistair was sitting on his hands and knees, examining an earthworm, and Penelope ran to join him.

Alone again, Jane took a deep breath. But when she wanted to rest her hand on her chest, she noticed it was trembling. So she clenched her fists and placed them on her lap.

Not for the first time, she questioned if coming to Paris had been the right thing to do. Would she soon be regretting her decision?

Chapter Ten

Agonisingly slow, the days crept by. The hours seemed unbearably long to Jane, as if time itself had decided to play a cruel trick on her. She felt trapped in a never-ending nightmare, and her heart was consumed with dread at the thought of another run-in with Lady Crawford.

Everywhere she went, she felt like she was walking on eggshells that threatened to shatter beneath her feet at the slightest misstep.

And all the while, she mistrusted everyone in the household. Every glance in her direction, and every word spoken to her – no matter how casual or trivial – her mind scrutinised everything, always searching for traps or hidden meanings.

The weight of all this tension was suffocating, leaving Jane feeling as if she was constantly gasping for air.

Eventually though, Sunday morning arrived. And once the family had attended church, Jane had the remains of the day to herself.

After her nerve-racking week, she was desperate to escape from the house and its oppressive atmosphere. She wanted to lose herself in some blissful distraction and, if only for a little while, forget about the constant pressure of Lady Crawford's scrutiny.

But what could she do, without the benefit of Georgie's company?

She sighed as she gazed out of the window in her small private room. High above in the clear blue sky, the sun shone down upon the world in all its glorious splendour. Jane could see people walking in the street below. They were dressed in their Sunday finery, intent on making the most of this lovely day.

Suddenly, the desire to join them gripped her.

"And why wouldn't I?" she asked out loud as a smile spread across her face. Breaking away from the window, she rushed over to the wardrobe and grabbed her hat and shawl.

If Georgie couldn't take her out because he was too busy at the patisserie, then by heaven, she would explore the city on her own.

Paris, here I come, she thought as she flew down the stairs in a flurry of eager excitement. In her mind, she could already see herself strolling along those broad boulevards. And by simply following her nose, she would happen upon charming, quiet streets lined with lovely shops and quaint little cafés.

She was so lost in these thoughts while she headed towards the servants' entrance that she didn't pay any notice at first to the sounds of animated chatter up ahead.

Until she spotted Marie among the small cluster of maids standing by the door. The girls also had their half day off, and just like Jane, they too were about to head into town.

A mean, derisive smirk appeared on Marie's face when she saw Jane. Immediately, the kitchen skivvy leaned closer to the girl next to her and whispered something in her friend's ear.

All the other girls now turned to Jane as well, and sniggered. Jane couldn't quite hear what they were whispering and giggling about. But she caught the gist of it.

They were commenting on her appearance and the way she was dressed. "So very English," she overheard one of the French girls saying. For some reason, this was a source of great mirth to them.

Jane decided that ignoring them was the best thing she could do. But their taunts and barbs still hurt. And as she headed out the door, their mocking stares felt like daggers in her back while their snorts of derision echoed through her mind.

Once outside though, the fair weather soon made her forget about the matter. She closed her eyes for a moment to let the sunshine warm her face. Then she opened her parasol and set off.

Paris was waiting for her, she told herself.

When Jane walked past the stables at the other side of the house, a smattering of young boys were playing in the street. One of them detached himself from the group and came running up to her, with a big smile on his face. It was, of course, Petit Jean.

"Bonjour, Mademoiselle," he said politely.

"Hello, Little John," she replied in French.

"Are you going out, Miss?"

"Yes, I am. It's my day off and I want to visit a few places."

"Which ones?"

"We have a saying in England," she chuckled. "Curiosity killed the cat."

"Oh, pardon me, Mademoiselle. I didn't mean to–"

"It's all right, Petit Jean. To be honest with you, I don't know yet where I'm going. But it's such a lovely day and I intend to make the most of it."

"On your own?"

She nodded confidently.

"But Paris is such a big place, Mademoiselle. And some parts of it are dangerous."

"London isn't exactly a peaceful little village either, you know. I'm sure I can manage." She smiled at him. His heartfelt concern for her was rather endearing.

"If you say so, Mademoiselle. But please promise me you will be careful."

"I will," she replied. "But only if you promise me that you'll stay out of trouble over there." She gestured towards the other boys, whose game sounded like it was becoming more rowdy.

"Them? Nothing I can't handle," he boasted, puffing up his scrawny chest.

"If you say so," she laughed. "Anyway, don't you have any family to be with? It's Sunday after all."

He shrugged. "You might say I have too much family. I have so many brothers and sisters, my parents prefer it when we stay away from home. Fewer mouths to feed that way."

"I'm so sorry to hear that." She pitied the poor lad and silently admonished herself for having broached the topic.

"No need for you to feel sorry, Mademoiselle. That's just how things are."

Jane looked at him, filled with respect and admiration for so much strength of character in such a young lad.

"You'd better get going then, Mademoiselle," he said. "Are you certain you don't want me to come with you?"

"Quite certain. I wouldn't want to keep you from enjoying your afternoon off. *Au revoir, Petit Jean.*"

"*Au revoir, Mademoiselle.*"

Having said their goodbyes, Jane set off again, musing about what an extraordinary boy he was.

Just before she rounded the corner, she looked back. Petit Jean was still standing there, watching her go. When he waved goodbye to her, she raised her hand slightly and wiggled her fingers at him.

I suppose I should count myself lucky that he doesn't follow me around like some faithful puppy, she giggled inwardly, giving her parasol a dainty twirl.

The Crawford residence lay in a neighbourhood that was chic and fashionable – and this showed in the sort of people who were prancing about. But it reminded Jane too much of Lady Crawford and the woman's haughty nature. And so she resolved that she would explore the 'real' Paris.

She would try to discover those secret corners and hidden places, away from the broad avenues and fancy façades. "That's where I'll find the true beauty of this city," she decided bravely.

Fleeing her troubles, she soon found a market in a less affluent neighbourhood. Its vibrant atmosphere caused her heart to soar with joy, and for a moment, it felt as if all of life's struggles had vanished. She bought a juicy pear and bit into it, savouring the taste with her eyes closed.

When she opened them again, a handful of raggedy looking children were staring at her.

"Please, Miss," one of them said. "Can you spare us a coin or two? We're very hungry."

Their eyes were wide and pleading, and set in gaunt faces that were caked in dirt. Their clothes were nothing but tattered rags, draped over thin frames.

Heartbroken, Jane reached into her purse for a few small coins. But the moment she did so, the beggar children pressed in closer – each crying out to her. Bony fingers tugged at her dress and clawed at her purse.

"Calm down," Jane said, starting to become a little frightened. She took a step back and tried to keep them at bay. But the children were relentless.

And when a sea of outstretched hands threatened to engulf her, she saw no other option than to use her dainty parasol as a means of defence against the onslaught.

One of the older ragamuffins snatched it from her however, and ran off with it – a trophy that would surely fetch him a few coins from the local ragman.

Tears of fear and frustration began to roll down Jane's face while the children continued their attempts to grab her purse.

"Leave the lady alone," someone suddenly shouted. "Get lost before I call the police."

Several well-aimed pebbles hit the street rats, who quickly decided to scamper off and disappear. With the threat gone, Jane burst out in sobs as her panic and anxiety were washed away by a wave of relief.

"Are you all right, Mademoiselle?" her saviour asked, coming closer. "Did they hurt you?"

Tears blurred her vision, but she recognised that voice.

"I'm fine, Petit Jean. Just a little shaken, that's all." She took out her handkerchief and dabbed it at the corners of her eyes. "Thank you for saving me. If it hadn't been for you..."

He shrugged. "I only did what was needed, Mademoiselle."

"What a stroke of good fortune that you found me," she said, tucking away her handkerchief. "Do you live around here?"

"Not really," he blushed. "But when you told me you were going to wander around Paris by yourself, I knew it was a bad idea. So I decided to follow you." He stared at his feet, slightly embarrassed by his confession. "Sorry, Miss."

Jane laughed. "Well, I'm very grateful that you did." Reaching into her purse, she said, "Please, let me reward you for your bravery."

"Oh no, Mademoiselle," he said, stopping her from taking out a coin. "I don't want your money. It wouldn't feel right, Miss."

She hesitated. "Then at least allow me to buy you something to eat."

A broad grin appeared on his face while he rubbed his hungry tummy. "That I couldn't possibly refuse."

Jane bought him a small meat pie, and he devoured it so quickly that she wished she had got another one for him.

"Shall I walk you back to the house, Mademoiselle?" he asked as he licked the last crumbs off his fingers.

"No," she replied, frowning at the thought of having to spend the rest of her day off cooped up indoors.

"No?! Haven't you had enough excitement for one day?"

"When I left the house this morning, I wanted to see Paris and enjoy myself. I still intend to carry out that plan."

Petit Jean looked at her as if she was stark raving mad. But Jane dug into her purse and produced a small business card.

Smiling, she said, "And I know just the man to help me."

Chapter Eleven

With Petit Jean in tow, Jane went to the Hôtel Faubourg, where Mr Dubois was staying according to his card. The young boy had insisted on accompanying her and she didn't have the heart to refuse. Not after he had saved her from that riff-raff at the market.

"Who is this man, Mademoiselle?" he asked on their way to the hotel. "Are you sure you can trust him?"

"Have you become my guardian angel now, Petit Jean?" she chuckled. "You don't need to worry though. Monsieur Dubois is a good man. He was most kind to me and very helpful when I met him on the boat from England to France."

"Do you always trust people so easily, Mademoiselle?"

"Certainly not, my cheeky rascal. But in Mr Dubois' case, he happens to be a perfect gentleman."

Petit Jean made his opinion known by letting out a short snort in derision. Before Jane could respond to his unspoken criticism, their hired cab arrived in front of the Hôtel Faubourg. She paid the driver and they got out of the carriage.

"He must be earning a pretty penny if he can afford to stay in a fancy place like this," Petit Jean said as they stared up in amazement at the impressive façade.

But when they wanted to enter, a doorman stopped them. The polished brass buttons of his uniform glittered in the sun.

"I'm afraid his kind aren't allowed inside, Mademoiselle," he spoke sternly, pointing at Petit Jean.

"But he's with me," Jane protested.

"With respect, Miss," the doorman smiled indifferently, "I cannot let him in."

"Why not?" she asked, even though she knew the answer already.

"Just look at him, Miss. Those clothes of his, and not to mention his smell, they would shock our guests. If I let him walk through those doors, I'd be out of a job in an instant. *You* are free to enter, of course. But it will have to be without him."

"It's all right, Mademoiselle," Petit Jean intervened quickly. "You go on alone. I'll wait for you outside." He smiled at her and said, "I'm not leaving until I've seen this Monsieur Dubois of yours with my own eyes."

Jane sighed, nodded reluctantly and walked towards the hotel entrance. She felt sorry for Petit Jean. But the boy didn't seem too bothered about the doorman's refusal. And by now she was dying for a bit of adventure in this dazzling city.

When she entered the lobby, it was as if she had stepped into another world. A world of luxury and excess, where money could buy anything and everything. The tiled marble floors were polished to a reflective sheen while a large crystal chandelier hung from the high ceiling.

Elegantly dressed guests milled about, trying to impress and outshine each other like peacocks. The ladies among them were decked out in a fortune's worth of jewellery that sparkled and glittered on their necks, wrists and fingers.

"How may I help you, Mademoiselle?" a clerk asked with an icy expression on his face when Jane approached the front desk.

"I'm here to see Mr Pierre Dubois. He's a guest at your hotel. Could you find him for me, please?"

"Certainly, Miss," the clerk replied, already visibly bored with her. He snapped his fingers at one of the porters and handed the young man a scribbled note.

While the porter went off in search of Mr Dubois, Jane took the opportunity to admire the lavish surroundings.

Dotted around the lobby, small tables and comfortable chairs invited the guests to sit down and enjoy a quiet moment of respite.

The walls were adorned with beautiful paintings in gilded frames. While a huge grandfather clock stood sentry in one corner, ticking away the time.

Fresh cut flowers further enhanced the beauty of the place, their delicate scent filling the air with pleasant aromas.

Somewhere, a piano and a small string ensemble were playing calm and heavenly music. Though where the sweet sounds originated from Jane couldn't tell.

For a moment she simply stood, drinking in the atmosphere and imagining she had been transported back in time – standing in a sumptuous palace of Louis the Great, when the Sun King was at the height of his reign.

This was the Paris she had dreamed of. The Paris of beauty, romance and delight. She sighed, a smile playing on her lips.

At last, an adventure. At last, escape from the dreariness of her daily life. She only wished Georgie could be here to share it with her.

For now however, the friendly Mr Dubois would have to suffice.

"Mademoiselle Lee, what a pleasure to see you again."

His smooth French accent interrupted her reverie. She turned to see Mr Dubois walking up to her, dressed in a tailored suit and silk cravat, a charming smile lighting up his face. "To what do I owe the privilege of your visit?"

"Monsieur Dubois," she beamed. "I hope you don't mind me dropping in on you unannounced. And on a Sunday, no less."

"Not in the slightest. How may I be of service to you? And where is that nice young man of yours? The one who was waiting for you at the train station when you first arrived?"

"Georgie? He had to work today, unfortunately."

"That's a shame," Mr Dubois replied with just the right degree of empathy. "Anything I can do for you?"

"I was rather hoping that you could, yes," Jane blushed. "I wanted to see Paris – the real Paris. But much to my regret, I have discovered that it's too dangerous for a woman by herself."

Briefly, she told him about the frightening incident at the market.

"You have made the right decision in coming to me, Mademoiselle," he said. "I will be honoured to be your guide and show you some of the beauty and magic of this extraordinary city."

A short while later, they stood outside the hotel, where Petit Jean was still waiting for her.

"Is this him?" the boy asked, looking Mr Dubois up and down.

"Petit Jean," Jane said admonishingly. "That's no way to greet a nice gentleman."

"I'm sorry, Miss," he replied meekly. "*Bonjour, Monsieur.*"

"Hello, young man," Mr Dubois smiled amicably. "I suppose I should thank you."

"What for, sir?"

"I hear you're the valiant hero who saved Miss Lee from a band of ruffians earlier today."

Petit Jean's little chest seemed to double in size with pride. "I did what I had to do, sir."

"Spoken like a true gentleman, my lad. I'm going to show Miss Lee some of the sights. Why don't you join us?"

"Can I?" the boy asked, his eyes widening with excitement. He looked at Jane, pleading for her to say yes.

"Of course you can," she replied with a smile. Fate seemed to have decreed that the two of them would be friends. So why wouldn't he come along? And the fact that Mr Dubois had suggested it first only spoke in favour of the man's good intentions, she felt.

"Then let's go," Mr Dubois said. "Today I will show you some of the wonders of Paris. You will fall in love with this city, Mademoiselle. I promise you that."

The three of them set off, embarking on a marvellous journey that offered as many twists and turns as the path they followed.

From grand cathedrals that towered above them like monolithic guardians of the faith, to quiet cobblestoned alleys filled with forgotten stories and secrets – every step seemed to bring them something new.

Stone monuments and towering obelisks stood testament to the great works of past generations, while sprawling green open spaces provided a welcome respite from the city's hustle and bustle.

And throughout the entire tour, Mr Dubois regaled them with interesting facts and wondrous tales about the people and the events that had shaped Paris into what it was.

"Is every Frenchman as knowledgeable and well-spoken as you, Mr Dubois?" Jane asked when they sat down for a much-needed rest and something to drink at a cosy bistro.

"I don't know if I'm either of those things, Miss Lee," he laughed. "But this city holds a very special place in my heart."

"I'm beginning to see why. It's all so incredibly beautiful. Like something out of a storybook." She sighed and gazed into the distance, while a waiter came to their table to take their order.

Mr Dubois asked for coffee, a selection of sweet pastries and a double helping of chocolate cake for Petit Jean.

"Forgive me for saying so, Mademoiselle," Mr Dubois said once the waiter had disappeared. "But you seem distracted to me. Perhaps even a bit sad. Is anything troubling you? I hope our afternoon together hasn't taxed you too much?"

"You are very perceptive, Monsieur. Yes, I must confess I'm feeling rather melancholy at the moment. But it has nothing to do with this afternoon."

"Then why the unhappy face, Mademoiselle?"

Jane hesitated. Mr Dubois had been kind to her on every occasion. But could she lay bare her worries to him?

"Forgive me if my question was too forthright," he said, sensing her reluctance.

Their conversation was interrupted when the waiter returned, carrying a tray with their order. After the man had placed their food and drinks on the table, Petit Jean attacked his two pieces of chocolate cake with great energy, while Jane and Mr Dubois sampled their pastries with a bit more self-control.

"I don't mind telling you," Jane said. She had decided she wanted to get the issue off her chest. Especially since she didn't have many other people to talk to in Paris. "Today has been simply wonderful. And I have you to thank for that, Monsieur."

He smiled and inclined his head. "It's what friends are for, Miss Lee. However, I sense that your next sentence will start with the word 'But...' Am I correct?"

She nodded. "I've had so much fun. But I wish Georgie had been here to share that joy with me." Staring at the half-eaten pastry on her plate, she said, "I wish he didn't have to work so hard. So he could spend more time with me."

Swallowing the last piece of his chocolate cake, Petit Jean asked, "Do you think you'll finish that pastry, Miss?"

Jane smiled and slid her plate towards the boy, who gratefully accepted it.

"Sometimes I wonder, you know," she said to Mr Dubois. "I wonder if, perhaps, Georgie doesn't *want* to spend more time with me."

"*Mais non, Mademoiselle.* You mustn't think like that. I'm sure Monsieur Georges has his reasons to work as hard as he does. Just like any decent man, he's doing it to build a better future for the two of you."

"You're right, I suppose. But I still feel that building a future shouldn't stop us from enjoying the present."

"Ah, Mademoiselle Lee," he chuckled. "I see you are already beginning to think more like the French."

Jane placed a hand over her mouth and giggled. It felt good to laugh. Like letting a weight fall off her shoulders.

"And in that spirit of enjoying the present," Mr Dubois said, "I would like to invite you to join me for dinner at my hotel. So you can have a taste of proper French cuisine."

"Dinner?" Petit Jean cut in. "That reminds me I'd better head home now. I don't want to miss supper."

"You're still hungry?" Jane asked, laughing. "After all that cake and those pastries you finished off?"

"A boy like me needs to eat in order to grow," he replied most sincerely before turning to Mr Dubois for support. "Isn't that right, sir?"

"Absolutely, my boy."

"Are you coming with me, Mademoiselle? Or will you be having dinner with Mr Dubois?"

"I don't know," Jane said, dithering. "I'm not sure if it's appropriate. I haven't got a chaperone. What will people think?"

"This is Paris, Mademoiselle," Mr Dubois replied with a grin. "And may I remind you of a famous motto from your own country? The Most Noble Order of the Garter that you British are so proud of says: *'Honi soit qui mal y pense'*."

"Shame on whoever thinks evil of it," Jane translated as a smile spread across her lips.

"You're right, Monsieur. I'll gladly accept your dinner invitation."

Because why wouldn't I? she thought to herself. After all, Mr Dubois himself had said they were friends. And there was nothing wrong with a pair of friends enjoying a good meal together.

Chapter Twelve

By the time they arrived at the hotel, Jane's spirits were soaring high, and a radiant smile adorned her face. During their carriage ride, Mr Dubois had once again proven to be a gifted storyteller.

It seemed like he could regale anyone with stories about times long gone in a way that made you feel as if you were right in the middle of it. Jane had gasped at his fascinating tales, giggled at the amusing ones, and blushed at his slightly saucier anecdotes.

She was still laughing when they entered the hotel lobby, the sound of her laughter mingling with the piano music into a harmony of pure joy.

Captivated by her giddiness, Mr Dubois cast an admiring glance in her direction. "You bring such life and vibrancy to every moment, Mademoiselle," he said, his eyes brimming with delight.

"On the contrary, Monsieur. It is you who has made the moments so delightfully enjoyable today. I feel like a happy songbird, twittering and flying through sunny skies without a care in the world."

"Wait until you have tasted the food," he joked. "Then you'll think you're in heaven."

As they approached the front desk, the clerk recognised Mr Dubois immediately and greeted them with a polite smile.

"I have a guest for dinner this evening," Mr Dubois said. "Could you arrange a table for two in the restaurant, please?"

"Certainly, sir," the clerk replied. "Oh, and Mr Dubois? There's a gentleman in the lobby for you. I told him you were out, but he said he would wait for you. He's been here for over an hour, I believe."

"It would seem I'm much in demand today," Mr Dubois quipped as he turned to Jane. "Please excuse me while I briefly attend to this mystery visitor. And then you and I shall indulge in some of the most exquisite delicacies French cuisine has to offer."

"You make it sound like another grand adventure," she smiled in reply. Standing by the front desk, she watched him go as he scanned the seats in the lobby for his visitor.

It didn't take Mr Dubois long to find the person he was looking for. The man had his back to them, so Jane couldn't see his face. But Mr Dubois seemed to know him well enough.

"Where the devil were you this afternoon, old chap?" the visitor grumbled, rising from his seat. "I've been sitting here for ages."

Jane's heart skipped a beat, and her entire being stiffened. A cold fear took hold of her as if icy fingers had wrapped themselves around her throat.

The man spoke in English. And she had recognised his voice even before she had seen his face.

Percy Yates, she gasped in silent horror.

His grandfather had been a money lender who had sent Jane and Abbie's father to prison over a bad debt. Their poor Papa had subsequently died in prison, plunging their happy little family into despair. To repay the substantial debt, the girls had been forced to work for Percy and his grandfather.

As charwomen, they had needed to clean, scrub, wash and cook from early morning until late at night – not just for the two Yates men, but for other families as well. And even then, they had barely been able to make ends meet.

The old Mr Yates had been a cruel and miserly penny pincher. But his grandson was far worse.

Percy used to make inappropriate comments and unwanted amorous advances towards Jane's sister Abbie. And he had always taken a wickedly sinister delight in doing so.

Luckily, with the help of the wealthy Joe Thompson, they had ultimately succeeded in defeating the brute. But before that happened, she and Abbie had suffered many moments of fear and terror.

Yes, Jane remembered Percy Yates and his evil games all too well. What on earth was he doing in Paris? And how did he know Mr Dubois?

The latter was talking to Percy, explaining how his plans for the day had unexpectedly changed. He made a gesture in Jane's direction to illustrate his point, and suddenly she wished that she could make herself invisible.

But it was too late.

When Percy turned his head, their eyes met. And he too recognised her instantly.

The initial look of startled surprise on his face quickly gave way to a broad and arrogantly amused grin. The sort of grin she remembered all too well, unfortunately.

"Mademoiselle," Mr Dubois called out to her. "Please come and meet my business partner."

Reluctantly, Jane dragged herself over to where the two men were standing. Business partners? She didn't like the sound of that. How could a nice man like Mr Dubois become entangled with a despicable villain like Percy Yates?

"Mr Yates, may I introduce Miss Jane Lee to you," Mr Dubois said kindly. "Miss Lee, please meet Mr Percy Yates. As you may have guessed already, Monsieur Yates is a compatriot of yours."

"Miss Lee and I have already met, old chap," Percy grinned while his eyes bore into Jane. "In fact, you could say we're old acquaintances. Isn't that right, Miss Lee?"

Jane nodded slowly. Perhaps she was merely dreaming this. Any moment now, she would wake up in the comfort and safety of her own bed and breathe a sigh of relief.

"Really?" Mr Dubois said, raising an eyebrow in wonder. "What a marvellous coincidence."

"Marvellous indeed," Percy agreed. "Although I must admit, Miss Lee is the last person I was expecting to meet here in Paris."

That makes two of us, she thought as her mind raced to figure out the meaning and the implications of this encounter.

When Mr Dubois frowned, Percy explained. "Miss Lee and I share a long and rather eventful history together, you see. And when we last parted ways, neither side was counting on seeing the other ever again."

Jane squirmed uncomfortably as the memories of that final confrontation with their tormentor came flooding back into her mind. By threatening to expose his dirty business dealings, they had pressured Percy into leaving London – for good.

"*Mon Dieu,*" Mr Dubois said. "Sounds like it must have been a dramatic farewell."

"Quite," Percy replied, his eyes gleaming with malice.

"And did this happen a long time ago?"

"It's been a while, yes. But I still remember – everything."

As do I, you vicious fiend, Jane wanted to hiss at him. She hadn't forgotten how he had doggedly attempted to have his indecent ways with Abbie.

Percy laughed. "Why, I even remember when the Lee sisters lived in my grandfather's attic and how they used to scrub our floors and do our washing."

Jane glared at him. Why did he have to bring up that particular detail in front of Mr Dubois? He was trying to humiliate her, she was sure of it.

"Speaking of whom," Percy continued brashly. "How is your dearest sister, Miss Lee? Married to that rich Thompson fellow, I heard?"

"Very happily married, yes," Jane replied, raising her chin defiantly. How she wanted to wipe the grin off his face. "But tell me, Mr Yates. What brings you to Paris?"

"I could ask the same of you," he replied with a hint of darkness in his voice.

"Miss Lee is working as a governess," Mr Dubois replied helpfully. "For Lord and Lady Crawford."

"Impressive," Percy nodded while his smile widened. "As for me, Miss Lee, after London I ended up in Paris. I'm a new man now – with a new life, as well as a new business." He gestured in Mr Dubois' direction. "Thanks to the help of my friend Pierre here."

Jane looked from Percy to Mr Dubois. How could two such vastly different men have become friends, she wondered? Somehow, she found it hard to believe.

"Miss Lee and I were going to have dinner," Mr Dubois said. "Why don't you join us, Percy? Then the two of you can reminisce and catch up."

Jane held her breath. *No,* she thought fearfully. Meeting her family's old foe was bad enough. The last thing she wanted was to sit at the same table with him for an entire evening, pretending to be nice to each other.

Thankfully, Percy appeared to have similar reservations. "I don't think that would be a good idea, old chap," he smirked. "It's likely to ruin Miss Lee's appetite. Mine as well, probably."

Relieved, Jane let out a discreet sigh. The sooner she was rid of him, the better. Perhaps she should feign a sudden illness and go home?

But there was no need for that. Because Percy picked up his coat and hat, and told Mr Dubois, "You and the young lady enjoy your dinner without me. Our business can wait until tomorrow."

"As you wish, *mon ami,*" Mr Dubois answered amicably. "*Bonne nuit.*"

"Good night to you too, old chap," Percy said, giving his partner a quick wink. Then he looked at Jane one last time, with that typical sneering grin of his on his lips, before shrugging into his coat and walking to the exit.

Jane kept staring at the door, even after Percy had left.

"Are you quite all right, Mademoiselle?" Mr Dubois asked, studying her with concern. "You appear distressed."

Jane hesitated, unsure about how much she could reveal of her history with Percy.

"Mr Yates and his grandfather caused a great deal of harm to my family," she said slowly. "It was... difficult, seeing him again so unexpectedly."

"I'm sorry to hear that," Mr Dubois said with all his usual warmth and charm. "Then let us talk no more of Monsieur Yates or things that are in the past. And let us instead enjoy a good meal, you and I."

He paused and added, tactfully as ever, "Unless of course, you prefer to return home?"

Jane shook her head. "No, let's have dinner, please. They say food can be like medicine for the soul." She smiled at him, weakly and unconvincingly.

To Mr Dubois' credit, he did his utmost best to be the perfect host, gracefully avoiding any mention of Percy Yates or how he himself came to be involved with the man.

But no matter how hard he tried, for Jane the mood never regained the cheerful heights that it had reached earlier that day.

She simply couldn't get Percy out of her anxious mind. His presence in Paris had disturbed her deeply. He was dangerous.

Part of the deal that he had been forced to accept, back when they had defeated him, was that he would never bother Abbie or her again.

But that was then.

Now however, through this odd twist of fate, their paths had crossed once more. And Jane's gut told her that Percy Yates was going to create trouble.

Chapter Thirteen

The days that followed had Jane in a constant state of fear and despair. Every waking moment, terrible memories haunted her mind. Memories of that dark and horrible time in their past, when she and Abbie had been caught in Percy's wicked clutches.

And the nights were no better, for she spent countless hours tossing and turning in bed, plagued by nightmares.

All because Percy Yates had resurfaced, materialising from the mists of the past like some evil spectre.

Curse that man, she caught herself thinking more than once. Why did he have to show up again, in a beautiful place like Paris? He should have just crawled underneath a rock, never to reappear.

She longed for Sunday, when she could meet up with Georgie and confide in him. Hopefully, he would know what to do and succeed in bringing some clarity to the tangled mess of her emotions.

The week passed by slowly and in an anxious blur. But finally, Sunday came along. As soon as she could leave the house, Jane hurried to their usual meeting spot in their favourite park.

I hope he's here, she thought, quickening her step even more when she passed the park gates. After a week of fretting and worrying, she really needed a listening ear and a soft shoulder to lean on.

She sighed with relief the moment she caught sight of him. He was sitting on a bench, engrossed in a book.

"Georgie!" she called out immediately.

He looked up from his book and greeted her with a warm smile, a sparkle of joy twinkling in his eyes. Snapping the book shut, he stood up and held out his arms for an embrace. They met in a warm hug, finding comfort in each other's presence.

"I'm so happy to see you," he whispered close to her ear.

"As am I," she said, nestling against his shoulder. "Oh, Georgie, you have no idea what I've been through this week."

He pulled back slightly, concern etched onto his face. "What happened, my darling? You seem troubled."

Taking a deep breath, Jane mustered her courage and uttered the words that had been echoing through her mind for days. "Percy is in Paris."

Georgie's eyes widened in surprise. "Percy? You mean Percy Yates? That vile man who tried to ruin you and your sister?"

Jane nodded. "Yes, the very same."

"How do you know he's here? Did you see him?"

"I met him, Georgie. I met Percy."

"What?! When?"

"Last Sunday. I didn't plan to run into him, but it just happened."

"How? And where? Please Jane, tell me everything."

"I will," she answered. "But can we sit down first, please? I've slept awfully bad all week long and my legs are so weak I'm afraid I might faint."

"Of course, of course," he said. Taking her by the hand, he gently guided her back towards the bench he had been sitting on when she arrived at the park.

When he smiled at her affectionately, she lowered her eyes. She felt guilty. Explaining to Georgie how she had met Percy meant that she would also need to tell him about the afternoon she had spent with Mr Dubois that day.

It had all been perfectly innocent, of course. She and Mr Dubois were merely friends, and he had simply acted as her guide. Nothing but a kind gesture of helpfulness towards someone who was still a stranger in the city he called home.

But then why was she feeling so awkward about confessing the matter to Georgie?

Taking a deep breath, she started telling the story, apprehensive of how he would react. "It happened last Sunday, late in the afternoon. Percy was waiting for someone in the lobby of the Hôtel Faubourg. He saw me before I could think what to do."

"Wait," Georgie said, frowning. "What were you doing in the Faubourg?"

"I'd been invited to dinner there."

"By whom?"

"Mr Dubois."

"Mr Dubois? That name sounds familiar."

"He's the French gentleman I met on the boat and who very kindly accompanied me on the train to Paris. You met him briefly at the station, remember?"

"Why did he invite you to dinner?"

"He was just being nice to me," she replied, becoming irritated by Georgie's obvious jealous tone.

"When did he invite you? Did he send you a letter at the Crawfords? He didn't come calling on you personally, did he?"

"Georgie, stop it," she bristled. Here she was trying to tell him about running into Percy and how it had upset her the whole week. And all he could think of was Mr Dubois.

"It was the other way around, if you must know," she said testily. "I went calling on him."

Georgie gaped at her. "What on earth did you do that for?"

"Because I had no one else to turn to. I was a sad and sorry wreck after having to deal with Lady Crawford all week long, and I was desperate to get out of the house. But you weren't available to take me out, remember? You were too busy at the patisserie."

She was feeling petulant and the words came flowing out of her angrily. She had done nothing wrong. If Georgie had been there for her that day, she would never have needed to set foot in the lobby of the Faubourg.

And then she wouldn't have run into Percy.

"What else was I supposed to do?" she continued. "I tried to go out on my own, but circumstances quickly made me change my mind. Then I remembered that Mr Dubois had very graciously offered me his card, and I went to see him at his hotel."

"And that's when you saw Percy?" Georgie asked. He sounded more subdued now, but there was still an undertone of mistrust in his voice.

"No, that happened much later. After Mr Dubois had taken me on a lovely tour of Paris."

Involuntarily, Jane stuck out her chin, as if she was daring him to take issue with this fresh piece of information.

Georgie sighed. "Darling, I told you to be careful with these Frenchmen. They're not always as honourable as they appear to be."

"It was all perfectly honourable and proper, I assure you," she bit back. "And besides, we had a chaperone the entire time."

She doubted whether Petit Jean could be regarded as a suitable chaperone. And the boy hadn't stayed for dinner. But she wasn't going to tell Georgie that.

Deeming she had the advantage over him now, she said, "Are you going to insist on being a jealous grouch? Or can I finally tell you about Percy?"

"Sorry," he replied, staring at his feet in shame. "Please continue."

"Thank you. So after our tour around Paris, Mr Dubois very politely invited me to join him for dinner at the hotel. And that's when I saw Percy."

"He recognised you as well?"

"Yes, he did. From the moment he laid eyes on me."

"What did he say to you? Was he unpleasant?"

"Percy Yates is always unpleasant," she replied. "He wasn't mean or angry with me. But you know what he's like: mocking grins and snide remarks all the time. And still full of himself."

Georgie nodded, gazing into the distance with a worried frown on his brow. "Did he seem resentful to you in any way? Do you think he blames you for the fact he had to leave London?"

"Who knows," she shrugged. "He's impossible to read. That scoundrel is an expert in putting up a shiny façade."

"We should tell Joe and Abbie. We ought to write them a letter and ask them for their advice."

"No," Jane replied in a heartbeat. "There's no need to get my sister involved."

"But don't you think they should be aware of the situation?" Georgie insisted. "Percy Yates isn't a man to be trifled with."

Jane shook her head. "If we tell them, Abbie will want me to leave Paris immediately and travel back to England."

"That might be the more sensible option, you know."

"No, I shan't have it! I've only just got here and I'm not willing to leave yet. Not on account of some bigheaded windbag like Percy Yates."

"He's a dangerous crook, Jane. Have you forgotten the things he tried to do to you and Abbie?"

"I haven't forgotten anything, don't you worry. But I refuse to turn tail and run off. Paris is much too exciting. And I want to see more of it before I'll even contemplate leaving."

"Is it Paris you find exciting?" he asked. "Or Mr Dubois?"

Jane gasped. "Take that back! What a mean thing to say, Georgie." Tears began to prick her eyes. But she refused to cry in front of him.

"I love you, and you alone," she said hotly. "But Mr Dubois has shown me more kindness in one single afternoon than you have in all the weeks that I've been in Paris yet."

Duly chastised, he lowered his head and mumbled, "You're right. I apologise. The fatigue from work got the better of me."

"Apology accepted," she said primly.

Lovingly, he took her hands, brought them to his lips and placed a soft kiss on each hand.

"What else did Percy say?" he asked after they had smiled at each other. "Did he give you any trouble at all?"

"Not really. He told me he had come to Paris to build a new life for himself. And after that, the conversation more or less ended. He said good night and left."

She decided not to mention the fact that Mr Dubois had initially asked Percy to join them for dinner. Or that the two men were in business together.

"Sounds like it wasn't too bad then," Georgie said. "Where was Mr Dubois during this time by the way? Was he with you?"

"Yes, he was right by my side," she replied, trying to sound casual.

"And what did he think of Percy? He must have noticed that you were upset?"

Bother.

Now she had no other choice but to tell him the whole truth. "Actually," she began, "Mr Dubois and Percy turned out to be business partners."

Georgie's jaw just about dropped to the ground. "Business partners? Now I'm even more worried. Jane, we need to inform your sister."

"No, we don't. The fact that Percy and Mr Dubois are business partners doesn't mean anything. It's just one of those odd and silly coincidences in life. That's all."

"I'm not so sure."

"Well, I am. Percy looked just as surprised to see me as I was to see him. If this meeting had been pre-arranged, he would have turned it into something much more dramatic."

Georgie sighed and relented. "If you say so, my darling. But what do you intend to do about Percy, if you don't want to involve Abbie and Joe?"

"I don't know," she said, biting her lip. "Maybe we won't need to do anything about him. It was just a chance encounter. An isolated incident that won't happen again. And don't forget, part of his agreement with Joe was that he'd leave us in peace. He gave us his word."

"I must say I'm doubtful," he replied, pursing his lips. "I don't place a lot of value in the word of men like Percy Yates. But if you insist, then I'll respect your decision."

"Thank you. I'm glad you see it my way."

"However," he said, taking her by the hands and giving them a squeeze. "For your own safety, you should stay away from Percy."

"Of course. I wasn't planning on inviting him to tea, you know," she replied, rolling her eyes.

"And that also means not seeing Mr Dubois any more," he added, giving her a look.

To avoid his gaze, she turned her head away, hesitating. Her afternoon with friendly Mr Dubois had been so much fun.

"Jane? It's too dangerous. If the two of them are business partners–"

"I know," she sighed. "You're right. We shouldn't tempt fate. I'll stop seeing Mr Dubois."

"Good girl," he said before planting a tender kiss on her forehead.

She let out a long and frustrated sigh. Just because Georgie was right didn't mean she had to be happy about it.

"So what have you got planned for us today?" she asked, trying to push all thoughts of Percy and Mr Dubois aside.

"I haven't got any plans per se. We can do whatever you wish. Do you feel like visiting some of the art galleries?"

"I'm more in the mood to have a quiet wander around, to be honest. Let's go somewhere romantic. The art galleries can wait until another time. Perhaps next week?"

"Ah, yes. About that," he began. "Bad news, I'm afraid. I'll need to work again next Sunday."

She glared at him. "Don't tell me," she responded sarcastically. "Another banquet? Who is it this time? The Tsar of Russia?"

"That's not fair, Jane."

"Oh, and what about you leaving me on my own then? Is that fair? Sunday is the only time of the week we can see each other, Georgie."

"I know, but–"

"Why don't you tell your precious Maître Leblanc that you can't work on Sundays? Don't you deserve a day of rest like everybody else?"

"I can't make demands like that. I'm only an apprentice. And besides, I'm learning so much."

She rose to her feet, fed up with his excuses. "It's a pity you're not learning to set the right priorities then."

"Jane, I–"

"Good day, Georgie," she said, turning to leave. "Hopefully, you'll be able to spare me half an hour in two weeks."

With an angry little huff, she marched away from him. Her heart was a confusing jumble of bitter sadness and hot anger. And by the time she was halfway home, she found herself beginning to regret her hasty departure.

Perhaps I should have given him a chance, she thought. *And perhaps I shouldn't have been so angry with him.*

But then again, she had her pride. Tears threatened to spill from her eyes, but she fiercely blinked them away. She would prove to him that she could be strong.

Chapter Fourteen

The following Sunday arrived, painting the clear Parisian sky with hues of vibrant blue. But the fine weather failed to lift Jane's spirits. Her heart remained heavy with the weight of the unresolved argument from the previous week.

And though she longed to reconcile with Georgie, her wounded pride held her captive within the confines of her own sorrow.

Dreamily gazing through the small window of her modest bedroom, she imagined herself going for a walk with Georgie. On a lovely day like this one, they could stroll through the park, admire the window displays of the expensive shops, and then sit down outside one of those lovely little cafés.

He would take her hand in his, gaze deep into her eyes, and tell her how much he loved her. Who knew, it might even turn out to be the moment when he asked her to marry him.

How adorably romantic that would be, she sighed happily, if he proposed to her right here in Paris.

"The mistress wants to see you," a sneering voice behind her said in French.

Startled out of her daydream with a nasty jolt, Jane spun round. Marie, the loathsome kitchen maid, stood in the open doorway, smirking at her.

"You could have knocked," Jane bristled. "It's very rude to enter someone's room without knocking."

Marie shrugged, before shamelessly letting her eyes wander around the bedroom. "Fancy having a room all to yourself. I have to share with three others."

That's because you're a simple kitchen skivvy and I'm a governess, Jane would have loved to reply. But she knew better than to antagonise someone like Marie.

"Anyhow," the maid continued. "As I said, the mistress wants to see you in the drawing room. And she seemed to be in a bad mood."

Lady Crawford is always in a bad mood, Jane thought. But she didn't say that out loud to Marie. Because the troublesome maid would tell everyone that Mademoiselle Lee had been gossiping about the mistress.

"Thank you, Marie," Jane said politely. "I'll go and see her ladyship at once." Then she paused and asked, "Why are you still in the house, by the way? It's Sunday. Shouldn't you be out with your friends?"

Marie scowled. "Even on Sundays they always want to have one or two of us around. In case milord or milady need anything. And it's my turn this week."

From the annoyed look on the maid's face, Jane could tell the girl hated it. "My sympathies," she said, hoping her smile would mask the sarcasm in her voice.

Marie simply turned up her nose at Jane and disappeared, leaving the door open. Jane watched her go, wondering what could have caused the girl's heart to be so bitter. Everyone had their own burdens to bear, she supposed.

With a sigh, Jane turned away from the open door and crossed her room. She smoothed down her modest dress, adjusting the collar and plucking at imaginary specks of fabric. She glanced at her reflection in the small, slightly tarnished mirror, taking a moment to gather her thoughts.

What could Lady Crawford possibly want to speak to her about this time? More likely than not, the woman was just bored and looking for a victim to have an argument with.

Lucky me, Jane sneered silently as she went down the stairs.

Approaching the grand double doors leading to the drawing room, she hesitated for a moment. Each encounter with Lady Crawford felt like stepping onto a battlefield. Taking a deep breath, Jane composed herself and knocked.

"Enter," Lady Crawford's chilly voice answered.

Jane turned the brass knob and pushed the door open. To her surprise, Alistair was present in the room as well. The young boy was looking gloomy, and he kept his eyes down.

The poor lad probably got another stern dressing-down from his mother, she thought. *Don't worry though, Alistair. I'll be next.*

"You asked to see me, milady?" she said politely.

"Indeed," came the reply, haughty and scornful as always. "I realise it's Sunday and all that. But this matter simply cannot wait until tomorrow."

Jane shot a concerned glance at Alistair, before turning back to Lady Crawford. "That sounds most serious, milady."

"Serious doesn't even come close, Miss Lee. My son's future is what's at stake here."

"Alistair's future? Sweet heavens, how may I help?"

Lady Crawford's cold eyes bore into Jane, as if they were trying to gaze into the depths of her soul. "It has come to my attention that Alistair has been devoting a considerable amount of time to the study of history lately. Is this true?"

"Yes, that's correct, milady."

"Ah! So you don't deny it?"

Jane frowned, not understanding what Lady Crawford was making a fuss about. "Alistair loves history, ma'am. It's by far his favourite subject."

"And you encourage him in this obsession?"

Sensing a trap, Jane decided she needed to tread carefully. "I try to provide the children with a balanced and well-rounded curriculum. But history is Alistair's passion. So I use it as a reward for him."

"A reward?"

"Yes, ma'am. I reward hard work and good behaviour by letting him read additional history books of his own choosing, for instance."

Jane sent a proud look in Alistair's direction, but the boy kept staring at his feet. "He's astonishingly knowledgeable for his age, I assure you," she smiled.

"I've heard quite enough, Miss Lee," Lady Crawford fumed angrily. "I won't have you turn my son into a bookworm. Alistair is destined for greatness, and he shall one day inherit his father's title. History is of no use to him."

"With respect, milady, I beg to differ." Knowing how much Alistair loved history, Jane felt the need to stand up for him. It was probably foolish of her to try, she realised. But the urge was too strong to resist.

"Surely, studying history can help to fuel his curiosity," Jane argued. "It will sharpen his thinking skills, and refine his understanding of the world around him."

"My son is to become a Lord, Miss Lee. Not some stuffy scholar." Lady Crawford's eyes narrowed, hardening her cruel aristocratic face even further. "This nonsense shall stop, here and now."

Jane's heart sank. How could she possibly expect someone as irrational and rigid as Lady Crawford to see reason? It was a lost cause.

Lowering her eyes, she didn't notice the mean little grin that spread across Lady Crawford's thin lips. "Furthermore," the heartless woman said, "I want you to be the one to tell Alistair."

Jane's head shot back up. "Ma'am?"

"You heard me, Miss Lee. I want you to tell my son that his foolish infatuation with history needs to end. He doesn't seem to respect his mother in this regard, but perhaps he will listen to you."

Jane wanted to lash out and wipe the insufferable smugness from her ladyship's façade. What a cruel, wicked and petty thing to do, she seethed inside.

She's jealous, Jane knew. *She's jealous that I have a better relationship with her son than she has.*

"Miss Lee? I'm waiting," Lady Crawford said. "Tell Alistair that history isn't good for him."

Hating herself for doing this to the boy, Jane said, "Alistair, history isn't good for you." Her words were flat, and devoid of any degree of conviction. But she thought she saw him wince nonetheless.

"Come now," Lady Crawford said. "You can do better than that, Miss Lee. Tell him history isn't a worthy pursuit for the heir to a Lord."

"But why?" Alistair suddenly demanded with angry tears in his eyes. "Why can't I study history? I like reading about people and places and discoveries from long ago."

"Darling," Lady Crawford said, her tone soothing but firm. "You must understand it's for your own good. Your father and I have great expectations for you. And we cannot have you burying your nose in dusty old books all day long."

"Those dusty old books are more fun and more interesting than you are," the boy snapped. "I hate you."

Jane gasped. "Alistair, you mustn't say that."

"Enough," Lady Crawford shrieked. "Go to your room, Alistair. And stay there until you've regained your senses."

Deliberately stomping his feet, Alistair headed for the door. Jane could see the tears rolling down his reddened cheeks.

"And no more history," his mother barked at his back. "None, do you hear? You've had enough to last you a lifetime."

Without bothering to reply, Alistair slammed the door as he left. In his wake, an oppressive silence took hold of the drawing room.

Jane waited for Lady Crawford to speak first. The lecture she was bound to receive would be unpleasant, she knew that much.

"This is all your fault, Miss Lee," Lady Crawford said, fixing Jane with eyes as cold as steel. "Alistair's behaviour towards me was unacceptable. And you're to blame for it."

"Milady, I–"

"I haven't finished yet! In our previous conversation, I warned you about this very thing. I told you that you were too soft with the children. Do you remember?"

"Yes, ma'am. I do."

"What transpired here today is the direct result of your unsatisfactory performance. A severe lack of discipline has caused Alistair to rebel against his own mother. Heartbreaking is what it was."

From a fold in her expensive dress, Lady Crawford produced a delicate silk handkerchief. She dabbed it elegantly at the crocodile tear that had appeared in the corner of her eye.

"My patience with you is running thin, Miss Lee. I consider myself to be a generous and forgiving employer. But if you are unable to keep the children under control, then you will leave me with no choice than to terminate your position. Is that understood?"

"Perfectly, ma'am," Jane replied with a modest nod.

"Leave me now," Lady Crawford said, giving her a dismissive wave of the hand. "I need peace and quiet to recover from this dreadful incident."

And a few glasses of sherry, no doubt, Jane thought as she bobbed a quick curtsy.

After she had left the room, with her nerves in tatters, tears sprang to her eyes, blurring her vision even as she rushed through the corridor.

How could Lady Crawford be so cruel towards her son? All poor Alistair had done was defend his love of history. But his heartless mother made it sound like he had committed the worst crime imaginable.

Lost in sorrow, Jane didn't notice the figure hiding in the shadows until it was too late. A foot extended itself just as she walked past, and she stumbled over it, barely catching herself before she fell.

"Marie," Jane growled when she recognised the culprit.

The French maid flashed an evil grin at her. "It sounds like you might be going back to England soon, Mademoiselle Governess."

"Have you been listening at the door?" Jane gasped, shocked at the girl's unabashed rudeness.

"*Et alors?*" Marie shrugged. "So what?" She stuck out her chin, arrogantly defying Jane to cause a scene in the corridor, where Lady Crawford might hear it.

Refusing to take the bait, Jane gritted her teeth and stormed up to her room, her hurried steps fuelled by anger and indignation.

Throwing open the door to her small bedroom, Jane quickly snatched her shawl and hat. She had to escape from this horrible household with its cruel tyrant of a mistress – if only for a little while.

She longed to be outside, where there was sunshine, fresh air and friendly people with smiling faces.

Dashing out of the grand house, she kept walking at a brisk pace until she spotted a cab. She hailed it and climbed into the carriage.

"Where to, Miss?" the driver asked.

"The Hôtel Faubourg, please," she replied before pressing her back against the old leather seat and letting out a long sigh of relief.

Chapter Fifteen

She knew it was dangerous to seek out Mr Dubois. Even though, so far, the Frenchman had proven himself to be perfectly trustworthy. His English business associate however was a different matter altogether. Percy Yates was evil through and through.

But Jane didn't care about Percy, or his dirty tricks, as she made her way to the Hôtel Faubourg. It was Mr Dubois she wanted to see. His wit and his charm would cheer her up.

Georgie's words of warning echoed through her mind, even as the carriage pulled up in front of the hotel. She had more or less promised him to stop seeing Mr Dubois. But that was before Lady Crawford and that awful Marie had ruined her Sunday.

Now she yearned for an escape – a few blissful hours spent bathing in the liveliness of Parisian street life. Guided by the man who seemed to know all the best sights, as well as the most interesting and unusual places.

"Ah, Mademoiselle Lee," he beamed as she walked into the lobby. He was sitting in a large leather wingback chair, enjoying a cigar and a glass of cognac. There was no sign of Percy, Jane was pleased to note.

"Mr Dubois, I sincerely apologise for troubling you again so soon. You must think me a troublesome nuisance."

"Not at all, Mademoiselle Lee. As a matter of fact, I was just thinking about you."

"You were?"

"Yes, I was contemplating how difficult it must be for someone as bright and spirited as yourself to live and work in that stuffy old house. You must be a remarkably strong young woman."

"Not half as remarkable or strong as you seem to think, I'm afraid. Lady Crawford can be quite challenging at times."

Mr Dubois chuckled. "Her reputation is well-known. And she's been the topic of many whispered conversations among the *beau monde* of Paris, I assure you."

"Really?" Jane asked, surprised to hear this. "That offers some consolation then, I suppose."

"And why is that? Have you been on the receiving end of Lady Crawford's infamous wrath?"

"On several occasions, unfortunately. The last one as recent as today, I regret to say."

"Ah, *ma pauvre*. You poor girl," he commiserated. "Is that the reason why you are here? To seek a moment of solace and distraction?"

"Is it that obvious?" she asked, smiling shyly. "Given the circumstances, I didn't know who else to turn to. Oh, I do hope you don't mind, Monsieur Dubois?"

"Not in the slightest, Mademoiselle Lee." Placing a hand over his heart, he declared, "As my name is Pierre Dubois, I promise to help you. We shall talk no more about this nasty English dragon lady."

Offering her his arm like a true gentleman, he continued, "Come, Paris is waiting. With me as your guide, this marvellous city shall heal your injured soul."

She couldn't suppress a short giggle as she accepted his arm. "Thank you, Monsieur. You certainly have a way with words."

If Mr Dubois had been younger and if Georgie hadn't already laid claim to her heart...

Instantly pushing aside that shameful thought, she let herself be whisked away – plunging into the warm, throbbing heart of the city, in the company of her trusted escort.

Soon, Jane's heart was dancing with joy as they embarked on their whirlwind tour. They ambled along lively streets and basked in the city's undeniable charm. Enveloped by the sights, sounds and scents of Paris, Jane forgot all about her worries.

Eventually, they reached the carefully manicured paths and lusciously green open spaces of the magnificent Tuileries Garden, next to the Louvre.

"For centuries, this used to be the palace garden – for the exclusive use of kings and queens and their nobles," Mr Dubois said, while Jane stood and stared in awe at the enormous park.

"Then we got rid of the kings and queens," he added with a grin. "And now everyone can enjoy this beautiful garden."

So at least some good has come from your revolution, she thought, keeping the words to herself to avoid any risk of causing offence.

A sudden burst of laughter caught her attention, drawing her gaze towards a young couple seated on a nearby bench.

Their fingers intertwined, their faces mere inches apart, the two lovers shared a fond kiss – a sight that caused a blush to creep up Jane's cheeks.

"Scandalous," she whispered under her breath. The word had escaped from her mouth almost as an instinctive reaction. Even though her heart yearned for the same kind of tenderness.

Oh, how she longed to be in Georgie's arms – and to feel the warmth of his lips against her own.

"Is something the matter, Miss Lee?" Mr Dubois asked, following her line of sight.

"Nothing, nothing at all," she stammered, forcing her eyes away from the enamoured pair. "It's just– Well, one would never see such a public display of affection in England."

"That is because the French are more passionate than the British, Mademoiselle," he said with an amused smile. "We embrace life, and we aren't afraid to show our emotions. Unlike the English. You are so dry, so repressed."

Jane was startled by the intensity of those last words of his. The way he had said them... Was that just his Gallic pride speaking? Or was there something more?

"Do you truly believe that, Monsieur?" she ventured carefully. "About all British people?"

He looked at her and smiled, "Not all of them, obviously. You, for instance, Mademoiselle – you are different. You possess a spark that sets you apart from the rest. And your vibrant spirit refuses to be confined by the conventions of society."

Jane blushed, feeling both flattered and apprehensive. "Thank you, Monsieur. I'm honoured that you have a high opinion of me. Although I'm not entirely convinced whether I'm actually worthy of so much esteem."

"But of course you are, Mademoiselle Lee. If only more people were like you. Ah, what a beautiful world we would live in then."

"Now you're really overdoing the flattery, Mr Dubois," she quipped.

"*Pas du tout,*" he assured her solemnly. "Not at all. The world is in dire need of good people who are pure in heart and noble in character. People like yourself... or Lord Crawford."

Jane's ears pricked up at the mention of her employer's name. "Do you know him?"

"I know *of* him. Unlike his wife, his lordship is a well-respected and much admired man."

"I must confess I have yet to meet him in person," Jane said. "I only ever deal with Lady Crawford, unfortunately."

"From what I've heard, Lord Crawford is a formidable figure. A man of vision." Mr Dubois gazed into the distance. "What I wouldn't give for a chance to have a few words in private with him."

"I thought you didn't like the British. Or the nobility," Jane said half-jokingly.

"But a man like Lord Crawford transcends all borders and titles, Mademoiselle. He stands far above such trivial details."

"You really mean it, don't you?" she asked as she watched his solemn face.

"Upon my word, yes, I am most sincere. To be able to exchange ideas with Lord Crawford?

Why, a conversation like that would benefit not just myself and his lordship personally. Both our nations as a whole would stand to gain."

Duly impressed, an idea took hold in Jane's mind. Clearing her throat, she said, "Mr Dubois, would you like me to introduce you to his lordship?"

His head whipped round to her, surprise and delight twinkling in his eyes. "You would do that for me, Mademoiselle?"

"I could certainly try," she replied somewhat hesitatingly.

"Such an opportunity would be extraordinary indeed." He paused and shook his head. "But no, I cannot ask this of you. It is too much. Please, do not go through such trouble on my account."

"Oh, but I want to," she said eagerly. "You have done so much for me. And you have been tremendously generous with your time. This way, I can finally repay you for your efforts."

"Mademoiselle, I give my time freely. And as for my efforts? What value do they have? Very little, no?"

"I insist. Please, Mr Dubois. You must let me return the favour. It's the least I can do for you."

Softly, he took her hands in his and smiled at her. "Miss Lee, your kindness and bravery are truly limitless."

With flushing cheeks, she returned his smile. His praise caused her heart to flutter and her spine to tingle with joy.

It feels good to be appreciated, she thought to herself. Especially after suffering so much unpleasantness at the hands of Lady Crawford.

"Very well then," she said. "I shall make the introduction. I don't know how yet, to be perfectly honest with you. But I'll do my best."

"If anyone can find a way, it's you," he replied confidently.

As they continued their stroll through the Tuileries in companionable silence, Jane's mind was teeming with fleeting ideas and conflicting emotions.

The blooming flowers and lush greenery of the park failed to capture her attention the way they had done when they first arrived. Instead, she was racking her brain to come up with a clever plan.

Or any old plan, for that matter.

How was she supposed to arrange a meeting between these two men, when she was nothing but a simple governess?

I've never even seen Lord Crawford, she realised nervously, making the prospect seem all the more daunting to her.

But she had made a commitment to Mr Dubois, so there was no more turning back. Not after he had revealed just how highly he thought of her. Failure simply wasn't an option.

He would lose all respect for her, she thought fretfully, if she proved to be the sort of person who couldn't keep a promise.

It was her duty to try. And to succeed.

The future of their friendship depended on it.

Even so, a small part of her wondered if perhaps this time she had got herself into something far too ambitious. Had she been too rash?

Don't be foolish, she told herself. Mr Dubois had said that Lord Crawford was different from his peers. Surely, someone like that would welcome the opportunity to exchange thoughts and ideas with a man as interesting as Mr Dubois?

The only thing she needed to do was come up with an excuse to actually meet the man. How hard could that be? After all, she worked in his own household, didn't she?

She would manage. One way or another.

Chapter Sixteen

In the end, after several days of contemplating the issue, Jane decided that the best plan was the simplest one. She would wander into Lord Crawford's study, pretending to be lost in the enormous house.

That way, she would be able to strike up a casual conversation with him – or so she hoped. Once they were talking, she would bring up Mr Dubois, sing her friend's praises and then suggest an introduction.

Easy.

It wasn't much of a plan, she conceded to herself. And she could plainly see the many flaws in it. But it was all she had. And even a poor plan was better than no plan at all.

It was actually Alistair who had, unwittingly, given her the idea. The boy had told a story about a pirate who managed to lay his hands on a treasure simply by marching into a coastal fortress and bluffing his way to the vaults.

She and Penelope had laughed, because it was a funny story – and probably one that he had made up all by himself. But something about the idea behind it had appealed to Jane.

Walking into a place under a false pretence and then achieving your goal with some fancy talk? She could do that, she thought.

"Children, can I trust you to keep a promise to me?" she asked in a hushed tone.

The pair of them drew closer and nodded.

"Of course you can, Miss Lee," Penelope said.

"*Especially* when it's you, Miss Lee," Alistair added.

"Splendid. Listen, there's an important matter I need to take care of downstairs. And I'd rather not let it wait." She felt slightly guilty about leaving the children on their own while she went on her stealthy mission.

But needs must.

"How can we help, Miss?" Alistair whispered, his eyes twinkling with excitement.

"I'd like you to promise me that you'll both be very sweet while I'm away. I shan't be long, but I don't want any mischief in the meantime."

"We promise to be on our best behaviour for you, Miss," Penelope said.

"I knew I could count on you," Jane smiled. "Penny, why don't you grab a history book off the shelf and read to your brother?"

Alistair's voice dropped to a barely audible whisper. "But Mama said I wasn't allowed to read any more history, remember?"

"It's your sister who'll do the reading," Jane replied with a grin and a wink. "You're merely listening. Your Mama didn't say anything about listening, did she?"

The children giggled with delight, so they quickly covered their mouths to muffle the sound – in case anyone was eavesdropping at the door.

"Right, I'm off," Jane said. "Don't forget your promise. I'll be back soon." Giving them one last reassuring smile, she left the nursery.

As she walked down the stairs to Lord Crawford's study, her stomach started to twist and turn with nervousness. She was about to take a huge gamble – and she knew it.

But she had made her choices, and that was it. If she changed her mind now and turned back, she wasn't sure if she would be able to work up the courage and try again once she had a better plan.

First though, she thought, *I'll have to find him.* She had no idea whether or not he was actually at home. And even if he was in, then she needed to catch him alone.

As luck would have it, Lord Crawford was in his study that morning. Through the open door she could see him sitting at his enormous desk, poring over some documents.

There didn't seem to be anyone else around.

Now or never, then.

Standing in the open doorway, she took a deep breath and walked in.

"Oh, pardon me, Lord Crawford," she said, pretending to be surprised to find him there. "I seem to have lost my way."

He glanced up from his work and looked at her. His gaze was calm and open.

Now there's a man who is used to being in control of any situation, Jane thought.

"I was on my way to the library," she explained. "In order to fetch a particular book for the children. But I seem to have taken a wrong turn."

"Down the hall, second door on your left," he said drily while his eyes drifted back to the papers on his desk.

"Thank you, milord. I admit I feel like a bit of a fool for getting lost indoors," she said, desperately trying to get some sort of conversation going. "But I've only been in my position as governess for a few weeks, you see."

He looked up again and smiled politely at her. "The house is rather big, isn't it?"

"It most certainly is, milord," she replied quickly. She tried to maintain eye contact with him, but his attention had already returned to his work.

Jane could feel a nervous heat rising up from her neck. And the palms of her shaky hands were beginning to sweat. But she kept her voice steady and pressed on.

"The children are doing well, by the way, milord. Alistair is showing great promise, and Penelope is a delightfully sweet girl."

This time, Lord Crawford didn't even look up. "That's nice to hear," he said flatly while he continued to study his paperwork. He reached for his pen and carefully scribbled a note on one of the sheets.

Jane hesitated. She had hoped that mentioning his children would have elicited more of a response from him. But he seemed more interested in his papers.

What else could she do? What more could she say? *Think, Jane. Think!*

"Now, if that will be all..." he said without as much as a cursory glance in her direction. Jane knew enough about the relationship between master and servant to understand that this was his way of ending the exchange.

"Yes, that's all, milord," she replied. "My apologies for troubling you."

He didn't reply. Not even with a little mumbling sound of acknowledgement. It was as if, to him, she wasn't in the room any more.

Her hopes of bringing up Mr Dubois were shattered, lying on the floor before her like invisible pieces of broken glass. Turning around, she left the study.

What a miserable failure, she muttered silently. *Why would I even think a brainless plan like that could have worked?*

"Miss Lee," a livid voice in the corridor hissed.

Jane froze. Lady Crawford stood before her, with glaring eyes that seemed to be firing bolts of pure hatred at her.

"What were you doing in there?"

"I–" Jane stammered, opening and closing her mouth, but not knowing what to say.

"To the drawing room," Lady Crawford snarled through gritted teeth. "This very instant."

Filled with dread, Jane followed Lady Crawford, who went stomping off to the drawing room with fast and angry strides.

"Close those doors," her ladyship ordered after she had burst into the drawing room like a furious whirlwind. She fixed Jane with a deadly stare.

"Now tell me. Why were you in my husband's study when you should have been with the children?"

"I was asking for directions, milady." Jane knew it sounded feeble the moment the words left her mouth.

"Directions? What sort of directions?"

"To the library. I was on my way over there, but then I got lost. And I wandered into your husband's study instead."

"You got lost on your way to the library?"
"Yes, milady." Jane was sure that her flushing cheeks were betraying her deceit.
"Do you expect me to believe that? You're a liar, Miss Lee."
"Milady, I–"
"Silence! You're a liar – and a hussy."
Jane gasped at the insult. Of all the horrible things to say...
"First you try to turn the children against me," Lady Crawford raged. "And now you're after my husband as well?"
Jane couldn't believe what she was hearing. That's why Lady Crawford was so angry with her? Because she assumed Jane was trying to carry on with Lord Crawford?
"Milady, that's ridiculous. I can assure you–"
"Ridiculous? You dare call me ridiculous, you disgraceful harlot? Have you forgotten your place? Do you picture yourself as the next Lady Crawford already?"
"Milady, please. That's not what I meant."
"Then what did you mean, pray tell?"
"I meant it was all perfectly innocent. Nothing improper took place between Lord Crawford and myself. Especially not... the sort of thing you wrongfully accused me of." Jane blushed at the mere thought of it. "I was only asking your husband the way to the library. I swear it's the truth."

Not the whole truth, she thought. But it wasn't a lie either. Not really anyway.

Through half-closed eyes, Lady Crawford glared suspiciously at Jane. The tense silence was mortifying, but Jane kept her shoulders straight.

"I suppose it's not inconceivable for someone as hare-brained as you to get lost on your way to the library," Lady Crawford conceded finally.

"Thank you, milady." She had never been so relieved to be called hare-brained before.

"But don't let me ever catch you going anywhere near my husband again," Lady Crawford warned her. "Or I'll scratch your eyes out. And then I'll personally drag you to the front door by your hair."

"I promise you that such drastic measures won't ever be necessary, milady."

"Let's hope not." Lady Crawford's gaze turned soft and drifted around the room. "And now I need something to mend my frazzled nerves. This nonsense of yours has rattled my sensitive disposition."

She went over to the drinks cabinet and poured herself a double sherry.

"Apologies for the distress I have caused you, milady," Jane said.

Lady Crawford dismissed her with an annoyed wave of the hand, while she downed her drink in one go with the other hand.

As Jane hurried to leave the room, she saw the mistress pouring out a second helping. The butler would soon be needing to refill that decanter, she guessed.

That was a narrow escape, she thought as she went back to the nursery while her cheeks burned with shame.

Pausing by the door, she rested her weary head against its smooth wooden surface. Inside, she could hear the children talking to each other. Penelope was patiently trying to read out loud from the book they had chosen, but Alistair kept interrupting her with questions and observations.

Sweet little angels, she thought.

Their innocent young happiness made Jane even more painfully aware of her own grief. Her plan had failed. And with Lady Crawford's blunt warning still ringing in her ears, she had little appetite for making another attempt.

How was she ever going to face Mr Dubois again?

And then of course, there was Georgie. She dreaded to think what he would have to say about this terrible fiasco.

Perhaps it's better if I don't tell him in the first place.

But the thought of keeping secrets from the man she loved brought a foul and bitter taste to her mouth. Her sister had done that in the past.

And Jane remembered all too well the misery it had caused.

Chapter Seventeen

The sun shone brightly in a cloudless sky, casting its glorious rays on the world below. It was a picture-perfect day, and the people of Paris – be they rich or poor – all seemed intent on making the most of this beautiful Sunday.

Inside Jane's heart however, a storm was brewing. She was on her way to meet up with Georgie in their favourite park.

And she hadn't forgotten how they had bickered the previous time. Annoyed by the fact that he needed to work on Sunday so often, she had walked away in a fit of anger.

In hindsight, it all seemed so silly and meaningless to her. Especially now, after the double Crawford disaster.

But had Georgie forgiven her in the meantime? Or would he be harbouring bad feelings towards her about their argument?

Not Georgie, she concluded. He wasn't the type to hold a grudge. On the contrary. Knowing him, she suspected he would be going out of his way to be extra nice to her.

It'll do me good to see him, she thought.

To hear his gentle voice talking sweet words of love to her. To watch his handsome face smiling at her. To feel the soft touch of his hands.

After her near disaster with Lady Crawford, Jane felt she needed all the tenderness she could get from Georgie.

And yet...

He was bound to sense her brooding unease. She wasn't a very good actress when it came to hiding her true feelings. And if he asked her what was troubling her, then what? She'd have no choice but to tell him about the sorry incident at the Crawfords.

But did that also mean she would need to confess she had gone to see Mr Dubois again?

And if so, would he understand? Would he sympathise with her, take her into his arms and speak soothing words of comfort?

Or would he be upset and tell her what an incredible fool she had been?

As she entered the park, she was hoping for the first. But her worried mind was better at imagining the second possibility.

Lost in her brooding thoughts, she didn't see him waiting for her by a statue up ahead. Georgie spotted her first and called out to her.

"Jane," he shouted happily.

She looked up and caught his fond smile. The sight of him temporarily chased away her anguish, and she quickened her pace to be with him.

"Georgie, thank heavens you're here," she sighed as they pressed hands.

"Why wouldn't I be here?" he laughed. "It's our Sunday together, isn't it? Look, I've even prepared something special for us." He picked up the basket that had been standing by his feet.

"What is it?"

"Why don't you see for yourself?" he said, lifting up a corner of the blanket covering the basket.

As soon as he did, the mouth-watering scent of freshly baked bread and cake reached her nose.

"You've made us a picnic? Oh Georgie, that's so sweet of you."

"There's bread and cheese and sausage; a bottle of wine too. Strawberries and some apples. And of course, cake. I baked that one myself. It's a special recipe I learned from Maître Leblanc."

"Then what are we waiting for?" she joked. "Let's find ourselves a good spot and enjoy all these delicious treats."

Beaming with joy, he offered her his arm and led her onto the grass, towards a small cluster of trees.

Satisfied that these would provide them with just the right amount of cool shade, he spread the blanket on the ground.

"Shall I help you?" she suggested.

"No, no," he said as he began to lay out their picnic. "You just sit there and relax, my darling. I want to spoil you silly today."

She rewarded him with a grateful smile, but inwardly, she winced with shame. Seeing all the effort he had put into this surprise only made her feel more guilty for what she needed to tell him.

"Any particular reason for all this?" she asked. "It's as if there's something to celebrate."

"Any opportunity to be with you is a reason to celebrate, Jane," he replied with a grin. "But as a matter of fact, yes, I do have some very good news to share."

"Oh? Tell me." She tore off a piece of the fresh bread and nibbled at it.

"I've had a talk with Maître Leblanc. About all these Sundays he wants me to work. Just like you told me I should."

She picked a strawberry and bit into its sweet, juicy flesh. "And? What did he say?"

"Well, it wasn't easy," Georgie replied. "And he wasn't too pleased at first. But..." He paused, deliberately dragging out the moment. Then a broad grin spread across his face. "I managed to convince him, eventually. He's giving me every Sunday off for the next three months."

"Georgie, that's wonderful."

"In exchange, I'll have to work longer hours most other days of the week of course," he added. "But that's a sacrifice I'm willing to make, if it means you and I can be together on Sundays."

Jane smiled, but the feeling of guilt that had been gnawing at her became even more painful.

"Are you happy, my darling?" he asked eagerly.

"Very happy," she said, putting as much conviction in the words as she could muster. Shame made her cheeks turn a rosy shade of red. But she was hoping that he would take that for a sign of excitement.

Seemingly unaware of her troubled mind, he took the bottle of wine and poured out two glasses. "A toast," he said. "To our love."

Awkwardly, she clinked her glass against his and took a sip while she tried to avoid his gaze.

"But now it's your turn," he said merrily. "How have you been? How is life at the Crawfords?"

Jane sighed and put her glass down. "Worse than ever, I'm afraid."

"I'm so sorry to hear that, my love. Are the children proving to be a handful?"

"No, Alistair and Penelope aren't the problem. They're so sweet, I couldn't have wished for a better pair of charges. It's Lady Crawford who's turning out to be more than a handful."

"What happened?"

Jane took another sip of her wine. She was going to need it to tell this tale. "She's just so...

difficult. A cruel and spiteful woman. And she does it on purpose, I'm sure of it. I think she actually enjoys making other people's lives miserable."

"Because she's such a miserable creature herself perhaps?" Georgie suggested.

"Probably. That would explain her drinking habit. I swear that woman guzzles more sherry than other people drink tea."

"So what did she do to upset you so much?"

"She accused me of trying to seduce her husband."

"What?! But why?"

"Simply because she saw me coming out of his study."

"Ridiculous!"

"That's what I said, too," Jane replied. "She didn't take it very well though."

"But you managed to convince her in the end? She didn't dismiss you from your position, did she?"

"I suspect she was very close to sacking me. But fortunately, she came to her senses – eventually, after I told her that I had only wandered into the study because I got lost on my way to the library."

"Good grief. You poor thing," he said as he grasped her hands and pressed a kiss on them. "It sounds like it must have been an awfully distressing ordeal for you."

"It was, believe me," Jane nodded. "She even said she'd scratch my eyes out if I ever came near Lord Crawford again."

"What a nasty woman," Georgie tutted. "Just because you got lost and accidentally entered the wrong room."

Jane hesitated. She had a choice to make. Leave it at that, carry on and enjoy their picnic.

Or...

Confess to him that the whole getting lost on her way to the library thing was just a ruse. But then she would have to tell him everything.

Blissful ignorance? Or the painful truth?

Pick your poison, Jane.

"The trouble is," she began, "I didn't *accidentally* wander into Lord Crawford's study. It was part of a plan. A foolish plan, I'll grant you that. But it was intentional nonetheless."

Georgie frowned. "I'm confused. Are you saying you actually meant to go into his study?"

"Yes."

"What for?"

"I wanted to talk to him."

"That makes sense, I suppose. After all, you're the governess of his children."

"It wasn't the children I wanted to talk to him about." Her breathing became more nervous, more shallow. "I wanted to try and arrange an introduction."

"To whom?"

Jane swallowed. "Mr Dubois."

Georgie's eyebrows shot up. "The Frenchman?! Why would you want to introduce him to Lord Crawford?"

Lowering her eyes, she replied, "Because he asked me to. He said he had some ideas he wanted to share with Lord Crawford. Ideas that could benefit both our nations."

"Jane, the man is Percy Yates' business partner, remember?"

"I know that. But he didn't mention Percy during–" She wanted to say during the time they had spent together, but that didn't seem wise to her. "During our conversation. Not even once."

"I bet he didn't," Georgie scoffed. "And when was this conversation? Did he come calling on you? At the Crawfords?"

"It was last Sunday," she replied, staring at her feet. "After I had gone to his hotel."

"Oh, Jane. I thought we had agreed you wouldn't see him again. On account of Percy. So why did you do it anyway?"

"Because Lady Crawford had been absolutely horrible to me and poor little Alistair that day." Tears began to roll down her cheeks as she remembered the scene in the drawing room. "And then Marie made things even worse. By pulling a dirty trick on me."

"Who's Marie?"

"She's one of the French maids. And she hates me. Just because I'm English and not a dressed-up tart like her and her dainty friends."

"But what have they got to do with you going to Mr Dubois?"

"Can't you see? I just had to get out of that house. I had to escape for a few hours and be with normal people. And the only one I could think of was Mr Dubois."

Georgie muttered something under his breath, which only added to her despair. Why couldn't he understand?

"He and I went for a nice long walk," she said, crying softly. "He took me on a tour of the city and we talked."

"And is that when he asked if you could introduce him to Lord Crawford?"

"Yes, but he was very polite about it. He even told me not to bother if it was too much trouble."

"How awfully thoughtful of him," Georgie sneered sarcastically. "But it did end up causing you trouble, didn't it? A whole lot of trouble, in fact."

His tone was becoming harsh and accusing.

"Yes, but that wasn't Mr Dubois' fault," Jane said, feeling the need to defend him. "If Lady Crawford hadn't seen me leaving her husband's study–"

"But she did see you, didn't she? Why did you take such a big risk, Jane – and jeopardise your own job – just so this Frenchman can rub elbows with his lordship?"

"I don't know," she said with a sobbing voice. Georgie's anger was beginning to frighten her. "I just wanted to do something in return for him. He's been so kind to me."

"Kind, bah," Georgie snorted. "Why do you insist on seeing that man, when we both agreed he's dangerous?"

"He isn't dangerous," she shot back. "Maybe if you spent a little more time with me on Sundays instead of at that confounded bakery, I wouldn't be in this mess right now."

"Don't go blaming the result of your own foolish decisions on me," he bristled.

"Why you inconsiderate beast! You have no regard whatsoever for my feelings or for the situation I'm in. Do you realise how hard it is to put up with someone like Lady Crawford or that abusive French maid?"

"If it's that hard, then perhaps you shouldn't have come to Paris in the first place. I've got enough problems on my mind already without having to play the part of a nursemaid catering to your every whim, you know."

Jane gasped. "What did you just say?"

He let out a frustrated sigh and shook his head. "Nothing. I spoke out of turn."

"You said I shouldn't have come to Paris. You don't want me here, is that it?"

"No, that's not what I meant."

"But you consider me to be a burden. You said so. Don't deny it, Georgie." Bitter tears of hurt and sorrow were streaming down her face.

"Jane, please–"

"I came to Paris because of us, Georgie. I came to Paris because I love you." She stood up, ready to leave. "But it seems you don't love me. So I guess this is adieu."

Bleary-eyed, she walked away from him.

"Jane, stop," he begged. "Come back."

Ignoring his plea, she started to run – aimlessly. She ran out of the park and into the streets of Paris. She had dreamt of this city once, thinking it would be a paradise of love and affection.

But that dream had been shattered. Destroyed by the words Georgie had spoken.

He didn't love her.

And that could only mean one thing.

Her life – together with the joy the two of them had shared these past few years – was nothing but a pointless lie.

Chapter Eighteen

"For once I wasn't too dissatisfied with your weekly report, Miss Lee." Lady Crawford sat on the sofa, looking at Jane as if she had just paid her the biggest compliment possible. And now she was expecting due gratitude.

"Thank you, milady," Jane replied flatly. She wasn't in the mood for these tiresome games. She wasn't in the mood for anything.

But she didn't want to provoke Lady Crawford's anger either. Because she was even less in the mood for one of her ladyship's furious rants. So she just played along.

"I was particularly pleased," Lady Crawford continued, "to note the absence of any History lessons last week."

Jane inclined her head politely in acknowledgement.

Nasty hag, she thought, remembering how mad and upset poor Alistair had been about being denied his favourite subject.

"Going forward," Lady Crawford said, "I feel the children could do with some more French. *N'est-ce pas?*" Finding that little addition at the end rather droll, she gave Jane a smug and self-important grin.

"Even more, milady? French is already part of their daily schedule. I make them read out loud and we have a short conversation in French every day."

"Then let's make that twice a day, Miss Lee. And in a more formal manner as well if you please: grammar and what have you. Reading out loud from a story book and having a simple conversation – that all seems a bit too playful to me."

"As you wish, milady," Jane replied simply. Inwardly however, she winced. Alistair and Penelope didn't like French very much. And they would outright hate it if she had to start teaching it the way their mother wanted it.

She suspected this was another one of those cruel and deliberate ploys of Lady Crawford, designed to make life harder for Jane and the children.

"Will that be all, ma'am?"

Lady Crawford didn't seem surprised by Jane's lack of fighting spirit. If anything, she looked rather pleased.

"Yes, that will be all for now, Miss Lee."

Jane wasn't sure, but she thought she saw a glimmer of triumphant glee on Lady Crawford's face.

She probably thinks she's finally broken me.

After a quick curtsy, Jane left the room and made her way back to the nursery – slowly, to give herself more time to gather her thoughts.

Inevitably however, her mind went to Georgie and the painful rift between them. Had their love truly ended? And if it had, then what use was there for her to stay on in Paris?

As soon as she had come back from their disastrous rendezvous at the park, she had started drafting her resignation letter. But before she got even halfway through it, she stopped and threw it away. Only to begin all over again an hour later.

This tiresome dance of doubt and indecision went on for days. The main thing that prevented her from tendering her resignation was the thought of the children: she would miss them awfully if she left.

Alistair and Penelope were such sweethearts.

As she reached the door to the nursery, she could hear them playing peacefully inside. The sound of their happy voices helped to soothe her own aching heart. Smiling, she quietly opened the door and then paused to watch them – unobserved.

They were both sitting on the floor, working on a jigsaw puzzle together while being the perfect vision of sweet harmony.

Jane sighed. Resigning would mean giving up moments like these. And what would she get in return? Nothing but loneliness back in England. And the dreadful prospect of slowly turning into an old spinster.

"Oh, hello, Miss Lee," Penelope said when she looked up and saw Jane standing by the door. "We're trying to put this jigsaw puzzle together."

"It's a dastardly big one," Alistair piped up.

"Ali," his sister gasped. "You shouldn't use that word."

"What word? Dastardly?"

"Hush! You're doing it again."

"But I've heard Papa say 'dastardly' many times."

"It's different for him," Penelope replied. "He's a grown-up. And a Lord."

"I'll be a Lord too someday. And then I'll be allowed to say all those words, like 'blast' and–"

Penelope quickly covered her brother's mouth with her hand, making Jane giggle.

"All right, you two," she said, stepping in before matters got out of control. "Time for your lessons."

"Will you help us finish the jigsaw first, Miss?" Penelope asked ever so nicely. "Please?"

"It's got a picture of HMS Victory," Alistair said proudly. "That's Lord Nelson's ship. He was the one who defeated the French and the Spanish at Trafalgar, you know."

Jane smiled. Even when he was playing, Alistair was obsessed with history. His mother would have hated it.

"Of course I'll help you," she said. "But after that we really must do some lessons. Starting with French."

"Oh no," he moaned. "Not French."

"I know you don't like it, but if you want to be a proper Lord someday, you'll be expected to be able to speak French."

"But why? We're British."

"It's considered to be *très chic,*" Jane explained with a wink.

"What if I become an admiral instead? I bet I wouldn't need to learn French then."

"Wouldn't you rather be a Lord?"

Alistair shrugged. "They made Nelson a Lord after he defeated the French fleet in Egypt. I could do the same. Then Papa and I would both be Lords at the same time."

"Admiral Crawford has a certain ring to it," Jane chuckled. "But how about we see to this puzzle first?"

"Aye aye, Miss," Alistair quipped.

Jane laughed and then the three of them sat down, huddled around the wooden pieces.

A little while later, just as they had finished their puzzle and were admiring the picture, there was a knock at the door.

Jane got up on her feet and went to open the door: it was Marie, carrying a large tray full of food.

"Lunchtime, Mademoiselle Governess," the maid said, her voice dripping with the usual disdain.

She peered over Jane's shoulder at the puzzle on the floor and then turned back to Jane with a smirk. "Must be a hard life, looking after two spoiled tots in a house like this. I don't know how you manage it all."

"Do you want to bring that in?" Jane asked, ignoring the taunt and gesturing at the tray in Marie's hands. "Or would you like me to do it for you?"

"You mean Mademoiselle isn't afraid of a bit of manual labour?" Marie sneered sarcastically. "*Incroyable.* Unbelievable."

"I'll just take the tray if you don't mind," Jane said starchily as she reached out to take the food from Marie.

"These plates are for the children," the maid said, nodding at the food on one side while she handed over the tray. "And this one's for you."

But instead of pointing at Jane's food, Marie spat in it.

"Bon appétit," she smirked.

Leaving a dumbstruck Jane standing in the open doorway, the French maid turned around and sauntered back to the kitchen.

How revolting, Jane thought as a shudder ran over her spine. She stared at her food on the tray, having completely lost her appetite.

"What's for lunch, Miss Lee?" Alistair asked from behind her. He and his sister hadn't witnessed the appalling incident.

And luckily, Marie hadn't spat in the children's food. *She wouldn't have dared to be that rude,* Jane realised.

"Cook has prepared a delicious selection of cold cuts for you," she replied as she carried the tray over to the table. "There's bread as well. Freshly baked from the smell of it."

"And cake," Alistair said, licking his lips while they took their seats.

The children tucked in, but Jane didn't touch any of her food. She just moved it around on her plate with her fork for a bit and then gazed at the window.

Who was she fooling but herself? She didn't belong here – not in this house and, without Georgie, not in this city either.

She simply didn't fit in. Alistair and Penelope were darling children, but the rest of the household were a nightmare. Lady Crawford despised her, and Marie downright hated her. And since the other staff sensed this, they tried their hardest to avoid Jane as much as they could.

If it's going to be like that, she thought, *I might as well write that resignation letter and head back to England. At least Abbie loves me.*

"Why are you looking so sad, Miss Lee?" Penelope asked. "You haven't eaten any of your food yet. Are you feeling unwell?"

Jane smiled at the girl. "No, I'm fine," she said. "It's just that..." She paused and sighed. How could she explain heartache to a child?

And besides, as their governess, she wasn't allowed to discuss her private life with them. On the other hand, lying to them didn't seem right to her either.

"I've had a rather serious argument with a dear friend recently," she explained.

Penelope nodded gravely. "Yes, it's sad when that sort of thing happens. But if it's a good friend, then you should always try to make up afterwards."

Simple, yet true, Jane thought.

"It's what Alistair and I do whenever we have a big row," Penelope continued. "Isn't that right, Ali?"

"Yes, it is," the boy said. "It's not always easy though. And sometimes I don't feel like making up at all. But then I remind myself that Penny is my sister and that I love her."

He shrugged and added, "Staying mad at someone you love doesn't make sense. So then I just stop being mad and try to be friends again."

If you put it that way, Jane thought, deeply moved by the innocence of their youthful view. Reliving the scene at the park, she could see how her actions would have hurt Georgie.

Could it be that he was just as broken-hearted about the whole affair as she was? Was he, even now, thinking about her? She imagined him kneading a ball of pastry dough at the patisserie, wearing a sad and forlorn expression on his tender face.

"I've been a silly fool," she muttered quietly.

The children giggled at her admission. "You should tell your friend that, Miss," Penelope teased. "Not us."

"I think you might be right, my little angels," Jane laughed. Then she paused and gazed at the window again.

The weather outside was perfect, she noticed, as a spark of excitement suddenly lit up in her heart.

"I have an idea," she said, turning to the children with a smile. "For your French lesson this afternoon, how would you like to go for a short excursion in the city?"

The children's eyes opened wide in surprise.

"Could we, Miss Lee? Please?" Penelope begged.

"Somewhere fun, Miss?" Alistair chimed in.

Jane grinned. "How does one of those French bakeries sound to you? I know just the place."

Chapter Nineteen

"Why a bakery?" Penelope wanted to know after Jane had asked the children to fetch their coats. "And what's so special about this place you have in mind, Miss?"

"Isn't it obvious, Penny?" Alistair said as a broad smile spread across his face. "They probably have the best cakes in the whole of Paris. And that's why Miss Lee wants to take us there."

"Yes, they do happen to have the most delicious cakes and pastries as a matter of fact," Jane replied. "And I personally know one of their apprentice bakers."

Tilting her head slightly, Penelope regarded Jane with an inquisitive look on her face. "Is this to do with you wanting to make up with your friend by any chance, Miss?"

"You're far too clever, aren't you?" Jane chuckled. "I admit: it's my friend who works at that bakery. And I'm so keen to make amends with him that I thought it would be a nice idea to turn this into an outing for the three of us."

She paused and grinned slyly at them. "Unless, of course, you think I should be more patient and wait until Sunday. After all, there's no need to drag you into this as well."

"But we want to be dragged into it," Alistair replied fervently. "Don't we, Penny? Especially when there's cake involved."

Penelope giggled. "Sounds like jolly good fun to me. And besides, I'd much rather go outside than be locked up in here on a lovely day like today."

"That's settled then," Jane said, clapping her hands in excitement. "But listen–" She drew the children closer to her and whispered, "It's probably better if we don't tell your mama about this, don't you think?"

"Like a secret?" Penelope asked, somewhat doubtful.

"More like an adventure," Jane said, hoping that made it sound more attractive and less naughty.

"An adventure," Alistair gasped, his eyes opening wide with awe. "No time to lose then. Let's go."

He dashed to the door, but Jane stopped him. "Not so fast, my fearless adventurer. Button up your coat first – both of you, please."

While the children did as they were told, Jane tried to think of how she would solve the next problem: getting them out of the house undetected. Or at least, without anyone informing Lady Crawford about it.

Leaving by the servants' entrance was out of the question. That route would take them past the kitchen. And there were too many watchful eyes there.

So she decided to go by the front door. A bold strategy perhaps, but in her view their best option under the circumstances.

"With any luck, we'll only have to deal with a footman," she explained her idea to the children.

"But what will we tell him, Miss Lee?"

"I'll think of something," she said. *I hope...*

Once they were ready, Jane led the children downstairs, her heart pounding nervously in her chest.

"Just follow my lead," she told them quietly. "Try to keep a straight face and don't say a word until we're outside."

When they reached the hallway, a surge of panic shot through Jane: just as she had feared, there was a footman by the front door. Tall and imposing, he seemed like an unyielding rock blocking their exit.

But Jane took a deep breath, held her head high and marched confidently towards him.

"Good afternoon to you, kind sir," she smiled. "I'm taking the children on a short cultural excursion. So if you wouldn't mind opening the door for us, please?"

He stood over a head taller than her. And in her anxious state, she thought he would be able to squash her like a troublesome bug if he wanted to.

"Pardon? A short what?" he asked, frowning.

"A cultural excursion. That's when we go for a walk in order to visit places, have new experiences and learn all manner of wonderful things."

"I see. Does Lady Crawford know about this, Miss? We're under strict instructions when it comes to the children, you know."

"My good man," Jane replied cordially. "Only this very morning, Lady Crawford personally instructed me to expose the children to the French language and culture more frequently. Double the amount of time, she said."

The footman hesitated. "So you're telling me... this is all right then?"

"Perfectly all right," she replied, gifting him with her warmest and most charming smile. Behind her, she heard Alistair suppressing a chuckle.

When the footman looked over at the children, Jane quickly added, "You wouldn't want to deny Lord and Lady Crawford's offspring such a unique learning opportunity, would you?"

The man threw up his hands as if to ward off any responsibility or blame. "I wouldn't dare deny them anything, Miss. You're their governess, so I suppose you know what's best."

He opened the door and stood to attention. "I wish you all a pleasant excursion."

Holding her breath, Jane slipped past him with the children in tow. Once outside, she headed for the nearest street corner so they would be out of sight as soon as possible.

And only then did she allow herself a long sigh of relief. They had made it.

"That was lots of fun," Alistair said. "What's next, Miss Lee?" He and Penelope were looking at her with twinkling eyes and smiling faces.

"Now we find ourselves a hansom cab," Jane replied. "And then we set off to Maître Leblanc's patisserie."

"Where we will buy a delicious piece of cake for each of us," Alistair said, rubbing his tummy.

"Yes, but on one condition," Jane cautioned. "You have to order your piece of cake yourself. And you have to do it in French." Smiling, she added, "This is a learning experience after all, remember?"

"In that case, I shall order two pieces of cake for myself," Alistair declared, making them all laugh.

Jane hailed a passing carriage and they clambered in, the children's faces alive with anticipation. As the horses started to trot, Jane felt a pang of anxiety.

Would Georgie be willing to speak to her? And if he was, then what would she tell him? She wasn't at all certain that a simple apology would do this time.

Soon, they arrived at their destination. Place Albertine was a lively and charming little square, where Maître Leblanc's patisserie stood nestled in between other shops and cafés.

The moment the horses came to a halt, Alistair jumped out of the carriage and ran straight inside the patisserie with Penelope close behind him.

"Miss Lee," the boy called out when Jane entered the shop as well. "Look at all these cakes and pastries. There must be hundreds."

"Then take your time and choose wisely, my little gourmand," she chuckled. Leaving the children to decide what they might like best, her eyes darted around the shop. Instead of cake however, she was looking for Georgie.

"*Excusez-moi,*" she said to one of the girls behind the counter. "Does Georges work here?"

"The young Englishman? Yes, he works in the atelier at the back, Mademoiselle."

"I'm a good friend of his. The children and I were in the neighbourhood, and since Georges has said so many nice things about this place, I thought we'd pay a quick visit. Do you think he would like to come out and say hello?"

"I'll go and ask him, Mademoiselle."

"Thank you," Jane said, mentally crossing her fingers. She would be mortified with embarrassment, she thought, if he refused to see her.

While she waited, Alistair and Penelope had made their choice. And just like Jane had asked them to do, they both very politely told one of the other shop assistants what they wanted.

Their pieces of cake had just been wrapped up carefully, when the first girl returned from the workshop. Jane looked up and stared straight into Georgie's face.

A confused frown creased his forehead. "I thought it was you," he said, not unkindly, "when Yvette told me there was an English girl in the shop who wanted to see me."

"Miss Lee?" Penelope asked as she appeared by Jane's side. "Is this your friend?"

"Yes, it is, my dear." Jane blushed and took out a few coins from her purse. "Here's some money. Be a good girl and pay the young lady for your cakes, will you?"

They watched as she skipped back to the counter.

"Are they–?" Georgie asked.

"My two charges, yes," Jane nodded. "Alistair and Penelope Crawford. Georgie, I'm really sorry to drop by like this, but I simply had to see you. Can we talk? Please?"

"Of course. I'll ask Maître Leblanc if I can have a short break. There's a nice café next door. We can go there and order coffee while the children eat their cake."

"That would be lovely," she sighed happily, relieved that he hadn't turned her away. Herding the children out of the shop and into the square, she picked a table for four outside.

By the time the waiter brought coffee and hot chocolate, the children had already devoured more than half of their cake, and Georgie had returned.

"I haven't got much time," he said apologetically. "But I told Maître Leblanc it was important."

"Thank you," Jane answered softly as a cautious glimmer of hope began to grow in her heart.

"He was giving me a black look though. So we'd better not make a habit of these surprise visits."

"Sorry," she said, casting down her eyes in shame. "I don't want to cause you any trouble. I've done enough damage as it is."

He smiled and tenderly took her hand. "I'm grateful that you've come, Jane."

His touch was almost magical, sending a warm glow through her entire being. She wanted to burst out crying, there and then, and tell him how awful she felt about the way they had parted.

But she couldn't do that with the children sitting next to them. So she bit back her tears and her sorrow, and merely nodded while she stared at her hand resting in Georgie's.

When Alistair and Penelope had finished their cake, Jane cleared her throat and said, "Children, why don't you go and feed your crumbs to the pigeons in the square?"

Penelope whispered something in her brother's ear and then the two of them ran off, laughing and giggling. Jane watched them as they went to a statue where a flock of pigeons were pecking around for scraps.

"They do seem like a loveable pair," Georgie said.

"I adore them," Jane replied, keeping her eyes on the children.

"You didn't just come here today for the cake, did you?"

"No, of course not," she said, turning her head to look at him again. "I came here for you. And for us. That is... if you feel there's still a chance for us?"

"Why wouldn't there be?" His voice was tender as he said it, and a slight smile graced his lips.

"Even after all the things we said last time?" she asked, gazing deep into his eyes, trying to fathom his true feelings.

"People say the silliest things sometimes."

They paused and stared at each other. In his eyes and in the way he looked at her, she didn't see any trace of blame – only love.

"Georgie, I don't know what to do anymore. Should I stay here in Paris, or go back to England?"

"Sweet Jane," he said as he gently traced the side of her face with his finger. "That's for you to decide. But I would love it if–"

Suddenly, a piercing scream filled the square.

It had sounded like Penelope, and when Jane's head snapped round to search for the children, her heart froze.

Three men had seized Alistair and Penelope, and now they were trying to shove them into a waiting carriage. The villains had pulled their hats low over their faces, while a neckerchief covered their mouths and noses.

"No," Jane shrieked in terror.

She jumped to her feet, but Georgie was already ahead of her and running towards the men with a defiant roar.

When he reached the kidnappers, he grabbed the nearest one by the sleeve. "Let go of those innocent children, you nasty brute," he growled.

But one of the others had a short wooden club in his hand and beat Georgie to the ground with a blow over the head.

And before anyone else could intervene, the villains bundled the struggling children into the carriage and jumped in after them.

"*Allez, vite,*" one of them shouted at the hooded driver. "Go, quickly!"

The horses squealed as the driver cracked his whip over their heads repeatedly and the carriage tore away at breakneck speed.

Jane came rushing over, but it was too late. Whimpering, she dropped down on her knees and cradled Georgie's head in her lap just as he regained consciousness.

"The children–" he murmured.

"Gone," she cried. "They're gone, Georgie."

A shocked crowd of people began to gather around them, while several voices shouted for the police.

"We should be going after them," Jane wailed. "Those poor little children. Alistair, Penelope! Somebody help them, please."

"There's nothing we can do for them now," Georgie said, slowly trying to get back on his feet. "The police will be here soon. They'll find those scoundrels."

"But how? It's too late. They're gone, Georgie. Gone." Jane was shaking and she felt like screaming from the top of her lungs.

"Calm down, my love," he said, holding her by her arms.

"It's all my fault," she wept hysterically. "I did this, don't you see? I should never have brought the children here. I should have waited until Sunday to see you."

"You couldn't have possibly known a thing like this would happen, could you? You're not to blame for this, Jane."

"And what will Lady Crawford say? She's going to be furious with me."

"Or maybe she'll be more worried about the safety of her children," Georgie said, trying to ease her fears.

"You clearly don't know her." Jane shivered and rubbed her own arms. "I never even told her I was taking the children out."

She started crying again, and so he wrapped her in his arms. Laying her head against his chest, she stared in the direction the carriage had taken.

"My darling little angels. They must be frightened to death. Who would do such a dreadful thing?"

Chapter Twenty

Jane watched the French policeman nervously twiddling the rim of the hat he was holding in his hands. The two of them had been shown into the sitting room by the housekeeper, Mrs Hill.

And now they would have to break the horrible news to Lady Crawford, who was sitting on the sofa and giving them her famously haughty stare.

"Tell me, Monsieur," Lady Crawford addressed the police officer in flawless French. "What is this news you bring? What's so important about it that you insisted on conveying it to me personally?"

She threw a mistrustful glance in Jane's direction. "And why is the governess of my children with you? Is she in some sort of trouble with the Law?"

"Madame," the policeman began awkwardly, "I have just come from Place Albertine – where, I regret to inform you, your children have been abducted by three unknown men."

"Abducted? What nonsense is this? My children are here at home, in the nursery, where they should be. Miss Lee, what's the meaning of all this?"

Jane cleared her throat. "I'm afraid it's true, milady. It happened before my very eyes."

Lady Crawford gasped in shock. The back of her hand flew up to her forehead and then she fainted. Or rather, she appeared to faint. Because Jane had never seen anyone lose consciousness in such a dramatic and graceful manner.

"Good heavens," Mrs Hill exclaimed before turning to the parlour maid who was standing quietly in a corner of the room. "Antoinette, go fetch the smelling salts. Quickly."

"I'll be all right," Lady Crawford murmured weakly, lying draped across the sofa with her eyes still closed. "Give me some sherry instead."

Mrs Hill nodded at the maid, who went to the sideboard to pour out a double measure.

Lady Crawford downed it in a single gulp.

"What happened?" she asked after waving her empty glass at the maid to signal for it to be refilled. "What were my children doing outside and far away from home? Why wasn't I informed of this?"

The policeman proceeded to recount the details of the incident, based on the official statements Jane and Georgie had given.

He had to pause several times, whenever Lady Crawford lamented loudly about the horror of it all. On each of those occasions, her ladyship's grief needed soothing with more sherry.

"We are doing everything we can to find your children, Madame," the policeman said, concluding his report. "And my superior will be coming over soon, to question the staff."

"The staff?" Mrs Hill asked. "Surely, you don't believe any of them would be involved in this?"

"We cannot exclude any possibilities," he replied. Jane thought she saw him giving her a quick sideways glance. "But at the moment we are merely gathering information."

Lady Crawford nodded. "Be as thorough and meticulous as you need to be in your investigation, Monsieur. You may use the library for your interviews. Mrs Hill?"

"I will make the necessary arrangements, milady," the housekeeper replied before turning to the policeman. "Monsieur? Follow me, please. You can wait in the kitchen until your superior arrives."

Jane held her breath as Mrs Hill and the policeman left the room. It was just her and Lady Crawford now – and Antoinette. But the French parlour maid could sense the tension hanging in the air too, and the girl made herself as inconspicuous as possible.

"How utterly scandalous of you, Miss Lee," Lady Crawford hissed as she rose up and went over to the sideboard – none too steadily, Jane noticed. "It's bad enough that you chose to secretly visit your lover during your working hours."

She poured herself a glass of sherry. "But to drag my innocent children along – why, that's immoral."

Lady Crawford put the glass to her lips and drained the sherry in one swift movement. "Don't you possess a shred of decency, you vile trollop?" Her eyes shot murderous glares at Jane.

"Milady, I assure you it wasn't my intention–"

"Silence, you despicable jezebel! I don't want to know what your intentions were. But I'm sure they were far from honourable."

Another sherry disappeared down her throat.

"Lady Crawford, please. If you would just let me explain–"

"What's there to explain? You absconded from this house with the children, and now they are gone. Because of you!" Her hands trembled as she poured herself one more glass, spilling sherry on the expensive rug beneath her feet.

"We tried to stop the villains, milady. I swear we did!"

"Then you didn't try hard enough, you coward. I would have fought them to the death. With my bare hands." She made a claw and lashed at the air in Jane's direction. "If those scoundrels do any harm to my children... Any harm at all–"

"I wouldn't be able to live with myself if that happened, milady."

"You wouldn't get the chance to live with yourself. Because I'd scratch your eyes out and then I'd strangle you."

Letting out a shrill cry, Lady Crawford threw herself at Jane. But she drunkenly stumbled over her own feet and promptly fell on the floor.

Jane and Antoinette wanted to rush over to her side to help, but Lady Crawford waved them away furiously.

"Leave me alone," she barked. "Both of you, get out. And Miss Lee? You're fired! I want you out of this house within the hour."

Tears running down her face, Jane fled from the sitting room and bounded up the stairs. When she reached her small private bedroom, she wanted nothing more than to throw herself onto the bed and weep.

But she couldn't. She had been told to leave and if she wasn't gone in an hour's time, she had no doubt that Lady Crawford wouldn't think twice about ordering a pair of footmen to forcibly remove her from the house.

Frantically, Jane began to pack. Her sobs echoed off the walls as she grabbed her clothes and personal belongings and stuffed them into her valise.

While she was busy gathering her things, images of the children's faces flashed through her mind – their laughter, their innocence, their trusting little hearts. It made her own heart ache with a pain so deep that it felt like it was tearing her apart.

A cold and cruel laugh behind her startled her. But even before she spun round, she knew who it would be. She had come to recognise – and loathe – that mocking tone.

"I hear you're leaving us," Marie said. The bothersome French kitchen maid was leaning against the doorframe of Jane's bedroom, her arms crossed and a smirk on her lips. "Tell me, how does it feel to be tossed out like a common beggar?"

Deciding to ignore Marie's taunts, Jane continued shoving her things in her valise.

"Some governess you are," the French maid sneered. "Going out gallivanting with your lover while you should be looking after those little tikes."

Jane glared at her. "I didn't mean for this to happen," she said through gritted teeth. "Those bandits appeared out of nowhere. We tried to stop them, but it all happened too fast."

"Oh, please," Marie snorted with derision. "You were probably too busy kissing to even notice when those men snatched the children away."

Jane refused to take the bait. Keeping her back straight, she fixed the maid with a cold stare and said, "Did you just come here to gloat, Marie? Because as you may have noticed, I'm rather busy at the moment."

Marie pulled a rude face and then replied, "Actually, I came to tell you that the police inspector has arrived. And he wants to speak with you."

Smirking at the look of fearful surprise on Jane's face, she added, "Who knows, maybe he'll arrest you. For criminal negligence or gross incompetence." With her nose in the air, the maid pivoted on her heels and slowly started back towards the kitchen downstairs.

"*Salut et bonne chance,*" Marie called out sarcastically.

"Yes, goodbye and good luck to you too," Jane muttered quietly. "And try not to break your pretty neck on those steep stairs."

Hurriedly, she finished packing her valise and closed it. With a slight grunt, she lifted it off the bed and took it downstairs with her, determined to leave the house as soon as she had spoken with this inspector.

"Mademoiselle Lee, I presume?" a middle-aged gentleman asked in French when she reached the bottom of the stairs. He had an air of calm authority over him, and he smiled at her. But Jane's guard went up nonetheless.

"I am indeed," she replied. "And you are?"

"Inspector Bouchard of the French police." He politely inclined his head to her. "I am leading the investigation."

"Let's pray you find Alistair and Penelope quickly, Inspector. I'm so worried about them. Do you have any idea who might have done this?"

"It's still too early to tell, Mademoiselle." He looked down at the valise in her hand. "I hear you have been dismissed?"

Jane sighed. "Yes, that's correct. Lady Crawford was very angry with me."

"Understandable, given the circumstances, wouldn't you say?"

"I suppose." Jane wondered how she herself would have reacted if she had been in Lady Crawford's shoes. Nowhere near as vicious, she hoped.

"Would you be so kind as to follow me to the library, Mademoiselle? I have a few questions I'd like to ask you before you go."

"Of course. Anything I can do to help."

When they entered the library, the policeman who had escorted her home was already sitting at a table, ready to take notes.

"Please, have a seat," Inspector Bouchard said with a friendly gesture at a chair near the table. "Coffee?"

"No, thank you."

"Biscuit?" he asked, holding out a tray with a large selection of biscuits to her. When she shook her head, he took one for himself, put the tray back down and casually perched on the edge of the table with one leg.

"This won't take long," he said amiably. "I have read the statement that you and your friend gave to the police after the incident. But I would like to hear from you, in your own words, what exactly happened."

Jane told her story and he listened carefully, interrupting her occasionally when he wanted more details.

Throughout the entire interview, he was perfectly courteous to her. But she was well aware that his eyes never once left her face while she talked.

"A sad affair, this is," he sighed when she had finished. "And what about you, Mademoiselle? What will you do now?"

Jane hesitated. "I haven't given that much thought yet. First, I guess I'll need to find somewhere to sleep tonight. And then in the morning–" She frowned and shook her head. "I just don't know."

"Whatever you decide, Mademoiselle, I must ask you not to leave the city. And while this investigation is ongoing, I want you to report to me every day. Here is my card, with the address of the police station."

"Report to you?" she repeated as she reluctantly accepted the card from him. "But why? I have already told you everything I know."

"Standard procedure, Mademoiselle," he said sympathetically. "The police need to remain informed of your whereabouts."

She gasped as the meaning of his request struck her. "Am I a suspect?"

Inspector Bouchard smiled ruefully. "We are exploring all possible avenues, Mademoiselle."

"But I'm innocent," she said, fear gripping her.

He didn't reply. Instead, he scrutinised her face, searching for any hint of deceit. After a few tense moments, he cleared his throat and stood up.

"I think this concludes our interview for today."

Jane stared in disbelief as he moved to the door and opened it silently, motioning for her to leave.

Slowly, in a confused daze, she rose to her feet, picked up her valise and left the library.

"*A demain, Mademoiselle,*" he said politely. "See you tomorrow."

When he softly shut the library door behind her, Jane got a sudden rush of goosebumps. How could the inspector believe she was a suspect?

I probably love Alistair and Penelope more than their own mother does.

The thought of Lady Crawford reminded her of the urgency to leave. She was no longer welcome in this house, and Jane didn't want to give anyone the pleasure of asking her why she was still here.

With her head held high, she marched to the servants' entrance. As she walked past the kitchen, she was sure Marie and her friends would be staring maliciously at her. But Jane pretended they weren't even there.

Taking a deep breath, she stepped outside. And then she closed the door for the final time.

Chapter Twenty-One

"Mademoiselle!" a familiar voice called out to Jane when she walked past the stable block of the Crawford residence. Petit Jean came running to her, his brow furrowed with concern.

"I heard what happened to milord's children," he said.

"Bad news travels fast," Jane smiled ruefully.

"It's all anyone was talking about in the kitchen."

"If that's where you heard the news, then I dread to think what they were saying about me."

"Not the nicest things, I'm afraid. But I didn't believe a word of it, Mademoiselle." He looked at the valise in her hand. "I see that this particular part of the rumours was true though: you are leaving us?"

"Lady Crawford didn't give me much choice in the matter. She blamed me for everything and sent me packing."

His eyes filled with sadness. "What will you do now? Where will you go? Back to England?"

"I can't go back just yet. The police told me not to leave the city until they have found the children and apprehend whoever took them."

She decided not to tell him that the police seemed to think she was a suspect.

"But then where will you stay?" he asked.

Jane sighed heavily and looked down at the young boy. Even though their time together had been brief, she had grown fond of him. His innocence and enthusiasm were a balm to her heart amidst the spiteful atmosphere of the Crawford household.

"I don't know, Petit Jean," she admitted softly.

"What about your friend? Maybe he can help."

"Georgie? No," she said, shaking her head. She didn't dare show up at the patisserie only a few hours after Alistair and Penelope had been abducted there. "I wouldn't want to cause him any more trouble than I already have."

"No, not him," Petit Jean replied. "I meant the French gentleman who's staying at that fancy hotel. The one who took us out and bought me chocolate cake."

"Mr Dubois?"

"Yes, he seemed like a decent man. I'm sure he would help you if you asked."

Hesitating, Jane bit her lip. In truth, she was reluctant to involve Mr Dubois in her troubles. But she saw no other option.

"Perhaps you're right," she said.

"If you want, I will accompany you to the hotel," Petit Jean offered, his face brightening at the thought of being able to assist her.

"Don't you have work to do here?" she asked, gesturing at the big house.

"I don't think anybody will be doing much work today," he shrugged. "They won't even notice I'm gone. Too busy gossiping, they are."

Despite the many doubts that filled her head, Jane nodded and agreed to let the boy join her.

"It's a long way to the Hôtel Faubourg though," she warned him. "We could hail a hansom cab, but–"

"Spare your coins, Mademoiselle. It's a lovely day. We'll go on foot."

Jane smiled gratefully at him. *So young and yet so wise in the ways of the world already.*

Maybe because he could sense her distress as they walked to the hotel, Petit Jean launched into a spirited monologue about his dreams and plans for the future.

He spoke of his desire to travel around Europe, visit the great cities and take in all the sights. Not simply for the fun of it, but to learn.

"I want to make something of myself, you see," he explained. "And I hope to have enough money one day to start my own business."

"For someone as brave, kind and clever as you, that shouldn't be too much of a problem," she said.

"Perhaps. The trouble is life isn't always fair – no matter how brave or kind or clever we are. Sometimes we also need a bit of plain old luck."

"True," she replied. And with a sigh she added, "Mine seems to have run out, unfortunately."

"Don't give up hope so quickly, Mademoiselle. Let's just get to Mr Dubois first. He'll know what to do."

Taking comfort from Petit Jean's words, Jane tried to put on a brave face. But even so, by the time they finally reached the hotel, she was feeling hot and flustered.

"I'll stay outside," the young lad said, knowing that the doorman wouldn't let him in anyway. "But I'll be right here waiting for you, in case you need me."

"Even as a boy, you're already more of a gentleman than some men of my acquaintance," Jane replied with a smile before walking up to the grand entrance and going into the hotel.

Peering round the brightly lit lobby, she soon spotted Mr Dubois sitting in one of the large leather wing chairs, reading a newspaper. She rushed forward, nearly colliding with another guest in her hurry.

"Mademoiselle Lee," Mr Dubois said, looking up from his newspaper with an expression of worried concern on his face. "What's the matter?"

"Apologies for the intrusion, Monsieur," Jane began, her voice trembling slightly. "But I find myself in desperate need of your counsel. There's been a tragic incident and–"

"Shh, my dear," he interrupted her, raising his hand. His eyes darted around the lobby. "This may not be the right place for that sort of talk." He stood up quickly and folded the paper. "Please sit down and wait here."

Before Jane could utter a single word, he vanished into the crowd. She stared after him in bewilderment, at a loss to understand his sudden departure.

Nervously settling into her chair, she waited – just like he had told her. But with every passing moment, her heart sank deeper and deeper into despair.

Coming here had been a mistake, she told herself after a while. *I must have looked like a madwoman the way I dashed over to him.* And now she had scared him off.

Just when she thought it would be better for her to leave, a bellboy appeared by her side.

"Mademoiselle Lee?" the young man asked cautiously.

"Yes?"

He held out a silver tray with a folded note on it. "A message for you, Mademoiselle."

Puzzled, Jane accepted the note and quickly read its contents.

'Meet me at the café of Madame Moureaux in Rue Fougasse. Come alone. And make sure you are not being followed.'

It was signed by Mr Dubois.

She blinked and read the message again. Then she glanced around the hotel lobby, but there was no trace of her friend.

How bizarre, she thought as she tucked away the note and went outside to look for Petit Jean.

"Rue Fougasse?" the boy asked after she had told him about the note. He let out a low whistle in dismay. "That's a rough neighbourhood, Mademoiselle. Are you sure you want to go there?"

"Do I have any other choice?"

"Perhaps not. But then at least allow me to take you there. That way, I can help you with the last part of Mr Dubois' message as well."

"Why would anyone be following us?"

"Shortly after you entered the hotel, a man went inside. And that very same man has just walked out again, trying very hard to look relaxed and casual. He may not be wearing a uniform, but I know a policeman when I see one."

Jane glanced over her shoulder. She didn't see anyone who struck her as suspicious or out of the ordinary among the busy crowd. But then again, she realised she wasn't anywhere near as streetwise as Petit Jean.

"Very well," she said. "I trust you. Please take me to Rue Fougasse. And let's lose this police detective along the way."

Petit Jean grinned. "With pleasure, Mademoiselle."

Chapter Twenty-Two

"Follow me," Petit Jean said as they set off. "And stay right behind me, please. It's for your own safety."

Jane thought his warning sounded ominous. And something about the seriousness of his tone told her that he absolutely meant it, too.

The pair of them embarked on a winding journey through the tangled alleys and backstreets of Paris. Holding on to her valise for dear life, Jane's heart pounded in her chest as they hurried along the narrowing streets.

Crowded tenement buildings towered over them, casting long shadows that felt like they were reaching out for her. And everywhere, the clamour of the city echoed off the walls, which soon caused her to lose any sense of direction – further adding to her anxiousness.

But Petit Jean was a skilled guide, leading Jane through a myriad of hidden passages that twisted and turned like a labyrinth. He moved with the agility of a cat, never once faltering or losing his bearings.

"I think we have lost him," the boy said after a while. "Finally."

Jane glanced over her shoulder. Petit Jean was right: the policeman was gone. She hadn't seen the man back at the hotel, but once they got underway, he had betrayed his presence quickly enough, even to someone as inexperienced as her.

He had been good, she had to admit, stalking them discreetly from the shadows. But an average looking man like him simply had no business going into some of the grubby streets that she and Petit Jean passed through.

Knowing she was being followed by the police had only given her more cause for alarm. So she was grateful for the relief that getting rid of him brought her.

"Good work, Petit Jean," she said in hushed tones while the boy kept up his pace.

"We're almost there," he replied. "Rue Fougasse is only a couple of streets further down. But please be very careful, Mademoiselle." He paused and looked at her. "The people who live here... Well, they are not like you. And some of them might want to do you harm."

Jane shivered, despite the warm evening air. But she nodded at him and then they pressed on.

After rounding a few more corners, they reached Rue Fougasse, where Petit Jean asked a pair of washerwomen if they knew where the café of Madame Moureaux was.

"Keep walking," one of them mumbled while pointing down the street. "You can't miss it. 'Chez Louise', her place is called."

"*Merci, Madame,*" Petit Jean nodded his thanks.

"Come here instead, *chérie,*" a man called out drunkenly to Jane. He and three of his friends were standing outside another café, grinning salaciously at her. "The company is better here. And the wine's cheaper too."

Laughing rowdily, the men beckoned her to come over. But Petit Jean tugged at Jane's sleeve and led her further down the street until they found themselves standing in front of Madame Moureaux's establishment.

From the outside, 'Chez Louise' didn't appear to be much better than the other drinking dens in the street. But at least there weren't any bawdy drunkards loitering by the entrance.

"I guess this is goodbye, Mademoiselle," Petit Jean said. "Mr Dubois asked you to come alone and I'd better head back anyway."

"Thank you, my young friend. For all your help. Promise me you'll be careful?"

"Of course," he smiled confidently. "But you must promise me something in return as well."

"And that is?"

"Don't walk these streets alone, Mademoiselle. Especially after dark."

Glancing around and hearing all the unsettling noises of inebriated revelry, Jane pulled her shawl tighter and nodded. She understood the wisdom of his advice. But she wasn't sure if she would be able to have a reliable escort.

"*Au revoir, Mademoiselle,*" he said as he ran off.

She waved goodbye to him and then went inside, not wanting to expose herself to any unnecessary risks on the street.

The café of Madame Moureaux was a rather seedy affair – with a squalid interior and rancid smells to match. The patrons looked up from their drinks as Jane stood by the door, nervously searching the smoke-filled room for Mr Dubois.

A voluptuous French waitress walked past carrying a full tray. The young woman eyed her up and down, as if Jane was some sort of exotic creature from a distant land.

Mr Dubois was sitting at a table towards the back, waiting for her. The moment Jane spotted him, he gestured to her to come over.

"You will have to forgive the unsavoury surroundings, Mademoiselle," he said when she joined him. "But Madame Moureaux is a trusted friend. And appearances notwithstanding, her café is a place where we can speak freely, away from prying eyes and curious ears."

Jane glanced around at the other patrons, who had already lost interest and gone back to nursing their drinks.

"I'll take your word for it, Monsieur. Although I must confess, it's a world removed from your hotel. I'm surprised you would frequent a venue like this."

"My business sometimes takes me to the oddest of places," he replied with a grin twitching at the corner of his mouth. "And the police hardly ever set foot in this neighbourhood."

Quickly changing the topic, he raised his hand to get the waitress' attention. "You must be hungry," he said to Jane. "Allow me to buy you a light meal."

Jane's first reaction was to politely decline the offer. But then her tummy reminded her that she hadn't eaten anything since breakfast. Perhaps if she had some food, she would be able to think more clearly.

"What'll it be, my lovely?" the waitress cooed flirtatiously at Mr Dubois, one hand on her hip to better emphasise her curves.

"Yvette, my dear," he smiled back. "Your special of the day for my young lady friend here, if you please. And some more wine as well."

"Of course," the waitress replied, throwing a casually mocking glance at Jane as she left.

"Now then," Mr Dubois said, giving Jane his undivided attention. "What is this tragic incident that you mentioned at the hotel?"

She started telling him about her ordeal: how she had taken the Crawford children on an improvised trip to see Georgie, only for them to be abducted right before her nose.

Jane paused only once, when Yvette brought the food and wine to their table. And then she continued her story while she ate.

Mr Dubois listened and sympathised with her plight, tutting when he heard about Lady Crawford's furious reaction and Jane's subsequent dismissal.

"This is grave indeed," he sighed after Jane had finished her woeful tale.

"I'm sorry for burdening you with my troubles, Monsieur," she apologised. "But I simply didn't know who else to turn to."

"You did the right thing coming to me, Mademoiselle. This is what friends are for, after all." Giving her an encouraging smile, he placed his hand over hers and patted it gently.

"First," he said, "we must think practically. Do you have any accommodation for the night?"

"No, not yet. And I'm afraid my funds are rather limited at the moment." Embarrassed, she lowered her eyes and stared at the well-worn wooden surface of the table. "I don't even know for how long I will be required to remain in Paris."

"Worry not, Mademoiselle. I shall speak to Madame Moureaux and ask her to give you one of the rooms above the café. Hardly luxurious by any standard, *hélas*, but affordable. Think of it as a temporary solution until help arrives."

"Thank you, Monsieur."

"Speaking of help," he continued, "I think you ought to write to your sister and ask for her assistance. In your unfortunate circumstances, you need all the support you can get."

Jane nodded. Initially, she had been reluctant to tell Abbie about her problems. But that was before Alistair and Penelope were kidnapped. Now, she wanted nothing more than to be close to her big sister.

"Wait here," Mr Dubois said as he rose to his feet. "And I will ask Madame Moureaux for pen and paper, so you can write your letter immediately."

"Oh, please don't trouble yourself on my behalf, Monsieur. I can write it once I'm in my room later this evening. Or maybe tomorrow, after a good night's sleep."

"It's no trouble at all, Mademoiselle. And I must insist, most humbly," he smiled with a slight bow of the head. "Time is of the essence."

She nodded her consent, knowing he was right. Already she had wasted too much time, and squandered too many opportunities to rectify her mistakes.

Nevertheless, the thought of writing to her sister made her nervous, the weight of her difficulties pressing down on her.

So she was very grateful to Mr Dubois, who upon returning with pen, paper and an envelope, helped her to write down her thoughts in a way that made some sense.

'My dearest Abigail,

'I pray this letter finds you well, even though, much to my regret, my words are likely to prove a source of great concern and distress to you.'

Jane then went on to recount the tragic events that had transpired, up to her dismissal as a governess, leaving her stranded in a foreign city, virtually homeless and destitute.

"And I haven't even told her about Percy yet," Jane said after she had reread the letter.

"One thing at a time," Mr Dubois advised her. "The news about the abduction of those poor children will come as enough of a shock to your sister, I should think."

"Once again you are right, Monsieur," she sighed. "Thank you for your guidance. I'd be absolutely lost without it."

"I shall personally post this in the morning," he said, folding the letter and sliding it into the envelope. "Hopefully, we will hear from your sister soon."

"A thousand times *merci*," Jane said, feeling an enormous sense of relief now the letter had been written. "You are a true friend, Mr Dubois."

"I am merely doing my moral duty, Mademoiselle," he replied, inclining his head in response. "I must, however, ask you to remain discreet about my assistance. As you have experienced for yourself, the police tend to jump to conclusions a little too easily. If they should hear about my involvement..."

"I understand, Monsieur," Jane rushed to say. "You may rest assured, I have no intention of causing you any more trouble than I already have."

"Most gracious of you, Mademoiselle." He rose to his feet. "I shall take leave of you now, so you may retire for the night. Yvette or Madame Moureaux will show you to your room."

Jane stood up as well and they shook hands. "Words cannot begin to express my gratitude to you, Monsieur."

"Take heart, Mademoiselle. All will be well in the end."

After Mr Dubois had left, Jane asked Yvette if she could go up to the room that had been arranged for her.

With a smirk on her painted lips, the French waitress led the way up the creaky stairs, swaying her hips as she went. At the end of a dark and narrow corridor, the girl opened the door to a dingy looking bedroom.

"*Bonne nuit,*" Yvette said as she handed the key and a candle to Jane, and then went back to her work in the taproom downstairs.

Jane slipped into the room, locked the door and looked around. The furniture consisted of only a bed with a thin mattress and an old wooden chest of drawers. The original colours on the walls had long ago faded, the carpets on the floor were beyond threadbare, and Jane spotted mould in several places.

But despite its dilapidated state, the room would do for a couple of nights, she thought. "Abbie will come," she whispered to herself.

Sitting on the edge of the bed, Jane's mind went to all the things that had happened that day. Inevitably, she broke down in tears.

A wave of exhaustion took her and she buried her face in the pillow, not bothering to undress for the night.

A few hours later, noises in the adjoining bedroom woke her up briefly from a restless and anxiety-ridden slumber. A woman was laughing and giggling, while a man mumbled softly.

Jane thought she recognised the voice of Yvette, leading her to assume that the waitress was engaged in money-making activities of a rather different nature after her regular working hours in the café.

Pulling the rough blanket over her head, Jane drifted off again. *Abbie will come,* she prayed silently.

Chapter Twenty-Three

Jane awoke with a start, her heart pounding as the echoes of her harrowing dreams still haunted her. She'd had terrible nightmares about Alistair and Penelope, imagining the pair of them being held in a dark cellar by a gang of demons wearing hideous masks.

Even now, the frightened screams and terrified faces of the poor children remained imprinted on her mind. Quickly, she folded her hands and said a prayer for their safety... wherever they might be.

Then she sat up, her fingers clutching the sheets tightly as she focused on her breathing, trying to calm the turmoil within her. Pale morning light filtered through the curtains, casting a soft glow that did little to hide the shoddy condition of the room.

Looking around, she hesitated. It was tempting to lie down again, pull the sheet over her head and simply hide from the world for the rest of the day.

But she knew that wouldn't do her any good. And it wouldn't bring Alistair and Penelope back either.

Gathering her strength, Jane forced herself to get out of bed. She would report to the police first, she decided. With any luck, they'd have news about the case. Maybe there had been some sort of development overnight, or even a breakthrough.

In her mind, she already pictured herself walking into the police station and being greeted by the smiling children. She would wrap her arms around them, crying tears of joy while raining down sweet kisses on their heads.

But that was just a fantasy.

Standing in her room above the café, Jane sighed and shook her head. "Stop daydreaming and get cracking," she told herself.

She didn't see a wash basin in the room, so a change of clothes would have to do. Choosing her simplest and most modest dress from her valise, she hoped her outfit would help her to stand out less in this rough neighbourhood. Although she feared it wasn't anywhere near tattered and frayed enough.

After she had combed and rearranged her hair, she closed her valise and slid it underneath the bed. Steeling herself for whatever the day would bring, she left and locked her room.

As she descended the creaky stairs down to the taproom, the nauseating smell of stale wine and cheap coffee greeted her. There were only a handful of customers in the café at this early hour: elderly men playing a muted game of cards.

"You must be Mr Dubois' friend," a slim and neatly dressed French woman in her early sixties said flatly when Jane walked into the public room. "I am Madame Moureaux."

A decades-long habit of wine and tobacco had made the woman's voice gruff and throaty. And when she spoke, her tone was indifferent, bordering on rudeness in that typical Parisian way.

Jane guessed that Madame Moureaux might have been attractive once – in the eyes of some men. But those days were long gone.

"*Bonjour, Madame,*" she replied politely.

"Would you care for some breakfast?" the landlady asked. "It's not included in the price of the room, of course. But it's not expensive either."

"No, thank you. I'm not very hungry this morning," Jane said. It was true that her stomach was too upset because of all the worries that plagued her. But she was equally conscious of her meagre finances. So skipping breakfast was an easy decision to make.

"Besides," she added by way of an apology, "I need to report to the police. And I'd better hurry, I suppose."

Madame Moureaux regarded Jane with a guarded curiosity. "Are you in any trouble? Not that it's any of my business, obviously. But I wouldn't want the good name of my establishment to be harmed by somebody else's legal issues."

Looking round the café, Jane wondered just what sort of reputation Madame Moureaux thought her establishment enjoyed.

Didn't the woman know about the lucrative activities Yvette appeared to be conducting on these very premises after hours?

Jane didn't see any sign of the waitress this morning however. *Probably sleeping it off,* she presumed.

"Your concern is noted, Madame," Jane replied, biting back the sarcastic remark that was on the tip of her tongue. "But my problems won't affect you. And I'm sure Mr Dubois would say the same."

Madame Moureaux shrugged. "Fine with me then. Speaking of Mr Dubois, he paid for your room, but only for one night. I assume you'll be staying longer?"

"Yes, I will. Although I don't quite know for how long exactly. The inspector didn't–"

"Doesn't matter," Madame Moureaux interrupted her. "But you'll need to pay for a whole week in advance."

"O–of course," Jane stuttered as she reached for her purse. There was something about this woman and her ungracious manners that unnerved Jane.

"No need to pay me now," Madame Moureaux said with a wave of the hand. "It can wait until after you have completed your business with the police."

When one of the old men at the card table called for more coffee, Madame Moureaux lost all interest in Jane and attended to her regular customers.

Grateful for the distraction, Jane quickly left the café and stepped out into the sunny Parisian morning.

Even in this poverty-stricken neighbourhood, the streets were already busy. People hurried past her on their way to work or whatever errand they were running. And hardly anyone seemed to glance in her direction. She was invisible to them – just another passer-by in an endless parade of faces.

Just as well, she sighed with some relief.

The air in the crowded streets was warm and muggy, making Jane realise just how tired and thirsty she was feeling.

"What I wouldn't give for a strong cup of proper English tea right now," she muttered quietly to herself. *With a thick slice of buttered toast,* her mind added hungrily.

Part of her was beginning to regret not having taken breakfast at the café. But then again, in her precarious situation, she didn't dare spend her money on such niceties.

And with some luck, she hoped, Inspector Bouchard would offer her something to drink when she reported to him.

Finally, after what felt like an eternity of trudging through the city, she arrived at the address mentioned on the inspector's card. The police station was a tall and intimidating building, with people walking in and out through its heavy double doors.

Her heart pounding in her chest, Jane climbed the steps to the entrance and went inside.

Wading through the busy rush of policemen, suspects and citizens, she approached the front desk, where a stern-looking sergeant with a thin moustache was scribbling something in a ledger. He glanced up at her, then returned to his writing without a word.

Clearing her throat, Jane spoke up. "Excuse me, I'm looking for Inspector Bouchard. Can you tell me where I might find him, please?"

The police sergeant looked up again, this time with a hint of annoyance in his eyes. "What's your business with him?"

"He told me to report to him daily. It's about the Crawford case."

"Ah yes, that nasty affair with the children." The sergeant turned to a younger colleague of his. "Go tell Bouchard the English girl is here to see him."

A few moments later, Inspector Bouchard came out of his office, walked over to Jane and politely shook her hand. "*Bonjour, Mademoiselle Lee.* How are you today?"

"About as well as might be expected given the circumstances, I suppose," she sighed. "Please, Inspector, tell me: is there any news about the children?"

"None, I'm afraid."

Jane's shoulders dropped even lower and she felt like crying as a horrible vision appeared before her mind's eye: a terrifying image of Alistair and Penelope lying dead somewhere cold and dark.

"We are doing everything we can, Mademoiselle," the inspector said. "But we haven't got much to go on yet. No leads and no traces. In the meantime however, there's someone who would like to meet you."

Jane looked up at him in surprise.

"Follow me to my office," he said, leading the way.

"Who is it?" she asked while trying to match his brisk pace. "Not someone I know, I take it?"

"No, but he is a compatriot of yours." Inspector Bouchard opened the door to his office and gestured for Jane to enter.

Hesitantly, she went inside.

A gentleman with a bushy moustache and an impressive set of whiskers was standing by the window. He looked to be in his late fifties and he was dressed in a tidy but unremarkable tweed suit. Everything about him exuded an air of Britishness.

Just as Jane entered the office, the man took a sip from the cup he was holding, and winced. "Blasted Frenchies," he grumbled in perfect Oxford English. "Can't even make a decent cup of tea."

He set down his cup and saucer and looked at Jane. "Oh, hello. You must be Miss Lee. I'm Inspector Hubert Woodcock of Scotland Yard."

"How do you do, Inspector," Jane greeted him, shaking the hand he held out to her.

"Inspector Woodcock has just arrived this morning," Inspector Bouchard explained as he took a seat at his own desk. "He's come all the way over from London to assist us with the investigation."

Jane thought she detected an edge of annoyance and sarcasm to the French policeman's tone, telling her he wasn't too happy about this 'cooperation'.

"Hopped onto the first available boat out to France," Woodcock said jovially, as if he was talking about a jolly jaunt abroad.

A cautious glimmer of hope stirred in Jane's heart. Surely, it could only be a good thing that

Scotland Yard were getting involved? And she wondered briefly whether her wealthy brother-in-law was behind this. Joe had connections in high places, after all.

But could her letter really have reached London so soon? She had only written it last night.

"That's marvellous news, Inspector Woodcock," she said. "And impressively quick as well."

"We don't like wasting time at the Yard, Miss," Inspector Woodcock beamed with pride. "It was all hands on deck once we received Lord Crawford's cable."

"Lord Crawford?"

"Yes, he sent a telegram to Scotland Yard yesterday. Caused quite the commotion, as you can imagine. It's not every day that someone snatches the offspring of an individual as important as his lordship. My superiors ordered me to pack a suitcase and travel to Paris immediately."

Jane couldn't hide her disappointment. Of course the inspector was here for Lord Crawford. How foolish of her to think that the British authorities would care about someone like her.

"By the by," Woodcock said, wiggling his moustache while fixing Jane with an inquisitive gaze. "Bouchard tells me he thinks you're a suspect."

"I would never do anything to hurt Alistair and Penelope," she shot back. "I love those poor little angels as if they were my own flesh and blood."

Woodcock nodded and turned to his French colleague. "See, Bouchard? Told you, didn't I? No respectable Englishman –or woman– would ever abduct the innocent children of a fellow countryman."

Inspector Bouchard rolled his eyes and shook his head.

"Do you have any idea who might have done this, Inspector Woodcock?" Jane asked.

"As a matter of fact, I do," he declared. "Russian spies."

Inspector Bouchard snorted. "A ridiculous notion."

"No more ridiculous than accusing this poor young lady of a hideous crime just because she's English," Woodcock said, wagging a finger at his French colleague.

"Very well. I'll humour you, Inspector," Bouchard said. "Why do you think it's the Russians?"

"Because that's just the sort of dirty game they like to play. Even now, after several decades, they still hate us for the beating we gave them back in the Crimean War."

Inspector Bouchard threw up his hands in frustration. "You must be joking, *mon cher homme*."

"Not at all, my dear chap. You wouldn't happen to have a list of known Russian agents lying around here, would you?"

Growing tired of the Anglo-French rivalry, Jane cleared her throat. "Excuse me, inspectors. Do you require anything more from me, or may I be excused?"

"You may go, Mademoiselle," Bouchard said. "But remember to report to me every day."

Jane nodded and turned to leave the office. As she closed the door behind her, she heard Inspector Woodcock say, "Perhaps I ought to disguise myself and visit some of the cafés that these warmongering agitators go to."

Her head throbbing with despair, she hurried out of the police station. How could there ever be any hope of finding the children when clowns like those two men were in charge of the case?

Chapter Twenty-Four

Jane glanced back at the police station behind her. The tall building seemed even bleaker now than when she had first entered it.

Inspector Bouchard didn't have any leads, or at least none that he was willing to share with her. She wasn't even entirely sure the man was actively and sincerely looking for clues.

And as for Inspector Woodcock with his wild theory about Russian spies? She frowned and shook her head in disbelief. No, it had to be something much simpler than that.

Hugging her arms around herself, Jane watched the busy street traffic rumble by: carriages, carts and omnibuses, all rattling along the wide boulevard. The noises and activity that usually marked the vibrant energy of Paris now felt distant and cold to Jane.

But somewhere in this bustling city, Alistair and Penelope were being held by a gang of vicious men.

"Where are you, my sweet darling angels?" she whispered, sending up her question to the blue sky above her head.

The very thought of them locked up in some darkened room, crying for their mama and papa, made her sick.

She should never have taken them along to see Georgie. How could she have been so careless? So reckless? If anything happened to those poor little souls, it would be her fault – and her fault alone.

Angry with her own wretched foolishness, Jane balled her fists. "If I'm to blame for this," she grumbled, "then I might as well try to do something about it myself."

It was clear that she couldn't rely on Inspector Bouchard's lacklustre efforts. And Inspector Woodcock seemed intent on chasing imaginary spectres.

Which left her with little other choice than to take matters into her own hands, she concluded. But how? And where would she start? She wasn't a police detective.

Still, it wouldn't hurt to start making a few enquiries here and there, would it? She could go back to Place Albertine, where the children had been abducted. Maybe if she asked around, she'd discover that one of the shopkeepers had seen or noticed something useful.

She knew it was unlikely to happen, but not doing anything would only drive her mad. And of course, going to Place Albertine also gave her the chance to pay a visit to the patisserie where Georgie worked.

He was sure to have some sensible advice for her, or to give her his honest opinion on the case. And at the very least, being with him – even if it was only for a little while – would provide her with a much-needed dose of comfort.

She wanted, no, she *needed* to hear his voice, to see his face, and to feel the gentle caress of his hand on hers.

"Next stop: Place Albertine," she said as she set off on foot with renewed vigour.

It wasn't long however before her body began to protest, reminding her sharply that she had gone without any food or drink for far too long.

Her steps faltered as a dizziness washed over her, forcing her to lean against the nearest lamppost for support. Her vision blurred and her legs felt as though they might give way beneath her.

Laying a trembling hand on her cold and sweaty forehead, she scanned her surroundings. She had to appease her grumbling stomach, and soon too, or she would risk collapsing.

Luckily, she spotted a small cluster of stalls on the far corner of the street. At least one of them was bound to have something to eat, she thought.

With a weak groan, she pushed herself away from the lamppost and mustered the strength to continue. By the time she reached the stalls, she didn't care any more what they were selling or if it was any good – as long as it satisfied her hunger and restored an inkling of vitality in her exhausted being.

"One of those, please," she croaked weakly as she pointed at what looked like a sausage roll.

The street vendor muttered what the price was, while he picked up the roll and held out his other hand to accept payment from Jane, who dug in her purse for some money.

Before she could find any coins though, a grubby young boy darted past and snatched the purse right out of her grasp.

"*Voleur,*" the street vendor cried out in alarm. "Thief!"

With a desperate burst of power, Jane gathered her skirts and took off after the experienced pickpocket as he wove through the crowded street.

But the boy was too quick and nimble for her. After only a few steps, Jane stumbled on the uneven cobblestones, skinning her knee and tearing a large hole in the hem of her dress.

Sprawled inelegantly in the muddy gutter, Jane could only watch helplessly as the thief disappeared around a corner.

"No," she lamented, feeling utterly drained.

Tears of frustration and pain welled up in her eyes. That purse contained the last of her money. She had been too afraid to leave anything of value back in her dismal room above the café.

As a result, she was penniless.

Ignoring the curious stares of passersby, Jane struggled to her feet. She did her best to brush the dirt from her skirts, but it was a lost cause. The once pretty floral cotton was now smeared with mud and splotched with blood from her injured knee.

"I'm very sorry for you, dear," the wife of the street vendor said. The kindly woman had come out from behind their stall, regarding Jane with sympathetic eyes. "Those pickpockets are a terrible pest. Will you be all right?"

Jane bit her lip and nodded, holding back a sob.

"Here, have this," the woman said, handing Jane the sausage roll. "Our treat."

"*Merci, Madame,*" she replied, gratefully accepting the free gift. She waited until the woman had returned to their stall before rapidly devouring the roll.

Then, with slow and painful steps, she made her way to Place Albertine. And even though the roll had taken the worst edge off her hunger, when she finally reached the patisserie of Maître Leblanc, she was dizzy and faint-headed.

Pausing in front of the window of the pastry shop, she caught a glimpse of her reflection. Her hair was a wild and tangled mess, while her face was smeared with sooty dirt.

As she entered the shop, her torn and filthy dress drew looks of disdain from the clientele. One elderly lady gasped and made a show of clutching her pearls while covering her mouth and nose with her expensive silk scarf.

But Jane was too tired to care about any of it. She dragged herself over to the counter and wearily leaned against it, her body begging for rest.

"Excuse me, Mademoiselle," she said to the shop girl through a hoarse and raspy throat. "Might I speak with Georgie?"

The girl's eyes widened at Jane's dishevelled appearance. She hesitated, then disappeared through the doorway leading to the bakery at the back of the shop.

Moments later, instead of Georgie, the imposing figure of Maître Leblanc emerged, his thick brows knitted in a scowl.

"*Sacré bleu!* What is the meaning of this?" the pastry chef thundered. "I'll not have vagabonds wandering in off the street!"

Jane shrank back, cringing. "Please sir, I only wish to see–"

"Monsieur Georges is hard at work, as you should very well know," Maître Leblanc interrupted. His voice boomed through the quiet patisserie. “Now see here. I’ll not have you tracking mud and... and heaven knows what else into my establishment.”

Jane’s cheeks burned crimson with shame as the other patrons turned to gawk at her.

“I’m sorry, it’s just... The children–” she stammered.

“Yes, yes, dreadful business, that,” Maître Leblanc snapped. “And now the police have been here asking questions, and people are gossiping. And you show up looking like... like–” He made an exasperated noise of disgust.

“Please Monsieur, I only need to speak with Georgie for a moment,” Jane pleaded weakly.

“I think not,” Maître Leblanc blustered. “We want none of your sort around here. Now be off, before I summon the police!”

Tears pricked Jane’s eyes. She gave a small, defeated nod and hurried from the patisserie, ignoring the scornful looks that followed her.

There had been no sign of Georgie, and she wasn’t sure if he was even aware that she had come into the shop to see him.

Outside, she slumped against the nearest wall and finally allowed the tears to fall. She had never felt more lost or deserted.

Jane wrapped her arms around herself, choking back sobs. Unsure where to go or what to do next, she simply sank down onto the ground, heedless of the dirt.

She didn't want to give up, not really – but the fight had gone out of her. And so, feeling utterly crushed, she rested her head in her hands while the weight of despair settled upon her shoulders.

She was alone, she had no money and she looked like a madwoman. Nothing could be farther removed from the dreamy fantasy life that she had imagined for herself and Georgie here in Paris.

The sobs she had been holding back now burst forth in wretched, heaving waves. Passersby gave her a wide berth, some shaking their heads in pity, others avoiding looking at her entirely. She was the very picture of destitution.

Jane didn't know how much more her heart could take. It felt near to shattering into a thousand pieces. She longed to curl up right there and surrender to the black pit of gloom that threatened to swallow her whole.

As the sun began to dip lower in the sky, a chill crept into the air. Or maybe it just felt like that to her.

Jane clutched her thin shawl around her tattered dress. Soon darkness would fall completely. And she didn't know if she should fear it, or welcome it.

Chapter Twenty-Five

The evening sky had faded to dusk when Jane dragged her weary body back to the café. She dreaded facing Madame Moureaux, knowing she had yet to pay for her lodgings.

As Jane approached the entrance, she could see the silhouette of the older woman through the window, hands on hips, deep in conversation with her waitress Yvette.

Jane slipped inside quietly, hoping not to draw attention. But Madame's shrewd eyes honed in on her immediately.

"There you are," the woman barked in her gravelly voice. "I was just about to let Yvette toss your belongings out onto the street, seeing as you've not paid your rent yet. I know this morning I said it could wait, but this is ridiculous. Do you know how late it is?"

"My apologies, Madame," Jane said, dipping her head contritely. "I did intend to come back sooner, but the day's events prevented it."

Madame Moureaux harrumphed. "That's what they all say. Meanwhile, I'm losing money. I'm not in the habit of housing freeloaders, you know. There's plenty of other people to whom I could rent that room."

"Once again, I do apologise for my tardiness, Madame." Jane's cheeks burned, but she pressed on gently. "I hesitate to ask, but might I trouble you for a small favour?"

She saw the woman's eyebrow shoot up in annoyed surprise, but Jane continued before Madame Moureaux had a chance to speak. "Could you send word to Mr Dubois, please? I find myself in dire straits and I require his assistance."

At this, Madame Moureaux arrogantly threw back her head and scoffed. "What am I, your personal courier? It's your mess, girl. Sort it out yourself."

Jane's heart sank. She had wanted to keep mum about the details of her misfortune, but now Madame Moureaux left her little other choice than to reveal the truth.

"Very well," Jane sighed. "Then I have a confession to make. I have no money at present to pay for my room."

Madame Moureaux blinked. "Pardon?"

"I was robbed," Jane explained. "Earlier today. A thief snatched my purse out of my hand. It contained all of my money."

The café owner gave her a cold, hard stare.

"Please, Madame," Jane begged. "I'm penniless and I'm desperate. Is there any chance you would let me pay my rent later?"

Madame Moureaux laughed. "You seem to mistake my café for a charity. I'm not stupid, you know."

"It wouldn't be for very long, I promise," Jane insisted. "Just until my sister gets here. I wrote her a letter, to ask for her help. And I'm sure that when she hears about this, she will repay you handsomely for your kindness."

"Of course she will," Madame Moureaux replied with a sarcastic sneer. "Save your breath, dear. I've been in this business for decades and I've heard all the excuses."

"But it's true! Abbie will–"

"Listen, it's very simple. If you want to sleep in that room tonight, you'll have to pay for it. And if you're hard up, then you'll need to earn your keep."

"W-why, naturally," Jane stammered. "I suppose I could work in the kitchen for you?"

"I already have a cook and someone to wash the dishes. No, a pretty girl like you can make more money offering physical services of a different nature."

Jane gasped. "You don't mean...?"

"It seems to work just fine for Yvette," Madame Moureaux shrugged. "Ask her about it. Who knows, she might teach you a trick or two."

"Never," Jane said, outrage and disgust roiling up within her. "I refuse to debase myself in that way."

"Then I hope your high morals and lofty principles will keep you warm," Madame Moureaux sniffed mockingly. "Because you'll be sleeping underneath a bridge tonight. Go gather your things at once and leave my café. You're no longer welcome here."

Fighting back tears, Jane turned and trudged up the narrow stairs to retrieve her valise. With trembling hands, she entered the small room and slid the valise from underneath the bed.

Once again, she was being tossed out on the street. And once again, she had no idea where to go or who to turn to. How had she fallen so far, so fast?

Her feet felt like they were made of lead as she descended the stairs back to the taproom. When Jane handed in her key, Madame Moureaux didn't say a word, which was probably just as well, Jane thought. She'd had her fill of insults and snarky remarks for a while.

Valise in hand, she left the café. Not knowing which direction to take, she paused on the doorstep and shivered. There was a crisp chill in the air and the night was promising to be a cold one.

I need somewhere to sleep.

Somewhere warm and safe.

Georgie would be able to help her. But it was late and he would already have left the patisserie by now. Cursing herself, she realised she had never asked him the address of his lodgings.

Her other option was Mr Dubois. But he too was out of reach to her. If she went to his hotel, the police might follow her again and then she would draw unwanted attention to her friend – which struck her as a poor way to repay him for all the kindness he had shown her.

And besides, even if she did go over to the hotel, the doorman would never permit her entry dressed as she was, bedraggled and torn.

Jane glanced down at her mud-spattered gown and ripped skirts. "I should have changed into something cleaner before I left the room," she muttered.

But it was too late for that now. She wasn't going to change clothes out here in the street. Being on her own was dangerous enough.

Just then, a light rain began to fall. Jane ducked into the narrow alley next to the café, seeking shelter. She slumped against a damp brick wall, as fatigue and despair threatened to overwhelm her.

The day before, she had still been gainfully employed as a governess, with a roof over her head. Now she was homeless and destitute, discharged from her post in disgrace.

Jane squeezed her eyes shut, hot tears mingling with the raindrops on her cheeks. She thought of her sister back home in England, blissfully unaware of her predicament.

How much longer before her letter reached Abbie and Joe in London, she wondered? Maybe a couple of days, at best. But for all she knew, it could take up to a week – or even longer. And she would need to stick it out until then.

Somehow.

The wind picked up, and Jane shuddered as rain drops trickled down her neck. She clutched her valise to her chest like a shield, though it offered little protection against the elements.

How was she going to survive this ordeal? What if it rained the whole time? She would catch her death from pneumonia before she got to embrace her beloved sister again.

If I don't starve first, she thought when her empty stomach growled.

The sound of hurried footsteps echoing through the alley startled her. As if exposure and hunger weren't bad enough, she thought with a racing heart. Out on the streets she would also need to contend with thieves, drunkards and all manner of unsavoury characters.

Would she ever see Abbie again? Or would her body be found floating in the Seine one morning, just another nameless victim in the dangerous City of Light?

Heaven help me.

Jane bit her lip, willing herself not to cry. She had to be strong now. Survival was all that mattered.

"Sweet and gracious Lord," she said out loud, casting her eyes up to the dark skies above her, "I have been foolish and vain in coming to Paris. But please, don't let me die here."

"Mademoiselle Lee?" a young voice called out hesitantly in the gloom. "Is that you?"

"Petit Jean?"

Could it really be him? Or were the cold and the rain already causing her to hallucinate?

A small figure came running into the alley from the main street. And when he stopped in front of her, a sense of warm relief coursed through Jane. At last, a friendly face.

"How did you find me?" she asked.

"I wanted to know how you were doing. So I came to the café earlier today. But Madame Moureaux said you'd gone out. And when I came back just now, she told me you had left. I was just about to go home when I thought I heard your voice."

She sighed and smiled at him. The young boy probably wouldn't be able to do much for her, but she was grateful to see him nonetheless.

"Why did you decide to leave the café, Mademoiselle? Was the room that bad?" Studying her in more detail, his eyes grew wide when he noticed the ragged state of her clothes. "What happened to you?"

Quickly, Jane told him of all her troubles: the ineffectual police, the stolen purse, the humiliation by Maître Leblanc. And she shared how Madame Moureaux had turned her out for want of payment.

"So you see," Jane said when she had finished her story, "I am beyond hope."

"My heart aches for you, Mademoiselle," the boy sympathised. "But the sun will rise again tomorrow, and then your troubles won't seem nearly so bleak."

"I'm sure you're right," she sighed. "But for that to happen, I need to get through the night first."

"Don't worry, I'll help you. I know a good sleeping spot where you'll be dry and sheltered."

"My guardian angel," she smiled.

"That's not what most people would call me," he shrugged. "Come, follow me. We still have some way to walk."

Allowing him to lead her through a maze of streets, Jane soon lost her bearings. But she was too tired to care, and she trusted her young friend implicitly.

And at least it stopped raining after a while.

Eventually, they reached the river and Petit Jean guided her down to the waterside, next to a large bridge. Beneath its sheltered arch, the ground was dry.

"Probably not what you're used to, Mademoiselle," he said apologetically. "But no one will bother us here. And the view isn't too bad."

He gestured at the river. Now that the rain had ceased, the slow moving water of the Seine was reflecting the moonlight. Under different circumstances, Jane might have said it was almost idyllic.

"It will do me nicely, Petit Jean. Thank you."

"I'll stay with you tonight, of course," he said as they sat down with their backs against the stone wall. "So you don't have to be afraid of being alone."

"That's very kind of you, but no," she refused politely. "I couldn't possibly expect you to keep me company. You ought to sleep in your bed at home, where it's warm and safe."

"Safe?" He snorted. "Not when my father's around."

He took something out of the inner pocket of his coat and unwrapped it. "Here," he said, offering her half of the piece of bread. I saved this for us."

She wanted to decline, but he insisted. And she really was very hungry. So she accepted the bread and started chewing it – slowly.

"How did you know about this place, Petit Jean? Have you been here before?"

"Oh, plenty of times. Some days I just prefer to sleep out here, far away from home."

"Why?"

The boy grimaced. "My father, you see, he likes his wine. And when he's had too much, well, his hands start flying." Petit Jean swished his own hand through the air twice, mimicking a double slap across the face.

Poor boy, Jane thought, resisting the urge to pull him into her arms for a comforting hug.

Once they had finished the bread, the two of them settled down for the night, huddled together for warmth.

"*Bonne nuit, Mademoiselle.*"

"Good night, Petit Jean."

As soon as he closed his eyes, Jane could hear the boy's breathing beginning to slow as he drifted off. For herself however, sleep wasn't coming that easily.

And when she heard angry shouting nearby, her body tensed in fear and panic.

"What's wrong?" Petit Jean asked drowsily.

"It sounded like a fight," she replied, her eyes scanning the surrounding darkness for danger. "Are you sure it's safe out here?"

"Drunk people having an argument," he yawned as he closed his eyes again. "Happens all the time. Nothing to be afraid of."

Jane tried to calm her pounding heart while Petit Jean fell asleep. He looked so peaceful, his chest rising and falling rhythmically.

But sleep continued to evade her, even after the yelling voices in the distance stopped. Shivering against the cold wall, she stared out over the water of the Seine.

Hurry up, Abbie, she prayed silently. *Before it's too late.*

Chapter Twenty-Six

Jane woke up slowly, her body aching and stiff from a night spent on the unforgiving stone ground beneath the bridge. A chill permeated her bones, made worse by the dampness of her tattered and dirty dress. Shivering, she tried to curl up into a tight ball in a futile attempt to retain what little warmth remained.

Beside her, Petit Jean began to stir as well. He rolled over to face Jane, rubbing the last remnants of sleep from his eyes.

"Good morning, Mademoiselle," he said through a yawn. "How are you this morning?"

Jane gave him a weak smile. "Not too bad, I suppose, given the circumstances."

In truth, she was feeling awful. But to tell him that would make it sound as if she was ungrateful for the unselfish support he had shown her.

"I must say though," she continued, trying to stretch her sore muscles without much success, "I don't know how you manage to sleep so well out in the open air and on these hard stones."

"You get used to it, I guess," he shrugged. "Are you hungry?"

She nodded. *Hungry... and cold.*

In her hazy mind, she pictured herself sitting indoors by a roaring fireplace, sipping a hot cup of tea while a plate of freshly baked biscuits stood within easy reach.

Out here by the riverside however, there wasn't a fire in sight. And she knew they had finished their crust of bread the previous evening.

"Come," Petit Jean said as he stood up and quickly patted down his clothes. "Let's go and put some food in our bellies."

"I'd like nothing more. But I haven't got any money, remember?"

"No need for money," he grinned. "There's a church not too far from here. They hand out free soup to the poor every morning."

"Won't they turn us away?"

Petit Jean chuckled. "We don't exactly look like a pair of wealthy *citoyens*, you and I."

Looking down at her torn dress, Jane knew he had a point. Picking up her valise, they set off together through the awakening streets.

The prospect of having to line up with the beggars, the needy and the infirm made her feel embarrassed and self-conscious. But the gnawing ache in her stomach drove her on.

"Welcome," a kindly nun greeted them with a smile when Jane and Petit Jean arrived at the church. "Pick up an empty bowl and a spoon from the table and then follow the queue."

"God bless you, Sister," Jane said in French.

"And you, my dear child."

It wasn't much warmer inside, but at least they were sheltered from the wind. And the promise of hot soup helped to soothe some of the chill in Jane's exhausted body.

The long queue progressed swiftly and when it was their turn, Jane and Petit Jean were each served a bowl of thin yet hearty vegetable broth that made her mouth water.

She breathed in the aroma of the steaming hot food and then took a careful first sip.

Heavenly.

With every spoonful, Jane felt a blissful warmth seeping down to her stomach, from where the sensation seemed to spread out to her entire being. Slowly, her spirits began to be restored.

Petit Jean ate eagerly, pausing every so often to peer up at Jane. "Feeling better?" he asked after he had licked clean his empty bowl.

"Much, thank you," Jane replied happily. The soup hadn't just revived her physically. It had also sparked a faint glimmer of hope within.

After handing in their bowls and spoons, they thanked the friendly nuns and left the church. Soaking up the warm rays of morning sun, Jane squared her shoulders as she tried to gather her resolve.

"I'm off to the police station to report to Inspector Bouchard," she said. "And then I shall see about exchanging one or two of my dresses for some coins to line our empty pockets."

"Sensible idea, Mademoiselle."

"And after that, I must somehow manage to speak to Georgie – without passing by that horrid Maître Leblanc."

"I'm sure you'll think of something," Petit Jean smiled encouragingly. "Me, I have to go to work. But let's meet under our bridge again this evening, shall we?"

"That would be lovely. Thank you, Petit Jean."

He tipped his cap to her and hurried off down the street. Jane watched him go until he disappeared around a corner.

Then, with a deep breath, she turned and headed in the opposite direction towards the police station. She steeled herself as she walked, determined to face Inspector Bouchard with as much courage as she could muster.

Which was more than yesterday, she was pleased to notice.

And who knew, perhaps today the inspector would have better news for her about the case. When she reached the police station, she sent up a quick prayer for the safe return of Alistair and Penelope, before entering the building.

Inside, the station was buzzing with its usual bustle of activity. Jane wound her way through the chaos and approached the desk. Manning it that morning was the same snooty police sergeant as the day before.

"Excuse me, Monsieur," she said. "I'm here to see Inspector Bouchard, please. As ordered."

The sergeant glanced up casually from his paperwork, but then froze when he laid eyes on Jane. His jaw dropped in astonishment, while the pencil he was holding fell out of his hand.

"M–mademoiselle Lee?" he stammered. "Mademoiselle Jane Lee?"

"Yes, that's me," she replied, surprised by his odd reaction to her. "I was here yesterday as well, don't you remember?"

A sudden hush fell over the station as all activity ceased and every policeman's head turned towards Jane.

She shifted uncomfortably under the weight of their stares, confusion and foreboding rising within her. Why were they all gaping at her as if she were a phantom?

The stunned silence lasted only a few seconds before the sergeant rushed off. "Inspector Bouchard," he shouted as he ran towards the offices further back into the building. "Inspector Bouchard, come quick! It's her. It's the English girl."

Inspector Bouchard came running out of his office and stopped short at the sight of Jane. Shock mingled with anger on his face.

"*Sacré bleu,*" he muttered.

"What's wrong?" she asked with a jittery voice. "Why is everyone looking at me like that?"

Bouchard quickly overcame his surprise and strode towards her. His expression was thunderous, causing Jane's unease to swell into fear.

"Thought you'd come to the lion's den to gloat, is that it?" Bouchard growled, looming over her. Before she could respond, he grabbed her arm with a grip as strong as iron.

"Jane Lee, I'm placing you under arrest."

"You're arresting me?! What for?"

"For the abduction of Alistair and Penelope Crawford."

"What?" Jane reeled, her head spinning. "You must be joking, Monsieur. What sort of travesty is this?"

"I assure you there is no joke and no travesty here, Mademoiselle," he replied. "I am most serious. Deadly serious, in fact."

"Then you are mistaken," she hissed, desperately attempting to wrench her arm free from his grasp. "I've done nothing wrong!"

Bouchard's lip curled up in a sneer. "Enough of your lies. Coming here was very brazen of you. But your foolish pride will be our gain."

He snapped handcuffs on Jane's wrists, the metal biting into her skin. The sudden pain caused a wave of terror to course through her as reality set in.

"Take her to the interrogation room," Bouchard barked at two officers. "We'll get the truth out of her soon enough."

Chapter Twenty-Seven

"I'm innocent," Jane cried out as the two policemen took hold of her arms and marched her down the hall. When they opened the door to the interrogation room, Jane's shocked confusion gave way to fear and despair.

None too gently, the officers shoved her into the small windowless room containing only a table and a set of chairs.

"Sit," one of them growled.

When Jane didn't comply with the order straight away, the other officer grabbed her and pushed her down onto the chair.

They're treating me like I'm a vile criminal, she whimpered silently. No matter how hard she tried, she could make no sense of this waking nightmare.

Inspector Bouchard entered the room, followed by his British colleague Woodcock, who looked at Jane with pity and disappointment in his eyes.

"Leave us," Bouchard told his two officers while he and Woodcock took a seat at the table across from Jane.

She gave a little start when the door slammed shut behind the policemen. Clenching together

her manacled hands, she tried hard to fight back her tears.

Why were they doing this to her? Had they decided she was a convenient scapegoat? Was Bouchard going to pin this crime on her, so he could tell his superiors and the press that he had solved the case?

Or were they playing a cruel game with her, trying to frighten her into a confession?

Jane ventured a fearful glance at the two inspectors sitting in front of her, but their faces didn't betray any hint of what was going through their minds.

Bouchard was the first to break the tense silence. "I'll give you one last chance to make this easy on yourself," he grumbled. "Just tell us where you're hiding the children, and maybe the judge will show you some leniency."

Jane's eyes widened. "Hiding the– But I don't know where they are," she cried. "If I did, I would have told you from the very start. Why in heaven's name would you think I kidnapped them?"

Woodcock leaned forward, sadness etched on his face. "Come now, Miss Lee. As your sole fellow countryman in this room, I urge you to cooperate."

Contrary to Bouchard's harshness, his tone was gentle. As if he was a kind and patient father talking to a child that had misbehaved itself.

"You'll only make matters worse if you don't admit to your crime."

"But I've committed no crime," Jane insisted. She turned desperately to Bouchard. "Inspector, you must believe me. I would never harm those children!"

Bouchard's expression hardened. "You can stop pretending, Mademoiselle. The jig is up. We have damning evidence, black on white, clearly implicating you."

Jane's pulse quickened. Evidence? What could they possibly have found?

The French inspector slid a piece of paper across the table. "Lord and Lady Crawford received this ransom note demanding money for the safe return of their children. Our experts have confirmed that the handwriting matches yours."

Jane grasped the paper with trembling hands, her eyes darting over the words. She couldn't deny that the handwriting did indeed resemble her own. To an uncanny degree even. But how was that possible? None of it made any sense.

"Lady Crawford was kind enough to provide us with the original letter you wrote to them when you applied for the position of governess," Bouchard explained. "Our experts have compared the handwriting on both of these documents. And there can be no mistake: you wrote that ransom note."

"But I didn't! I swear." Panic swelled within Jane. "Inspector, you have to keep searching for the real kidnapper."

Bouchard slammed his fist on the table, causing Jane to jump. "Do not take me for a fool, Mademoiselle," he bellowed. "You penned that note, and you have the children stashed away somewhere. This charade ends now. Tell me where they are!"

Jane shrank back. "Inspector, please. I beg you, listen to reason–"

"Perhaps she's a Russian spy," Woodcock mused calmly, persisting in his far-fetched conspiracy theory.

"I'm not a spy," Jane bristled irritably.

"Come now," Woodcock said. "Then perhaps they forced you into this villainy against your will?"

"Nobody forced me to do anything. Please, Inspector, is this really necessary?"

"Don't be afraid, my dear," Woodcock smiled amicably. "You can confide in us. We're your friends. What pressure did they put on you to betray your country? Was it blackmail? Vicious threats to harm your loved ones? Tell us, so we may rescue you from their evil clutches."

"I've never met any Russians in my entire life. And I don't know who took the children or where they are." Exasperated tears burned in Jane's eyes. "All I want is for Alistair and

Penelope to be found and returned home safely."

"Enough of these lies," Bouchard shouted, pounding his fist on the table again, much closer to Jane this time. "Give us the names of your accomplices, and the hiding place of the children. Or you'll regret it."

Glaring darkly at her, he growled, "I ought to lock you up in a cell and throw away the key."

Jane shrank back, any further protests dying on her lips. The inspectors' minds were clearly made up. With no proof of her innocence, how could she make them see the truth? She blinked back tears of frustration and fear, utterly powerless against the incriminating weight of that mysterious ransom note.

Inspector Bouchard got up from his seat and began pacing the room. He had quieted down, but his frustration was still palpable.

"You strike me as an intelligent young lady, Mademoiselle," he said. "Someone who wants to live life to the fullest. Respectable, well-educated girls like you? They dream of falling in love, meeting the right man and starting a happy family."

Calmly, he placed his palms on the table and leaned in closer to Jane. "Don't throw away such a beautiful future, Mademoiselle – I implore you. Confess, and your punishment will be lighter."

Jane's vision blurred with tears. "I have nothing to confess, Inspector," she whispered.

Bouchard let out a long and disappointed sigh. "Most regrettable. But..." Pausing, he removed his hands from the table and rose up to his full length.

"If you will not talk willingly, we have ways of extracting the truth from you."

Jane paled at this veiled threat. She turned to Inspector Woodcock, her teary eyes pleading for his help.

The Scotland Yard inspector smiled at her and uttered a bunch of words in a harsh and garbled language.

"I– I don't understand, sir," she replied. "What are you saying?"

Woodcock spoke again, in that same foreign tongue that she couldn't make heads or tails of.

"Your Russian is impressive, *mon ami*," Bouchard said to his British colleague. "But save yourself the effort. Mademoiselle seems intent on denying everything."

He opened the door and barked an order in French into the corridor. Seconds later, his two officers reappeared in the interrogation room.

"Take her down to the prison cells," Bouchard said. "Let her stew in there for a bit, until she comes to her senses."

Deflated and defeated, Jane offered no resistance when the policemen led her away.

"Poor child," she heard Woodcock saying behind her. "Much too young to be caught up in the dirty games of foreign politics."

"British imbecile," Bouchard muttered under his breath as he followed his men out of the room.

Thoroughly ashamed of herself, Jane kept her eyes downcast while they marched through the police station towards the holding block.

Her sense of humiliation turned into sheer dread however, the moment they reached the cellar where the cells were located. The place reeked of unwashed bodies and all manner of human waste.

Somewhere a madman cried out drunkenly. "Just you wait until the Emperor hears about this, you filthy coppers."

"Shut up," a prison guard shouted back. "Napoleon's been dead since ages in case you'd forgotten."

The man took his bunch of rattling iron keys and unlocked an empty cell for Jane. Her escorts pushed her inside.

"Please," she begged, turning around to face Inspector Bouchard. "I've done nothing wrong."

But the French inspector's face remained stony. "You've brought this upon yourself with your refusal to cooperate. I suggest you use this time to search your conscience."

Gesturing at the guard to close the door, he added, "We'll continue our discussion tomorrow, Miss Lee."

The cell door banged shut with a resounding clang and then someone turned the key in the lock.

A cold shiver running down her spine, Jane looked round her tiny cell. There was a grimy bucket in one corner and a simple bed with a straw mattress. A single barred and narrow window high up in the wall was the only source of light in this dismal hole.

Sitting down on the lumpy bed, Jane dropped her head into her hands. How had everything gone so horribly wrong?

Just this morning, her world had still held a small glimmer of hope. But now here she was, accused of a terrible crime she did not commit.

Who wrote that ransom note?

Why did they do it in her handwriting?

And how?

As tears began to roll down her cheeks, Jane realised she didn't have any of the answers. There was only one thing she was certain of...

Her life, as she knew it, was well and truly over.

Chapter Twenty-Eight

Harsh noises of rattling keys and heavy footsteps echoed through the corridor of the prison block at the police station, rousing Jane from her shallow slumber.

She blinked, willing her foggy mind to come back to life. A narrow shaft of light shone down from the small window near the ceiling.

Must be morning then, she assumed as her thoughts sluggishly began to pick up pace.

How many mornings had it been now since she was locked up in this dreadful place? Three? Four? The days and nights had blurred together in a haze of fitful sleep, endless questioning by the inspectors, and the gnawing ache of hunger in her belly.

She shivered, her rough blanket providing little comfort or warmth on the hard wooden bed with its bug-infested straw mattress.

Jane sat up, slowly, every muscle in her body protesting. She had lost weight in her time here, her dress hanging loosely off her famished frame. Sleep had eluded her most nights, her mind spinning in circles trying to make sense of it all.

Why would anyone want to take those poor children? And why did the French police insist on accusing her?

Outside her cell, the guard suddenly rapped his baton against her door, causing Jane to jump in fright.

"Time to wake up," he said in his usual uncaring tone. He turned the key in the rusty lock and opened the door. "No breakfast for you this morning, princess. There's someone here to see you."

When the man stepped aside, Inspector Bouchard strode forward and paused just outside her cell. Jane tensed.

"Come with me," the inspector said gruffly. "To my office."

With hesitant steps, she followed Bouchard down the gloomy corridor. The world swayed around her, and she had to grasp the damp walls for support. Lack of food and sleep had left her lightheaded.

But she persevered, concentrating on putting one foot in front of the other. The inspector set a brisk pace, clearly impatient.

To his office, he had said. She'd heard that correctly, hadn't she? Normally, they interviewed her in the interrogation room. So why this change?

Perhaps it was nothing but an insignificant detail. The result of a trivial practical matter.

Or perhaps the inspectors had decided to change tack. Were they going to try to elicit a confession out of her by putting her at ease in the relative comfort of Bouchard's office, with a cup of English tea and a ginger biscuit?

Or could this be the start of a far more sinister phase in her ordeal? Maybe they were sending her somewhere even worse.

Jane's heart quickened as they approached the door to his office. She whispered a silent prayer, hoping against hope that by some miracle, this nightmare might end.

She was fully expecting to find Inspector Woodcock waiting for her. But when she and Bouchard entered the office, it was a very different familiar figure that stood beside the desk.

"Abbie," Jane cried, rushing into her sister's open arms.

Abbie embraced her tightly, stroking Jane's limp hair.

"Oh Jane, look at you," she murmured. "So pale and thin." Abbie's voice caught with emotion as she held Jane's gaunt face between her hands.

Jane drank in the sight of her dear sister through a film of grateful tears. "You came for me," she whispered.

Abbie turned fiery eyes on Inspector Bouchard. "Is this how you treat innocent young women in your custody, Monsieur?" she demanded. "My poor sister is skin and bones!"

Bouchard shifted on his feet, looking uncomfortable. "We are running an investigation here, Madame. Not a hotel," he muttered.

Jane sank into a chair, her legs too weak to support her. "How did you know I was here?" she asked Abbie.

"Georgie sent us a telegram when he read about your arrest in the local papers," Abbie explained. "The moment we got his cable, I packed up and came straight here from London. Joe is coming too, just as soon as he wraps up some business."

"Georgie?" Jane asked, her miserable heart lifting at the mention of his name. "He's the one who sent you a message? Is he here?" She glanced round the office. But the only people present, apart from herself, were Abbie and Bouchard.

Abbie nodded. "He's waiting outside. Very impatiently, no doubt. Joe has sent Bill along too, as my escort."

Jane blinked back more tears, overcome with gratitude. Standing beside them, Inspector Bouchard cleared his throat awkwardly.

"Your brother-in-law must have some very influential friends," he told Jane, trying to hide his irritation. "I have been ordered to release you into your sister's custody."

"I'm being released?" Jane gasped incredulously.

"For now, yes," Bouchard replied. Raising his finger as a stern warning, he swiftly added, "But this is only a temporary measure. You are still our prime suspect. And as such, you are required to stay by your sister's side at the hotel at all times."

Jane turned to Abbie in distress. "I didn't take those children, I swear."

Abbie took hold of Jane's hands and gave them a gentle squeeze. "I know that, my darling. Don't you fret. We'll get to the bottom of this."

Turning her cool eyes on Bouchard, she said, "Come, Jane. Let's get you out of this horrible place."

Jane rose unsteadily, holding on to her sister. She was afraid that, any moment now, she would wake up and discover this was just a dream.

"We shall be keeping an eye on you, Mademoiselle," Inspector Bouchard said when Jane and Abbie left his office. "Sooner or later, you will have no choice but to lead us to wherever you are hiding young Alistair and Penelope Crawford."

Ignoring his remark, Jane grasped her sister's arm for support as they made their way outside.

The pale morning sun nearly blinded her and she wavered on her feet. How long had it been since she had felt fresh air or seen the sky?

"Jane," the sweetest voice in the world exclaimed. Georgie bounded up the broad steps outside the police station. Jane released Abbie and flew into his embrace.

They clung to each other wordlessly, tears flowing.

"I was so worried for you," Georgie finally choked out. "After I read the news report about your arrest, I came here every day. But the police wouldn't let me see you."

He pulled her into his arms again and sighed, "Thank heavens you're out of there. It must have been gruesome for you."

"I'm all right now," Jane managed through her sobs. "Now that you're here."

After a long moment, they drew apart and Jane saw Bill standing nearby. The tall young man touched two fingers to his temple in a casual salute.

"Good to see you still kicking, Jane," he said with a grin.

"Hello Bill," she laughed, wiping the tears from her face and touching his arm affectionately. "It's great to have you here as well."

Bill was a young business associate of Joe's, and a force to be reckoned with. Jane knew that

Bill had once been a member of Joe's street gang, many years ago, before her brother-in-law had mended his ways.

Forever leaving his life of crime behind, Joe had used his natural charm and wit to become a legitimate and very successful investor.

And then he had met and fallen in love with Jane's elder sister.

"Let's go to the hotel, shall we?" Abbie announced to the group. "Jane, you'll have to share my suite with me, I'm afraid. But don't worry," she chuckled. "It's as big as a house."

Arm in arm with Georgie, Jane felt like she was walking on clouds as they went to the carriage that stood waiting for them. After days of despair in her dark cell, this tasted sweeter than any dream.

"Let's get you bathed and into some fresh clothes," Abbie said after the carriage had deposited them all safely at the hotel. "Because quite frankly, my dear baby sister, you smell dreadful."

Jane looked down self-consciously at her rumpled dress. "That would be lovely, thank you."

Next, Abbie turned to Georgie and Bill. "You two go and see what more you can learn out there. Ask the police what leads they are following. Revisit the scene of the crime and talk to any witnesses. Jane and I will freshen up and meet you back here in a few hours."

The young men nodded. Georgie touched Jane's shoulder. "We'll find Alistair and Penelope," he said. "And the villains who took them."

Jane managed a small smile in return. Did she dare hope for such a perfect outcome already? She was only just beginning to believe that her release from police custody was real.

Once upstairs in their suite, Abbie arranged for a hot bath to be drawn. Jane peeled off her soiled dress and gratefully sank into the tub. She sighed in pleasure, feeling her body relax for the first time in days.

Before long, the water had turned grey as the dirt and grime washed away. Abbie helped Jane wash her hair and then laid out a fresh dress on the bed.

"It's one of mine," she said. "But I'm sure it'll fit you nicely."

Jane emerged from the bath feeling reborn. As she slipped into the clean clothes, the soft linen shift and Parisian blue day dress caressed her skin.

"Much better," Abbie declared after having inspected her younger sister. "Now, how about we go downstairs and get some food in your tummy? I hear they have excellent scones and macaroons in the hotel lounge."

Jane placed a hand over her rumbling stomach. “That sounds perfect. I’m famished.”

Their arms linked, whispering and giggling like back in the days when they were happy little girls, the two sisters made their way to the grand hotel lobby.

The hotel lounge was furnished with plush divans and armchairs, occupied by well-heeled ladies chatting over tea. Jane lowered herself onto an emerald velvet sofa while a waiter promptly appeared to take their order.

“A pot of your finest tea,” Abbie instructed. “Scones, macaroons, little cakes. Fresh butter, obviously. Just bring us a bit of everything, there’s a good man.”

She turned to Jane with a smile. “We need to put some meat back on those bones of yours.”

Soon, an array of delectable treats appeared before them. Jane’s mouth watered at the sight. She bit into a still warm scone slathered in clotted cream and nearly swooned.

“This is heaven,” she sighed while she slowly chewed the scone with her eyes closed.

Abbie chuckled, pouring the fragrant tea. “Prison food not quite up to these standards, was it?”

“Hardly,” Jane snorted. The exquisite delicacies and the warm tea helped to revive her spirits. She was almost feeling human again.

While Jane continued to devour the food, Abbie recounted all that had happened after receiving Georgie's shocking telegram. She had rushed off to Paris by the next available boat, while Joe worked to secure Jane's release through his connections.

"I'm indebted to you and Joe for the rest of eternity," Jane said, pinching back a few tears of joy at the corner of her eye. "It must have taken some doing. Inspector Bouchard sounded none too pleased about having to let me go."

"Let's just say Joe can be very persuasive," Abbie smiled vaguely. "Eat another little cake, love."

Jane happily complied, the sweetness replenishing her depleted body. As she finished the last scone, she hesitated.

"Abbie, did you... Did you receive a letter from me, asking for help?"

Her sister blinked. "A letter? No, Georgie's telegram was the first we knew of any trouble."

Jane's brow furrowed. Mr Dubois had promised to post her letter after she had written it. Had he lied? Or did it simply take that long for a letter to reach England from France?

"Why?" Abbie asked. "Did you send us a letter? When?"

"After the trouble started. But I suppose it's all irrelevant now," Jane said, dismissing the matter. "What's important is that you're here."

"Thanks to Georgie," Abbie added with a smile.

Yes, Jane thought. *Thanks to Georgie.*

She let out a long and sombre sigh. "We've had quite a few terrible quarrels, you know – Georgie and I. We've both spoken in haste, and we've flung hurtful accusations at each other."

Abbie reached out and patted Jane's hand. "You mustn't be too hard on either of you, dear. Men sometimes need a little help understanding matters of the heart."

Jane bit her lip. "But I was so awful to him. What if he doesn't forgive me?"

"From what I saw earlier, that young man is still utterly smitten with you." Abbie smiled and squeezed her hand. "All will be well, Jane. You'll see."

The comforting food and sisterly chat had restored Jane's spirits. But she could not fully relax knowing that the true villains were still at large.

Who had taken the children? And why?

Stifling a sudden yawn behind her hand, Jane felt gripped by a wave of fatigue, brought on by the copious amounts of sweet treats she had consumed.

"Come," Abbie said. "You need to rest." She signed the bill and began escorting Jane upstairs. "You can have a nap for a little while. And then hopefully, by the time you wake up,

Bill and Georgie will have returned with some good news."

Back in their lavish suite, Abbie opened the door to the bedroom. Jane immediately froze in the doorway, shock rooting her to the spot.

There, lounging casually in an armchair, was Percy Yates. He looked up from examining his nails and grinned wolfishly at them.

"Well, well. Look who's here. The charming Lee sisters, reunited at last."

By the window, brooding and keeping his back turned to them, stood Mr Dubois – gazing out over the street below.

Chapter Twenty-Nine

"You," Abbie seethed, glaring at their nemesis with fury etched on her face. "What are you doing here?"

"Come now, dearest," Percy grinned. "That's no way to greet an old friend." He remained seated in his chair, looking completely at ease.

"You're not a friend," Abbie replied. "How did you get into my room?"

"It's amazing what a bit of money can accomplish, you know. In exchange for a handful of coins, one of the maids kindly let my business associate and myself in." He chuckled. "Don't be too hard on the poor girl though. It's pathetic how little these people are paid."

Jane glanced over at Mr Dubois. But the Frenchman still hadn't turned around and kept staring outside instead. Not a trace of his usual charm and warmth. Only sombre silence. It uneased her.

"Money can buy all sorts of useful information, too," Percy continued smugly. "Like the name and address of the hotel you were staying at."

"Who gave you those details?" Abbie growled.

"A special friend at the police force," Percy said, the corners of his mouth curling up in a sarcastic smile. "That's also how I knew you were coming to Paris before you had even set foot on French soil."

"You're bribing a police officer?" Jane asked. "Let me guess: Inspector Bouchard?"

"That crusty old fool," Percy laughed. "Far too decent to be swayed by bribes. He may seem like the gruff and grumpy type, but he's infuriatingly honest."

Then he turned his attention back to Abbie. With a sinister twinkle in his eyes he asked, "But why are you acting so surprised to see me, dearest? Surely, your darling baby sister already warned you I was in Paris?"

Abbie's head whipped round to Jane. "You knew?"

Jane nodded, her stomach twisting into a nervous knot.

"Then why didn't you tell me?" Abbie demanded.

"It slipped from my mind."

Abbie bristled. "It's not as if it's a minor detail, is it? Have you forgotten the things this man tried to do to us? The misery he put us through?"

"No, but–"

"When did you find out he was in Paris?"

Jane swallowed. Her throat felt dry. "It happened a week or two after I arrived. Mr Dubois took me on a brief tour of the city. And when we returned to his hotel, Percy was waiting for him in the lobby."

"So you've known all this time, yet somehow you failed to mention it to me?"

"I had other things to worry about, you know," Jane answered defensively.

"My, oh my," Percy chuckled. "The loving Lee sisters are having a bit of a quarrel. How delightful!"

Immediately, Jane and Abbie stopped their bickering. With a wordless apology in their eyes, they reached out and held each other's hand, giving it a gentle squeeze.

Turning back to Percy, Abbie drew herself up, eyes blazing defiantly. "Leave this room – now. Or I will call for a member of staff and have you removed."

"So soon? I've only just got here," Percy said sweetly. "Don't you first want to hear what I have to say?"

"I have no interest whatsoever in anything that comes out of your vile mouth."

"But we have so much to talk about," he insisted in that insufferably smug tone of his. "It's been ages since we last saw each other."

"Not nearly long enough," Abbie said. "May I remind you that you gave us your word to stay away? Or do I need to refresh your memory?"

"I remember the circumstances and the details perfectly well, I assure you," he replied in a low growl as a dark cloud seemed to come over his face.

But his moment of anger passed quickly, after which his usual mocking grin promptly returned. "How could I forget, when your husband was so persuasive?"

"Then why are you here?" Abbie demanded to know.

"For old times' sake?" he quipped.

"This is obviously a laughing matter to you. Jane, hurry on down to the hotel lobby and ask them to fetch the police. Tell them a pair of vagrants have intruded into our suite."

Percy calmly raised a hand to stop Jane in her tracks. "No need for threats, my lovelies. It's all very simple, really. You see, I never had any intention of renewing our acquaintance."

He paused to let out a dramatic sigh. "But then, by pure chance, Jane and I bumped into each other again. And that's when a plan began to formulate itself in my mind."

He looked at each of them in turn, deliberately drawing out the moment.

"What plan?" Jane asked, unsure whether she would like his reply. She could sense that he was up to something.

"A very wicked plan," Percy said with visible glee. "Involving revenge of the sweetest nature."

Another pause. He glanced at his sleeve and brushed away a speck of dust that wasn't there. "Dreadful what happened to those Crawford children, isn't it?"

Jane inhaled sharply. "Alistair and Penelope. What do you know about them?"

"Everything," Percy replied, looking Jane square in the eye. "Because you see, it was I who orchestrated the whole thing."

A short shriek escaped from Jane's lips before her hand flew to her mouth in horror. Beside her, Abbie paled.

"Why?" she whispered hoarsely.

"Not for the obvious reasons," Percy replied lightly. "And certainly not for the money. I did it solely and in such a way that the blame would be pinned on you, dear Jane."

She gasped for air. But her chest felt too constricted, her nerves and muscles too tight.

"And just imagine," he continued, "what will happen once the police find the cold, dead bodies of those poor little children."

"They're– Are they dead?!"

"Not yet," Percy grinned. "At the moment, they are still very much alive and unharmed.

But not for long any more. And then you will hang for their murder."

Jane swayed on her feet, the room spinning. Just in time, she felt her shoulders being grasped by her elder sister to steady her.

"Monster," Abbie hissed at Percy.

"Do I detect a hint of disapproval there, my dearest?" He laughed. "Good. Because I'm doing it all for you."

"For me?" Abbie asked.

"You'll be helpless to save your beloved baby sister. You'll watch her swing from the gallows. And then you'll spend the rest of your days devastated by grief."

He sat up straight and came leaning forward, his eyes glittering darkly with hatred and malice. "You'll never be happy again, no matter how much more money that filthy-rich husband of yours makes."

Smiling, he calmly sat back again. "It's an infinitely sweeter form of revenge than if I had dealt the fatal blow to you directly. A bit more complicated to pull off perhaps. But most gratifying."

"You're mad," Abbie said. "Only a deranged madman would dream up such a demented scheme."

"You ruined my life when you banished me from London," Percy snarled. "So now I'm ruining yours."

Having found her voice again, Jane cut in angrily. "I should've known you were lying when you told me you had changed."

Emboldened, she turned to Mr Dubois. "And you, Monsieur. Don't just stand there. What do you have to say about all this?"

Mr Dubois turned round to face her, stiffly clasping his balled fists behind his back.

"You told me that you and Percy were business partners," Jane said. "How exactly does snatching innocent children fit into that picture?"

She could see him nervously clenching his jaw, while his chest expanded with the breath he was holding.

When Mr Dubois hesitated, Percy jumped in. "You mustn't judge my associate too harshly," he said. "His intentions with you were much simpler."

Spotting the alarm on Jane's face, he laughed. "Oh, nothing of *that* sort, I assure you. It's true Pierre and I are business partners. We just happen to be in the business of relieving rich people of their money – subtly and tactfully, so they don't blame us for their loss."

"So you're swindlers," Abbie grumbled.

"That's a terribly harsh word, dearest," Percy quipped. "I like to think of it more as an art form."

"Call it what you like," Abbie said. "It's still fraud and it's still a crime."

Percy shrugged. "Foreigners are our favourite target. Something about the magic of Paris lowers their guard," he chuckled. "Pierre has a special preference for swindling the British. He detests most of us with a passion."

Jane stared at Mr Dubois, who immediately lowered his gaze to the floor. "He was friendly enough with me," she said. "Why, Monsieur? Was it all just an act?"

"He was merely using you to gain access to Lord Crawford, my dear," Percy explained, revelling in the hurt and the pain caused to her pride. "But then, as fate would have it, you and I crossed paths again. And I just couldn't let an opportunity like that slip past me."

"You gave us your word," Abbie said bitterly.

"And I kept it," he barked. "I abandoned my life in London, and I even left England. But when your sister showed up here in Paris–" Regaining his composure, he smiled. "Well, that made her fair game, didn't it?"

"Fair game," Jane huffed. "Like that ransom note you forged?"

"A true work of art, that was," Percy replied proudly. "Pierre never posted the letter he asked you to write, obviously. We gave it to an acquaintance of ours, who happens to be an expert in these things. Falsifying documents is a rather useful skill in this line of business. Our friend studied your handwriting and then wrote that ransom letter: the perfect piece of evidence, pointing the finger of guilt directly at you."

He grinned, extremely pleased with how clever he thought he had been. Unable to bear Percy's smugness, Jane looked at Mr Dubois.

"I trusted you, Monsieur," she said. "But you betrayed me. What a dishonourable coward you are."

"My, my. Look at the time," Percy said after a quick glance at the clock on the mantelpiece. He rose to his feet, smoothing down his clothes. "What do you say, Pierre old chap: shall we make our way and leave these two lovely ladies to it?"

"You won't get away with this," Abbie growled. "We'll go to the police and tell them everything."

Percy snorted. "By all means, please do. They won't believe you. After all, like you said: only a deranged madman would dream up a scheme as demented as mine."

With an exaggerated hand flourish, he bowed to them and sauntered off – Mr Dubois following him in shameful silence.

When the door closed behind the two villains, Abbie turned to Jane, her eyes blazing with furious determination. She started saying something, but Jane couldn't hear the words. Everything was turning into a distant haze.

Overcome with emotions, Jane's legs buckled and she collapsed on the floor.

Chapter Thirty

"Jane!" Abbie's voice came drifting into Jane's mind, seemingly from far away at first, but then with more urgency. "Jane, can you hear me?"

Slowly regaining consciousness, Jane's eyes fluttered open. She was lying on the plush carpet of their hotel suite. Her sister Abbie sat kneeling beside her, gently patting her cheek.

Jane let out a soft groan as the room swam into focus. An instant later, her mind was flooded with the horrific memories of what had just transpired: Percy's gleeful admission that he had abducted Alistair and Penelope, his intention to kill them... and leave Jane to take the fall for it.

It all came crashing down on her like a tidal wave.

"Oh Abbie," Jane cried, sitting up and clutching her sister's hands. "This is all my fault. If anything happens to those dear children–"

"Hush now, don't speak like that," Abbie soothed, though her voice trembled slightly. "At least we know now that they're still alive."

"But for how much longer? You heard what Percy said. That horrible snake is going to kill them." Her voice broke over the awful words, while a tear traced down her cheek. The thought of Alistair and Penelope being murdered was intolerable – even more so than the looming threat of her own demise.

Abbie's jaw set with determination. "Which is exactly why we must go to the police straight away and tell them everything. They will track down Percy and put a stop to this hideous scheme."

Jane looked at her dubiously. "Do you really think Inspector Bouchard will believe such a wild tale? He seems convinced I'm guilty."

"We'll make him believe," Abbie said firmly, her tone allowing no room for argument. "You mustn't give up hope, my darling."

With Abbie's help, Jane rose to her feet. She swayed unsteadily, her head still swimming. Taking deep breaths, the floral scent of Abbie's perfume cut through the fog in her mind. She wanted to believe her sister, but doubt kept gnawing at her soul.

"Come," Abbie said, gently grasping her by the shoulders. "There's no time to wait for Bill and Georgie to return. We must go directly to the police."

She took Jane's arm and led her from the suite. Jane's knees felt weak, and her stomach churned with dread. But she took courage from her elder sister's commanding presence. Abbie had always been her anchor in times of distress.

With Abbie by her side, perhaps this nightmare could still be resolved.

Putting one foot in front of the other, Jane followed her sister down to the hotel lobby. Lives hung in the balance, she realised. And the police were their only hope.

Outside the hotel, they hailed a hansom cab and set off. But the streets were busy in the late afternoon, and their progress was vexingly slow.

Willing herself to remain calm, Jane prayed with all her heart that Inspector Bouchard could be made to believe the truth.

"Finally," Abbie sighed when they arrived at the police station. After they had hurried out of their carriage and into the building, an officer duly showed them to Inspector Bouchard's office.

Jane was startled to find Inspector Woodcock sitting across from his French counterpart. *Or maybe that's a good thing,* she thought. After all, the Scotland Yard man had proven himself less inclined to view her as the main suspect.

"Back so soon?" Bouchard said, his eyebrows shooting up in surprise. "We released you only this morning, Mademoiselle. You weren't due to report to me until tomorrow."

His tone turned wry. "Unless of course, you've decided to finally start telling the truth?"

Jane gathered her courage. "I have come to tell you the truth, Inspector. But it's not what you think."

She threw a quick sideways glance at Abbie, who nodded and gave Jane's hand a reassuring squeeze, urging her to go on.

As she launched into their astonishing account, Bouchard and Woodcock listened, stone-faced. But with each word that passed her lips, she could see the scepticism growing on Bouchard's face.

"Preposterous," he snorted when she had finished. "Villains lying in wait in your hotel suite? An old enemy plotting against you? Do you really expect me to believe this absurd tale of vengeance and intrigue?"

"She speaks the truth," Abbie insisted. "Percy is a beastly scoundrel. The lives of those two poor children are in mortal danger."

Bouchard raised a sceptical eyebrow. "So you say. But can others corroborate this story?"

Jane shook her head. "There was no one else present."

Bouchard sighed. "Then I have nothing but your word to rely on. And you must admit, Mademoiselle, your tale sounds rather... fantastical."

"Inspector, I swear on my life: every word is true," Jane cried desperately. "Please, you must find this man before it's too late!"

"Very well," Bouchard sighed deeply. "I will humour you and make some enquiries. If this Percy Yates of yours truly exists–"

"He does exist, Inspector," Jane interrupted. "And he's going to commit a dreadful murder if you don't act soon."

Bouchard held up a hand to silence her. "If he exists and he is here in Paris, then my colleagues at Immigration will have a record of him. I'll go and ask."

Scribbling a note, he grumbled, "Don't let it ever be said that Inspector Bouchard should leave any stone unturned."

He tore off the piece of paper and rose to his feet. Pausing by the door, he gave Jane a stern look. "But I must warn you, Mademoiselle. I do not like being played for a fool."

Jane nodded before watching him disappear into the corridor. Wringing her hands, she started pacing the room while they anxiously awaited his return.

"See?" Abbie smiled at her. "We did the right thing in coming here. As soon as the inspector finds Percy's file, we'll be one step closer to resolving this dreadful business."

Jane sighed, wishing she could feel as confident as her sister seemed to be.

"Percy Yates, you said, eh?" Inspector Woodcock mused. The sound of his voice made

Jane halt her frenetic pacing. She had nearly forgotten he was still there.

"I do wonder..." he said.

"Yes, Inspector?"

"Just a notion I had." Woodcock tugged at his moustache. "Percy Yates... Hmm, yes. Sounds remarkably similar to Pyotr Yadenski."

Jane stared blankly at him. "I'm afraid I don't follow."

Woodcock leaned forward eagerly. "Pyotr Yadenski is a Russian master of espionage. Highly elusive chap. My colleagues and I have been after him for years. But the fox always evades capture. The fellow is so slippery we don't even know what he looks like."

"I beg your pardon?" Abbie spoke up, looking askance at him. "How does a Russian spymaster come into any of this?"

"The inspector is convinced Alistair and Penelope were taken by Russian spies," Jane clarified awkwardly. "On account of Lord Crawford being such an important peer of the realm."

Abbie blinked several times in perplexed disbelief. "My dear Inspector, surely, you're not suggesting–"

"Oh no," Woodcock hastened to say. "I'm not suggesting anything at all." He gave an airy wave. "Still, quite the coincidence, eh?"

Jane shook her head emphatically. "Inspector, I assure you, Percy is as English as they come. This is merely about his personal vendetta against my sister and I."

Woodcock stroked his chin thoughtfully. "Hmm, unless that's just his cover story. A clever way to disguise his true identity."

"But we knew Percy years ago," Abbie objected. "His grandfather was a moneylender in London. Our poor Papa – may God rest his soul – borrowed too much money from him and was sent to debtor's prison for it."

"You'd be surprised at the lengths these chaps go to," Woodcock replied stubbornly. "And our man Pyotr is probably the most cunning of them all."

Ignoring Jane and Abbie's exasperated sighs, he stood abruptly. "I must alert headquarters. Wire the Yard immediately. Coded messages and all that."

He bustled out of the office, nearly colliding with Inspector Bouchard. "Sorry, old chap," Woodcock murmured. "I'm in a bit of a rush. Can't waste time, you see. Not when the crafty Yadenski himself could be lurking in Paris."

Bouchard entered the office, while making his opinion of his British counterpart obvious by rolling his eyes.

"Inspector," Jane said, breathing a sigh of relief. "What have you uncovered about Percy?"

"Not much, I'm afraid," he replied. He plumped down in his chair and stared at her. "We have no record of any Englishman by the name of Percy Yates entering France in recent years."

"That's impossible," Jane bristled. "He must have paid someone off to cover his tracks. He boasted to us about bribing a policeman, you know."

Bouchard's expression darkened. "So now you accuse the police of corruption, Mademoiselle? Are you becoming that desperate?"

"I only meant–"

"My sister intended no offence, Inspector," Abbie cut in tactfully. "But isn't it possible that Percy entered the country under a false name?"

Bouchard shrugged. "What would you have me do, Madame? Track down every Englishman in Paris and bring them in for questioning? Perhaps I ought to let your Inspector Woodcock join me. So he can ask everyone if they are a Russian agent."

He made a derisive noise and shook his head. But Jane wasn't through with him yet.

"What about his business associate?" she said. "Mr Pierre Dubois. Don't you have any records about him?"

"Pierre Dubois is a very common name, Mademoiselle. A bit like John Smith or Jack

Johnson in English. There must be thousands of people called Dubois."

"But this one is staying at the Hôtel Faubourg. I've visited him there on several occasions."

"Have you now?" Bouchard smiled knowingly. "So you admit to associating freely with one the people whom you accuse of having committed this crime?"

"What? Why, yes. But that was before I realised who he really was."

"I see."

"No, you don't," Jane replied, raising her voice in frustration. "Just go to the Faubourg and ask for Pierre Dubois. Then you will have to believe me."

"Enough!" Bouchard slammed a fist on his desk. "Don't tell me how to do my job, Mademoiselle Lee. And stop wasting my time with these outlandish stories of yours."

He stood, pointing sharply to the door. "Until you decide to speak truthfully, we are finished here."

Jane reeled, stunned by his abrupt fury. Tears pricked her eyes. "Inspector, I beg you–"

"Now," Bouchard thundered. "Before I arrest you both for attempting to pervert the course of justice."

Defeated, Jane turned toward the door.

Abbie gripped her arm, casting a scathing look at Bouchard. "For shame, Inspector. Can't you see that she is a victim here, too?"

Bouchard's glare didn't soften. "I see only a young woman intent on obscuring the truth. Good day, Madame Thompson."

With no choice left to them, the two sisters departed from the police station. Outside, the sun had already set.

"Come, sweetheart," Abbie spoke softly, wrapping an arm around Jane's shoulder. "We'll find a hansom cab and return to the hotel. Bill and Georgie should be back by now. Perhaps they'll have found new information."

"No, they won't," Jane said. "They won't have found anything. You know that as well as I do, Abbie. Percy is just too clever."

Abbie pulled her a little closer still. "We can't give up hope, Jane."

"But what hope is there? Tell me that. Percy is going to kill those children, Abbie. I'll get the noose for it, and you'll be broken for the rest of your life. That fiendish weasel will have his revenge and there's nothing we can do about it."

Unless...

As a sudden idea struck her, Jane instantly made a decision. Breaking free from her sister's grasp, she backed away, her face pale but set with grim resolve.

"I'm sorry, Abbie," she murmured through her tears.

Then she whirled and took off down the street, heedless of her sister's cries. Knocking startled pedestrians aside, she ran as if the devil himself pursued her.

This nightmare will end tonight.

She only prayed her sacrifice would not be in vain. And that Alistair and Penny might still be saved.

Chapter Thirty-One

Jane fled along the cobbled streets of Paris, tears streaming down her cheeks. The night air was cold against her skin and her breath came in ragged gasps as she ran, but she did not feel the burning in her lungs. All she felt was an icy terror clawing at her heart.

Her mind was awash with turmoil, Percy's sinister plot echoing in her thoughts. She had to stop him – tonight.

And she knew just how.

Even though the cost to her seemed steep.

But if her own life could somehow save Alistair and Penelope, then she must pay that price. It was better for her blood to stain the cobblestones than for the tender souls of the children to be extinguished forever.

Driven by grim determination, her feet carried her all the way to the river where she slowed to a halt, her shoulders heaving with sobs.

As the inky waters of the Seine flowed past, dark and foreboding, Jane gazed at the swirling currents, imagining their deadly embrace.

She removed her shoes, placing them neatly aside. Beneath her stockinged feet, the rough stones of the embankment were cold.

Then, after taking a deep breath, Jane willed herself to climb onto the stone parapet lining the river.

It must be done, she told herself silently while the black waters churned hungrily before her.

She pictured Alistair and Penelope's faces, so innocent and bright. If her sacrifice could preserve their precious young lives from peril, she would leap gladly into oblivion's arms.

It was a desperate plan, she realised. But in her strained mind, only drastic measures could defeat a madman consumed by hate and jealousy.

The way she saw it, she was nothing but a pawn in Percy's sick game of vengeance. So what if she eliminated herself from his chessboard?

Percy wanted her dead.

It's why he had abducted the children and was planning on murdering them: just so that Jane would be tried and executed for the crime. Which would ruin Abbie's life forever – the true goal of Percy's cruel and twisted plot.

So if Jane took her own life instead, then she would steal the wind out of Percy's sails. And there would be no more use for him to kill the children.

Or so she hoped.

Abbie would still be devastated, of course. But that might satisfy Percy's lust for revenge to some degree.

And at least Alistair and Penelope would live.

"Forgive me, Abbie," Jane whispered into the night. Trembling, she prepared herself to step forward and disappear forever underneath the pitiless waves.

But some invisible force held her back, as if a loving hand were clasped around her wrist, keeping her from the brink. Jane wavered, tears spilling down her cheeks.

The cold waters called invitingly, promising an end to her sorrows. Yet Jane found herself paralysed, unable to take the final plunge.

Was there another way?

She sank to her knees on the embankment, sobs wracking her body. The silence of the night held no answers. Jane buried her face in her hands, lost in indecision and desperation.

Suddenly, before she could gather her resolve once more, a fearful shout sounded through the quiet night. Cries for help echoed from beneath the nearby bridge that spanned the river.

Jane froze, listening intently.

Again the desperate pleas rang out: a child's frightened voice that Jane now recognised as Petit Jean's.

In an instant, she was on her feet and racing along the embankment toward the bridge.

The scene she arrived to was horrific. Petit Jean lay cowering on the ground as two heartless drunks loomed over him, their fists already bloodied from beating the boy.

"Leave him alone," Jane shrieked, as a red hot fury ignited within her.

Without any thought of her own safety and caring only about protecting her young friend, she hurled herself at the drunken brutes. With a wild cry, she started raining down blows upon them in a frenzy.

The men were much stronger and bigger than her. But her attack was so unexpected, and so fierce, that initially they stumbled back in surprise.

Jane scratched and clawed like a hellcat, heedless of the punches aimed her way. When one man grabbed her hair, wrenching her head back painfully, Jane simply sank her teeth into his hand with all her might. The drunkard howled in pain, releasing her to nurse his wounded hand.

Spitting blood, Jane whirled round to confront the other attacker. The man took his half-empty bottle of wine by the neck and smashed it against the wall, instantly creating a mean-looking weapon. Grinning viciously at her, he wielded the broken bottle in front of Jane's face.

But she danced out of reach of his wild swings, before landing a swift kick between his legs that dropped him to the ground with a groan.

The first man, cursing at the bite mark on his hand, grabbed his companion. "Come on, this doxy is mad. For all we know, she might have rabies or something. Let's get out of here!"

The two drunks fled into the night, leaving Jane breathless and dishevelled. Petit Jean gazed up at her with awe. "You saved me, Mademoiselle!"

He scrambled to his feet and threw his arms around her waist in a tight embrace. When he let go of her again, he looked up in concern. "But those men were so strong. They could have killed you."

Jane simply shook her head. "That wouldn't have mattered much." In truth, she hadn't cared whether she lived or died.

As the fury seeped out from her veins, the full import of what she had nearly done at the river's edge began to dawn on her. She sank to the ground beside Petit Jean, suddenly feeling faint.

"What is it, Mademoiselle?" the boy asked worriedly, grasping her hand in his smaller one.

Jane managed a wavering smile. “Just a spell of dizziness, that’s all.” She got back up and gently touched his cheek. “Come, let’s walk for a short while.”

Holding hands, they moved away from the bridge and strolled past the spot where Jane had nearly lost herself to despair. Her shoes were still there, and she picked them up.

Providence had stayed her hand, she admitted to herself, forcing her to recognise that she must cling to hope, even though the path ahead was still as unclear as before.

Jane shivered.

“Are you cold, Mademoiselle?” Petit Jean asked.

“Tired, mostly. Why don’t we sit down over there,” she said, gesturing at a little alcove that promised to shelter them from the wind.

Once seated, Jane put her shoes back on. Petit Jean looked at her, his young face furrowed with concern.

“Why did you say it wouldn’t have mattered if those men had killed you? You fought them like a lioness.”

Jane hesitated. But the earnest worry in the boy’s eyes compelled her to honesty. Haltingly she told him of Percy’s vile scheme, and of Inspector Bouchard’s refusal to believe in her innocence.

"I thought if I ended my life, it would ruin Percy's plan," she confessed. "Then perhaps he would have no more reason to..." Her voice broke as tears spilled down her cheeks.

When the meaning of her words dawned on him, Petit Jean turned pale and pressed himself against her side in a fierce hug.

"Oh Mademoiselle, please don't ever do such an awful thing to yourself," he cried. "Life is too precious to be thrown away. And you are probably the nicest person I've met in my entire life."

Jane stroked the boy's hair as he wept against her shoulder. His distress at the thought of losing her seemed absolutely genuine, making her heart ache.

"Hush now," she murmured. "I won't do anything rash."

Petit Jean pulled back to look earnestly into her eyes. "Do you promise that?"

"I promise," she nodded. "I had a moment of weakness back there. But that's passed now."

Satisfied that she was speaking the truth, he let out a short sigh of relief. "You'll find a way to save master Alistair and mistress Penelope, just you wait. In the end, good always prevails over evil. But you must have faith, Mademoiselle."

His simple conviction brought fresh tears to Jane's eyes. She pulled him close again, overwhelmed with love for this dear child.

There was a special bond between them, destined by fate perhaps. It had been there right from the start, back in the kitchen at the Crawfords when that nasty bully had tried to take Petit Jean's apple from him.

For a while, they sat huddled together in silence as Jane's tears slowly abated. The boy's quiet acceptance soothed her wounded spirit. For the first time since Alistair and Penelope's abduction, she felt a cautious spark of hope.

"What will you do?" Petit Jean finally asked.

Jane sighed. "I honestly don't know yet."

"Let me help you," he pleaded sincerely. "Whatever you need, I will do it."

"You've already helped me more than you know, my faithful little friend." She smiled and stroked his hair. "I have to search my own heart for the right way forward. But I'm glad that you will be nearby if I need you."

Petit Jean nodded, looking solemn. "I will always be here for you, Mademoiselle."

Jane kissed his forehead, drawing strength from his steadfast loyalty. However dark or difficult the road ahead might be, she understood that she would never have to walk it alone.

"It's late," she said. "And you ought to be in bed. Shall I accompany you home?"

"That's kind of you, but no. I came here tonight because I wanted to sleep outside."

"Do you think that's safe, after what happened earlier?" Jane asked with concern.

Petit Jean chuckled. "Don't worry, Mademoiselle. Those cowards won't dare to return. Not when they know a wild woman with sharp fangs guards the bridge."

"I'll become the stuff of legends next," she quipped. "The savage she-beast of the river."

They laughed and said a fond goodbye to each other, after which Petit Jean went looking for a good place to sleep while Jane wandered off alone into the night.

She found herself being pulled to the park where she and Georgie had shared some of their better moments together – precious few as they were.

Though it was the middle of the night, Jane went to their favourite spot, beneath a group of chestnut trees. She was bone-weary, her mind and body utterly spent. Leaning her head back against the bark of a tree, she let her eyes fall shut.

At first her thoughts swirled chaotically, echoes of the day's turmoil chasing each other in circles. But slowly they began to settle, like silt sinking to the bottom of a pond.

Jane allowed herself to drift in that hazy realm between waking and dreaming, senses dulled. She knew there was danger in falling asleep here. Being exposed to the elements, the night's chilly air could prove fatal to her weakened body. And then there was the risk of a cutthroat ending her life while she slumbered, unaware.

But Jane didn't have the strength to worry any more, so she placed herself in the hands of fate, come what may. If dying tonight brought some solution to this tangled mess, so be it.

And if morning light found her still breathing, then she would rise to do what had to be done.

As she sank deeper toward sleep, she fancied the brush of feathers against her cheek. Strong yet gentle arms encircled her, lifting her from the ground.

Surrendering to the softness, she nestled against it like a babe in its mother's embrace. The heady scent of chestnut blossoms surrounded her as she floated, weightless as a cloud.

Had the angels come to bear her home?

Even as slumber overtook her, she thought she heard a voice murmur lovingly, "I've been searching everywhere for you. No, don't open your eyes. Rest. It's all right."

Jane sighed, letting go of all earthly cares as she slipped into sleep's sweet oblivion.

Chapter Thirty-Two

Slowly, Jane's senses returned to the world of the living. She had dreamt of being taken to heaven by an angel, and then of sleeping between fluffy white clouds with the moon watching over her.

Now however, it felt as if her mind was coming up from the murky depths of the ocean, trying to reach the bright surface up above. When she lazily moved her arm, it brushed against soft pillows and smooth bedsheets.

"Jane?" a woman's voice whispered sweetly. "Are you awake, dear?"

She opened her eyes, blinking against the daylight that streamed in through the sheer curtains. "Where am I?" she rasped, her throat dry.

"In our suite, at the hotel," the voice replied softly.

"Abbie?" Fully awake, Jane lifted her head and saw her sister sitting on the side of the bed, looking down at her with a fond smile.

"Good morning, my darling," Abbie spoke. "Or should I say, good afternoon? It's past midday already."

"That late? What happened? How did I get here?"

"Georgie found you, sleeping in the park. He carried you here." She smoothed a stray lock of hair from Jane's face. "You gave me such a fright last night, running off like that. Where on earth did you go?"

Jane flushed. But she could hear no hint of blame or accusation in Abbie's tone, only heartfelt concern.

"I was just... upset. And confused." She averted her gaze, unwilling to burden her sister with the truth of her desperate intentions the night before. "I wanted to clear my head, I suppose."

Abbie patted Jane's hand. "Well, I'm glad we found you, and that you're unharmed. We were so worried, especially after... after everything that's happened."

Her sister's allusion to those horrible recent events caused a heavy weight to settle upon Jane's chest. Percy still had Alistair and Penelope bundled up somewhere. How much time did they have left before he would go through with the next phase of his evil plan?

Jane felt like crying. Nevertheless, for her sister's sake, she managed a small smile. "I wasn't thinking straight yesterday. Sorry."

"There, there now. Let's get you washed and dressed," Abbie said, ever the practical thinker. "You'll feel so much better afterwards, I promise. Georgie will be eager to see you awake."

"He's here too?"

Abbie nodded with a smile. "He and Bill are waiting in the sitting room next door. Those two were out for hours searching for you, until Georgie found you underneath some trees at the park."

Jane tensed. The thought of facing Georgie after all that had transpired between them made her stomach twist into an anxious knot. But she couldn't hide away forever.

Taking a deep breath, she rose from the bed to ready herself. Abbie helped her wash and dress, brushing out her hair until it shone.

Fully restored and refreshed, Jane entered the sitting room with her sister close behind her. Georgie leapt up at the sight of her, relief washing over his handsome features.

Despite everything, a spark of happiness fluttered in Jane's heart. Perhaps their troubles were not insurmountable after all.

Crossing the room in a few quick strides, Georgie stopped in front of her and took her hands in his. "Jane dearest, I'm so happy to see you."

He had dark circles underneath his eyes from fatigue and worry, but his smile was radiant.

"Georgie," she murmured, lowering her gaze to the floor in shame. "Please forgive me, I've been such a fool."

"You have nothing to apologise for," he said, tilting up her chin with a gentle finger. "All that matters is that you're safe now."

His eyes searched hers, and she read the depths of his caring there. His lips were so tantalisingly near, she thought. If she moved her face just a little bit closer...

A discreet cough in the room quickly made her cast aside any romantic stirrings. Jane glanced round and saw Bill lounging in a chair, smiling at her.

"Morning, Bill. Abbie tells me I owe you and Georgie my gratitude, for bringing me here."

"Our pleasure," the brawny young man said with a reassuring nod. "Seemed a bit chilly to be spending the night outside underneath the stars. Did you sleep well, in the end?"

"Like a baby, thanks to all of you." She turned back to Georgie and frowned. "Shouldn't you be at the patisserie?"

"I resigned."

Jane's eyes widened in dismay. "Your apprenticeship, your dream... Why?"

"After you were arrested, I asked Maître Leblanc if I could have some time off. But he refused." Georgie shrugged. "So I quit on the spot."

"Oh, Georgie." Jane's heart sank. She knew how much that position had meant to him. "It's all my fault. I'm so sorry."

"Don't be. You're far more important to me than that apprenticeship," he said firmly. "Maître Leblanc is a pompous old windbag. All I care about is clearing your name and keeping you safe."

Jane felt herself blushing from the neck up, moved by his devotion. *He loves me,* she thought as a tender warmth enveloped her heart. *He truly loves me.*

She hesitated, trying to find the right words to express her feelings for him. "Georgie, last night, I–"

A sudden knock at the door interrupted her.

Abbie, who had taken a seat on the sofa after entering the room, glanced over at Bill and Georgie with a puzzled expression on her face. "Did either of you order room service by any chance?"

Bill silently shook his head that they hadn't, and then moved to answer the door. His gate and the tension in his shoulders betrayed his alertness.

"Yes?" he asked after opening the door. From the sitting room, and with Bill standing between them and the person at the door, Jane couldn't make out who it was.

But she recognised the voice the moment the caller spoke up. “Apologies for troubling you,” he said politely. “Might I come in for a moment, please?”

It was Mr Dubois.

Chapter Thirty-Three

Jane froze, hardly believing her eyes. The sight of the treacherous French businessman standing by the door sent a ripple through the room.

Bill had never met Mr Dubois in person, so of course he didn't recognise the visitor. But the look of shock and terror on Jane's face told him all he needed to know.

Georgie moved to position himself protectively between Jane and the door, flexing and balling his fists as he did.

"You've got some nerve showing your face here," he snarled at their unexpected visitor.

Mr Dubois held up his hands. "I have only come to talk. And to offer you my help."

Bill blocked the doorway, awaiting the others' response. Jane looked to her sister. Mr Dubois had shown himself to be a traitor who had abused Jane's trust. As he stood there by the door however, his humble demeanour seemed sincere.

Or was she merely being naive to believe that?

"Let him in," Abbie said calmly.

Bill stepped aside and allowed Mr Dubois to enter. But he made sure to remain one step behind the Frenchman, ready to intervene at the first sign of trickery.

Mr Dubois looked round to everyone in the room, his face etched deeply with remorse.

"First, I must apologise for the sorrow I have caused you all." He turned to Jane. "You in particular, Mademoiselle. I am ashamed of my role in this ugly business." He paused and bowed his head.

"Bit late for apologies, isn't it?" Georgie snapped.

"I understand your anger, Monsieur. And I am certain I would feel the same way if I were in your shoes. But I have come to make amends, if you will permit it."

Jane studied him. So far, he wasn't showing any signs of deceit. But then again, she had been sorely mistaken about him before.

"Why the change of heart?" she asked.

"Or have you simply come here to tell us more lies?" Georgie sneered.

"Early this morning," Mr Dubois began after a heavy sigh, "I received a visit from your young friend Petit Jean. And I was most distressed when he told me about... what you attempted to do last night, Mademoiselle."

Jane inhaled sharply. Sensing everyone's eyes on her, she burned with embarrassment.

"Jane, dear?" Abbie asked kindly. "What is Mr Dubois talking about? What really happened out there last night?"

Realising it was wrong to hide the truth from them, no matter how much she regretted her temporary weakness, Jane swallowed.

"I wanted to take my own life yesterday," she confessed. Abbie and Georgie gasped with shock. And even Bill tensed up visibly.

"It was a moment of madness," Jane added quickly. "I thought if I killed myself, instead of allowing Percy to send me to the gallows, I could thwart his plans and save the children."

"Oh, Jane," Abbie said with tears in her eyes. "That's a horrible idea."

"I agree," Mr Dubois cut in. "Your suicide would have been a tragic and unnecessary loss, Mademoiselle. When your young friend Jean told me the story... Well, I shall not hide from you that it caused me to search my conscience. And to recognise the error of my ways."

"So you have a conscience, do you?" Georgie snorted. "You could have fooled me."

Mr Dubois took the snide comment in good grace and inclined his head to Georgie.

"What is it you want from us, Mr Dubois?" Abbie asked coolly.

"To make a new alliance, Madame. I wish to switch sides and help you, if you will accept my assistance."

"Help us?" Georgie laughed derisively. "As if any of us would still trust you."

Mr Dubois did not rise to the bait. "You are right to doubt me, Monsieur. I am a scoundrel in many ways. But I draw the line at murder. This has gone too far." He shook his head, looking genuinely dismayed.

"Then why did you go along with Percy's scheme in the first place?" Jane asked.

"Originally, this was merely supposed to be another one of our usual swindles. Through you, I would win Lord Crawford's trust and relieve him of his money."

Jane nodded pensively. She remembered all too well her disastrous attempt at making an introduction.

"But then," Mr Dubois continued with a sigh, "Mr Yates began hatching this mad abduction plan of his. And of course, he conveniently forgot to mention his real intentions for the children."

"He didn't tell you he wanted to murder them?"

"When he revealed his true plan to you, that's the first I heard about it." Mr Dubois shook his head. "I fear his thirst for vengeance has turned him insane."

Jane sensed the sincerity in his words. She was convinced there was still good left in Mr

Dubois. "Tell us what you know," she said gently. "Can you help us find Alistair and Penelope?"

"I can do better than that," he replied, brightening somewhat. "I will take you right to them – *if* we strike a bargain."

Georgie bristled and crossed his arms, but Jane silenced him with a look. Now wasn't the time for anger or resentment. Lives hung in the balance.

"What sort of bargain do you propose, Monsieur?" Abbie asked.

"It is simple, Madame. I will share all I know, including the name of the policeman Percy has been bribing. And I will personally guide you to the children."

Jane's pulse quickened at the thought of rescuing Alistair and Penelope. But Abbie was more cautious.

"And what do you want in return, Monsieur?"

"You must swear not to inform the police of my involvement in any of this. I want no part in Mr Yates' vile scheme, but in the eyes of the Law I would still be viewed as an accomplice. And I'd rather not be sent to prison."

"You scoundrel," Georgie growled. "It would be what you deserve. You ought to rot in a prison cell and go straight to hell afterwards."

"I am Catholic, Monsieur," Mr Dubois grinned sarcastically. "As long as I confess my sins to a priest before I die, I won't need to go to hell."

Georgie rolled his eyes, but before he could say anything, Mr Dubois continued, "Jokes aside, it was never my idea to abduct the children. It's not my style. But please, let us stop this bickering. I have explained my offer to you all. What is your response?"

"It sounds reasonable to me," Abbie said. "But I think Jane ought to have the final word in this."

Jane swallowed as all eyes turned to her. "I want the children to be safe, whatever the price. We accept your offer, Mr Dubois."

"You can't be serious," Georgie bristled. "This blackguard belongs in prison."

Jane gave him a stern look. "Our priority is saving Alistair and Penelope. If this is our only route to finding them, then we must take it."

Seeing Georgie's stubborn expression, she softened her tone. "I don't like it either, my love. But we have no time to waste on pride."

Georgie wrestled with this before giving a begrudging nod. Jane smiled at him and placed a soft hand on his arm in consolation. However unsavoury they might find the bargain with Mr Dubois, they had to pursue this opportunity.

"Tell us where the children are being held," Jane said, turning back to the Frenchman.

"There's an old warehouse at the Rue Mauregard in the 5th District. Mr Yates uses the top floor as his hideout. That's where the children are too."

"Right," Georgie said resolutely. "We'll go there straight away."

"I must caution you however," Mr Dubois warned. "Mr Yates has three men guarding the children at all hours."

Georgie cracked his knuckles. "We can handle a few thugs. Can't we, Bill?"

"But there's Mr Yates himself to consider as well," Mr Dubois said. "He's a dangerous and unpredictable man. And he has a pistol. I've seen it with my own eyes."

"So we storm the warehouse," Georgie scoffed. "We rush in, crack a few skulls and grab the children."

Jane and the others however hesitated.

"You are brave, Monsieur," Mr Dubois conceded. "But an approach as bold and direct as yours is fraught with peril."

"I'm afraid Mr Dubois is right, Georgie," Jane said. "We mustn't risk jeopardising the children's lives."

"If only we could involve the police," Abbie sighed.

"No police," Mr Dubois reminded her politely.

"See?" Georgie said. "Rescuing the children ourselves is our only option. Abbie, when is Joe arriving in Paris?"

"Tomorrow or the day after. Why?"

"With him, me, Bill and Mr Dubois, I'm convinced we'd stand a decent chance against those four villains."

"Yes, perhaps we would," Mr Dubois said. "Unfortunately, I'm not sure we can afford to wait that long. The children..."

He left the horrible thought unspoken, but they all knew what he meant. Percy could be plotting to kill poor Alistair and Penelope at any moment.

"Then we must strike now," Georgie said, punching his fist into the palm of his other hand. "I say we wait until the cover of darkness, and go rescue those little ones. Alone."

A heavy silence fell over the room. Georgie's plan was perilous, bordering on recklessness. But what other choice did they have? They had no friends or allies in this city. No one who could come to their aid in defeating this sinister nemesis and his henchmen.

Suddenly, Jane perked up. "I might have a better idea," she said. "Abbie, there's someone you and I need to talk to."

"Mademoiselle," Mr Dubois objected. "If you are thinking of going to Inspector Bouchard behind my back–"

"No, not him," Jane said. "You have my word that we will keep your name out of the conversation. Abbie, grab your purse and coat. We must hurry."

She realised her idea was crazy. But then again, the person she had in mind was no stranger to absurd flights of fancy.

Chapter Thirty-Four

Stalking through the night like silent phantoms, four figures rounded the street corner and turned into Rue Mauregard. In the shuttered buildings lining the deserted lane not a soul stirred. The only sounds were the echo of the four's soft footfalls and the occasional scurry of rats.

As they approached an old warehouse, one of them gestured to the others to halt. "That is the place we seek," he whispered in a French accent. "Just ahead."

"Thank you, Mr Dubois," the sole woman in the group replied quietly. She peered into the gloom at the building looming dark and foreboding before them. "That's where Percy is keeping the children?"

"*Oui, Mademoiselle.* On the top floor. That's his lair."

Invisible to the others, Jane gave a rueful smile. *Lair,* she thought. What a fitting word for the hiding place of a monster like Percy.

"There appears to be a light burning up there," Georgie said. "So that probably means someone is still awake."

"One or more of the guards," Mr Dubois confirmed. "Or possibly Mr Yates himself. He often stays up late and then sleeps half the day away."

"Right," Georgie said, flexing the muscles in his neck. "What's our next move then?"

Jane touched his arm. "We wait," she said. "For Inspector Woodcock and his men to arrive."

Bill tipped his cap back, scanning the empty street. "I'll keep watch." He melted into the shadows as the others drew back into a doorway.

"Are you sure Woodcock is coming?" Georgie asked, leaning against the brick wall to settle in for the wait. "From what you've told us, the man sounds like he's half mad."

"Oh, he'll come, don't you worry," Jane said confidently. "He was thrilled when Abbie and I told him we'd discovered where Pyotr Yadenski was hiding."

Mr Dubois shook his head. "I'm still not sure I understand. This British inspector of yours really believes Monsieur Yates is a Russian spy?"

"He does."

"But why?"

"As far as I can tell, it's a matter of mistaken identity," Jane explained. "Inspector Woodcock has been chasing a Russian agent named Pyotr Yadenski for years. And now he's convinced that this spy is here in Paris under a false name."

"Which happens to be Percy Yates?"

Jane chuckled. "I suppose the name Percy Yates does sound a little bit like Pyotr Yadenski. Especially to a man as zealous and obsessed as Inspector Woodcock seems to be."

"The English are mad," Mr Dubois sighed. And with an apologetic glance towards Jane and Georgie, he added, "That is to say, some of you are. But please, tell me: there is no truth to this idea of Mr Yates being a spy, correct?"

"None whatsoever," Jane said firmly. "Percy is English, born and bred. But Inspector Woodcock presented us with an opportunity we couldn't ignore."

"And so you pandered to the good inspector's misguided fantasy about Russian spies?"

"Exactly. It was our only chance of securing additional help for tonight," Jane said. "Brave as you gentlemen are, just the four of us storming that warehouse would be dangerously reckless."

Mr Dubois nodded, but Georgie looked sceptical. "What makes you think Woodcock's men will be of any use to us? Even if they're only half as mad as him, they could still prove to be more of a liability."

"I saw them myself when Abbie and I went to speak to him. There were just a handful of them, but they had the look of well trained and experienced men to me."

"And how did you say Woodcock got hold of them?"

"They're reinforcements from Scotland Yard. The inspector sent a coded telegram to London after he began to suspect this Russian plot."

"I'm certain these Scotland Yard men will perform adequately," Mr Dubois cut in again. "The men Mr Yates has hired aren't exactly the finest either, you know. What troubles me more though is what happens afterwards..."

"What do you mean?" Jane asked.

"At some point tonight, Inspector Woodcock is going to realise that Mr Yates is not a Russian spy, yes? What happens then?"

Jane shrugs. "That's not important. Because by then we'll have rescued Alistair and Penelope, and that's all that matters to me."

"Fair enough," Mr Dubois conceded.

"Oi oi," Bill's voice suddenly whispered from the shadows. "There's a bunch of men coming up the street. No uniforms, but I think it's Woodcock."

Jane held her breath. The moment of truth was finally drawing near. She prayed all would go well. As long as they got the children out, unharmed, she didn't care much about the rest.

Bill stepped out into the light and gave a short wave at the approaching men, who silently acknowledged his gesture. Moments later, the two groups converged and a hurried round of greetings and introductions followed. Then all eyes turned towards the warehouse. Light was still glowing faintly from the windows on the top floor.

"So that's the place then, is it?" Inspector Woodcock asked, gazing at the building like a man eyeing the treasure he's been hunting all his life.

"Yes," Jane replied. "Top floor. That's where we'll find our man, Inspector."

Woodcock nodded pensively. Then he tore away his eyes from the warehouse and frowned at Jane. "As much as I appreciate your assistance, Miss, I must say I don't like having a young lady mixed up in this sort of operation. These things often have a blasted habit of taking a messy turn."

"I appreciate your concern for my safety, Inspector," she replied. "But we agreed it was better for me to be there when you liberate the children. They'll be frightened out of their wits. A familiar face will provide some comfort."

It had taken a good amount of reasoning from Jane and Abbie before the inspector had finally given in on that point. Initially, Abbie had wanted to join them as well. But as a compromise, Jane's sister had promised to stay at the hotel.

"Yes, yes," Inspector Woodcock grumbled now. "The feminine touch and all that rubbish."

Turning to his men, he rubbed his hands together. And with a keen glimmer of excitement in his eyes, he said, "Right then chaps, let's go nab us a Russian spy."

Chapter Thirty-Five

Remarkably more nimble than Jane would have given him credit for, Inspector Woodcock led his men towards the warehouse across the street. Bill and Georgie followed right behind them, with Jane and Mr Dubois bringing up the rear.

After having located a side door, one of Woodcock's men picked the lock and carefully eased it open to avoid any loud creaks.

Jane felt her heart thudding as everyone slipped inside one by one. When she entered the building, Inspector Woodcock and his team were already waiting at the bottom of a large winding staircase.

"Up we go," he whispered. "Quiet and light-footed like a mouse."

Slowly, they made their way up the stairs, ears peeled for noises. The boards occasionally groaned under their feet, making Jane wince. But they reached the top floor undetected, and Jane wondered if perhaps the villains had fallen asleep.

The muffled voices that drifted across the landing soon told her otherwise however.

Inspector Woodcock held up his hand, signalling everyone to halt.

He pointed at a closed door on the other end of the landing. A light was burning in the room behind the door. And within, a mightily heated argument was taking place.

"We want the money you promised us, Yates," came a rough, angry voice. "A small fortune, you said."

"And you'll get it," Percy's voice snapped back.

"How you plannin' on paying us then?" a second voice demanded. "If you kill the little'uns now, like you said you would, there won't be no ransom money."

Jane clapped a hand over her mouth to hold back a horrified gasp. Beside her, Georgie tensed and took a step towards the door before Woodcock grabbed his arm.

"Yeah, explain that one, Yates," the first man in the room said. "You told us we were kidnapping those nippers because their father's loaded. Not because you have some stupid old score to settle."

"D'you know what we should do, boys?" a third voice grumbled. "I say we get rid of this English lunatic and collect that ransom money ourselves."

The other two made rough consenting noises, until the metallic click of a pistol being cocked could be heard.

"I'm in charge here," Percy growled menacingly. "And anyone who disagrees with my plan will get a bullet between the eyes. Is that clear?"

"Don't be stupid, Yates," one of the men scoffed. "It's three against one. You'll never be able to take down all three of us."

"No, but I bet I can kill at least one of you. Possibly two. So who wants to try first? Eh? Is it you, Louis? Or maybe you, André?"

As Jane pictured Percy waving a gun at his own henchmen, her blood turned to ice in her veins. She looked over at Woodcock. Was the inspector going to let the argument blow up into a nasty fight? That might save him having to deal with one or two of the troublemakers perhaps. But at what cost? The children's lives were at stake.

Fortunately, Inspector Woodcock seemed to reach that same conclusion. He gave a curt nod to one of his men, who immediately went and kicked the door open.

Woodcock was one of the first to burst into the room. "Police," he bellowed. "Put that weapon down."

Percy spun around, aiming his pistol at the intruders. For a long, terrifying moment, no one moved a muscle.

Jane hardly dared to breathe. She wanted to enter the room as well, to see where Alistair and

Penelope were. But Mr Dubois held her back and shook his head.

"Who the devil are you?" Percy spat at the policemen.

"Scotland Yard," Inspector Woodcock declared dramatically. "Finally we meet, Yadenski."

"Who?" Percy's brow furrowed in confusion. "What on earth are you talking about, old fool?"

"Oh come now," Woodcock scoffed. "It's no use pretending, Yadenski. The game's up."

"Yadenski?" Percy narrowed his eyes and tightened the grip on the pistol in his hand. "I don't know whether you're drunk or simply stupid, old boy. But you have the wrong man. My name's Yates. Percy Yates."

"Really, Yadenski," Woodcock snorted. "Did you honestly believe we wouldn't see through such an obvious deception?"

"I'm growing tired of this travesty," Percy bristled. "You've rudely interrupted the business dispute I was having with my three associates here. So if you would kindly leave now?"

Fearful that her gamble might begin to fall apart, Jane decided to jump into the fray. "Stop playing games, Pyotr," she said. "It's over."

"You?!" Percy's nostrils flared with anger at the sight of her. "I'll make you regret this."

"Tut-tut... Pyotr," Jane teased. "Inspector Woodcock tells me he has been chasing you halfway across Europe."

"Sure have, Miss," Woodcock said. Grinning triumphantly, he turned to Percy. "But we have you this time, Yadenski. You won't be slipping through our fingers like you did in Cairo."

Percy looked utterly bewildered. "Have you all gone mad?"

"Enough already," Jane said defiantly, while casting her gaze around the otherwise empty room. "Your little ploy has failed. Where are the children?"

Percy's lip curled. "Tied up in the other room," he replied, his eyes blazing with fury. "But they're not going anywhere. And neither are the rest of you." He waved his pistol in their faces.

Jane tensed, twitching to rush over to the room where the children were being kept.

"Stay away from that door or you're dead," Percy threatened.

Woodcock held up a hand. "You're greatly outnumbered, Yadenski. Don't be a fool. Put down your weapon and surrender."

"Never," Percy shrieked. The pistol wavered dangerously as he swung it between his adversaries. "You'll all rue this day, I swear."

Jane's pulse quickened at the growing lunacy in his eyes. They had to end this confrontation soon, before he became even more volatile. She took a cautious step forward. "Percy, be reasonable–"

"Don't come any closer," he screamed, aiming the gun right at her. Jane froze. "One more step and I'll shoot you dead, wench."

Mr Dubois edged forward, palms raised imploringly. "*Mon ami,* please. Do as the Inspector asks. Let us end this without violence."

"Silence, traitor!" Percy hissed, glancing feverishly around the room. There was no way out for him. Inspector Woodcock's men had quietly moved to block the exits.

"It's over, Yadenski," Woodcock repeated firmly. "Now for the last time, lay down your weapon."

Realising that his defeat was inevitable, Percy let out a roar of angry frustration.

"You and your wretched sister ruined me once before," he seethed at Jane. "But I will have my revenge. Mark my words!"

With a feral cry, he aimed the pistol at Jane and pulled the trigger.

Everything slowed. Jane saw the muzzle flash, and heard the deafening report. Then Mr Dubois crashed into her from the side, knocking her down. The bullet ripped through his shoulder in a spray of crimson.

"No!" she cried as she watched her saviour collapse to the floor.

Percy cursed and took aim at her again. But two of Inspector Woodcock's men tackled him. Swiftly, they wrestled the gun from his grip and pinned him down.

"Unhand me, you brutes," Percy spat and struggled furiously. But the policemen had him firmly restrained.

Woodcock's other men moved in on Percy's hired thugs, who seemed too stunned by the situation to put up much resistance.

Jane scrambled over to where Mr Dubois lay slumped on the ground. Bill was already by his side as well, applying pressure to the wound.

"It's– it's just a scratch," the Frenchman grimaced in pain. "Rescue the children. Go."

Jane met Georgie's gaze for a split second before they both sprinted for the closed door on the opposite wall. Georgie threw it open and they rushed inside.

"Alistair! Penelope!" Jane exclaimed as she hurried to untie the ropes that bound them to the chairs they were sitting in. The children were gagged, their wrists raw from the coarse hemp – but they seemed unharmed otherwise.

When she and Georgie had removed the gags, Jane pulled the children into a fierce embrace. "Thank heavens you're all right," she breathed, tears of relief welling up in her eyes.

"Miss Lee," Penelope cried, flinging her little arms around Jane's neck. Alistair wiped his eyes and joined the hug, letting Jane envelop him too.

"It's over," Jane soothed, holding them close as their young bodies shook from sobbing. "Hush now. Hush, my darling babies." She looked up at Georgie, seeing her own joy mirrored on his face.

They had succeeded. The children were safe.

When the four of them returned to the main room, Inspector Woodcock was firing off orders to his men. "Get those three Frenchies in irons and down to the wagon." With a chuckle, he added, "They're nothing but small fish anyway, so we'll toss them to Bouchard and keep the main prize to ourselves."

Jane went over to Mr Dubois first. The Frenchman was looking terribly pale.

"It's not as bad as it seems," he whispered hoarsely. "I don't think the bullet hit anything vital."

"Nevertheless," Bill said, kneeling by his side. "We must get you to a hospital. That wound of yours needs cleaning and stitching."

"No hospital," Mr Dubois replied faintly. "They might involve the police."

Jane pulled out a small purse that was fat with coins. "Abbie gave me this. In case we needed to grease a few palms. Take it," she said, handing the money over to Bill. "Use it to reward the hospital staff for their discretion."

Bill gave her a knowing grin and then helped Mr Dubois to his legs. "I'll see to it. You and Georgie focus on the little ones."

After a quick goodbye to Mr Dubois, Jane turned her attention back to Alistair and Penelope. The children had been standing by Georgie's side, but now they came rushing back to her, clinging to the folds of her dress.

"What happens next, Inspector?" Jane asked when Woodcock joined them. "What will you do with Percy– I mean, Yadenski?"

Her nemesis was still being held to the floor by his captors, who had gagged him to stop the crook from shouting and cursing the whole time.

"We'll whisk that villainous scoundrel off to England," Woodcock said. "Find ourselves a nice secluded location, where we can extract every last bit of information out of him."

Jane suppressed a wicked grin. It sounded like Percy was in for a thoroughly unpleasant time. "And after you're done with him?"

"Then we'll send him back to Russia. But I doubt his masters will be happy to see him. They'll probably dump him in one of their penal colonies in Siberia."

"Very good, Inspector. Though I confess the thought of exile seems almost too merciful for the likes of him," Jane said darkly.

"Rest assured, Miss. The frozen wilds of Siberia don't offer much of a holiday," Woodcock laughed. "It's as good as a death sentence."

Georgie raised an eyebrow. "It all sounds rather cloak-and-dagger to me, I must say. I didn't know Scotland Yard engaged in that sort of activity?"

Inspector Woodcock drew himself up. "Yes, well, the activities of my department are not commonly known to the public," he replied loftily. "I am part of the Yard's Secret Branch, you see. Hush-hush high-level affairs and all that."

He winked and tapped the side of his nose.

"Scotland Yard has a Secret Branch?" Georgie asked, his eyes widening in surprise.

"Naturally," Woodcock nodded. "But mum's the word, my dear boy. Wouldn't be much of a secret if we went round telling everyone about it, eh?"

"Indeed," Georgie murmured.

Next, Woodcock turned to Jane with a smile. "You needn't worry about the French police troubling you further, Miss. I'll make certain you and your companions are absolved of any wrongdoing in this affair."

"You are too kind, Inspector," Jane said earnestly. "But what of Lord and Lady

Crawford? Surely they will require an explanation?"

"Leave that to me as well," Woodcock declared. "I shall call on his Lordship in the morning and inform him the Russian spy Pyotr Yadenski was to blame for this whole debacle."

Jane nodded and wanted to thank the inspector, but then Alistair tugged hesitantly at her sleeve.

"Miss Lee?" the boy asked softly. "I'm awfully tired. Might we go back to Papa now, please?"

"Of course, my darling," she replied. "I'll take you home myself. Your Papa and Mama will be so very happy to see you."

A brief pang of worry reared its ugly head when Jane thought of Lady Crawford. The woman could be cruel beyond reason. But surely, her ladyship would be able to show some tenderness to her own flesh and blood in this case?

"I'll come with you," Georgie said. "Let's just hope we'll be able to find a carriage at this late hour."

"No need for that," Inspector Woodcock said. "I've arranged transportation back to his lordship's residence for you and the children. My men will see you there safely."

Outside, true to the inspector's word, a coach awaited them. Georgie helped Jane and the drowsy children inside before climbing in as well and taking the seat opposite.

Penelope nestled into Jane's lap, while Alistair slumped heavily against Jane's side. Overtaken by exhaustion, both of the children were fast asleep shortly after the carriage set off.

Jane too felt the fatigue pulling at her weary mind, and she rested her head against the tufted back of the seat. Relief washed over her now that the terrible danger had finally passed.

When her eyes met Georgie's, she gave him a tired but joyful smile. Georgie gazed back lovingly and answered her smile with a matching grin. Neither of them needed any words to convey what they were feeling in their heart.

Jane knew the coming days would bring fresh trials and conversations – about her own future and her relationship with Georgie for instance.

But those worries could wait until sunrise.

For now, Jane thought only of how happy she was, while the gentle sway of the carriage rocked her into a contented doze.

Chapter Thirty-Six

Three days later, Jane once more found herself in a carriage heading towards the Crawford residence. This time however, she was accompanied by her brother-in-law. Joe had arrived in Paris the day after the children's rescue, and his calm strength had done much to put Jane's mind at ease: the evil had well and truly passed.

This particular morning unfortunately, nerves were getting the better of her again. Because Lord Crawford himself had requested to see her. And although Jane had been absolved of any blame or suspicion, the thought of coming face to face with his lordship filled her with dread.

She hadn't seen him the night when she and Georgie had safely returned the children to their home. Due to the late hour, Mrs Hill had refused to rouse Lord and Lady Crawford from their sleep, choosing instead to rush Alistair and Penelope off to bed.

"I shall inform milord and milady of the good news in the morning," the housekeeper had promised her. And that was the last Jane had heard of it.

Now, as the hansom cab clattered over the cobblestone streets of Paris, she fidgeted with her gloves.

"Stop worrying, Jane," Joe smiled kindly. "I'm sure Lord Crawford only wants to make things right with you."

"I hope so," she sighed. "It's just... Well, I've only ever met the man once. My dealings were always with his wife. And she was–" Jane hesitated, looking for a polite way to describe Lady Crawford.

"A right cow?" Joe supplied helpfully.

"I was going to say 'less than genial' perhaps," she grinned.

"That's putting it too mildly if you ask me," he snorted before giving her a roguish wink.

Despite herself, Jane smiled. Dear Joe. Ever since he had married Abbie, he'd been like the protective older brother Jane had never had.

"Do you think she'll be present as well?" Jane asked. "Lady Crawford, I mean?"

"I don't know. But one would hope that, as the mother of those two poor children, she'd be grateful to the person who played such an important role in their rescue."

"The woman is so alien to the idea of gratitude that she probably can't even spell the word," Jane scoffed. "And heaven only knows what she's been telling her husband about me during this dreadful business. Oh Joe, what if

Lord Crawford hates me just as much as she does?"

"He won't. From what I hear, Lord Crawford is a perfectly reasonable man. And besides, you've done nothing wrong. On the contrary. You're the hero who saved his children, remember?"

Joe patted her hand reassuringly and Jane nodded, putting on a brave face for him. Even though she didn't feel like a hero in any way, she supposed he was right. Her name had been cleared and she didn't have anything to be ashamed of. So that would have to be enough.

As the carriage rolled to a stop before the imposing façade of the Crawford residence, Jane gathered her courage. Come what may, she would face Lord Crawford with dignity.

Joe stepped out first and offered Jane his hand. Before they reached the top of the marble steps leading to the house, a footman opened the heavy front door and bid them welcome. In the foyer, a second footman stood waiting to escort them to his lordship's study.

"Mr Thompson and Miss Lee to see you, milord," the man announced stoically.

Lord Crawford rose from his desk to greet them. "Mr Thompson, Miss Lee. How very good of you to come." He shook Joe's hand, then took Jane's hand and bent his head over it in a brief, polite bow.

After she had returned his greeting with a short curtsy, Jane cast a quick glance around the room. There was no sign of Lady Crawford yet.

"Please, have a seat," his lordship said, gesturing to a small seating area in the corner. "Can I offer you some tea?"

"That would be lovely, thank you," Joe responded politely as they all settled themselves on the velvet chairs.

Soon a maid appeared with a silver tea service and she began pouring out a cup for each of them. Lord Crawford let the silence stretch until the maid had left the room.

Finally he spoke, his voice grave.

"Let me first say, Miss Lee, how deeply I regret this entire business. It was an abhorrent affair, made worse by my wife's abominable behaviour towards you." Solemnly, he met her eyes. "Please accept my most sincere apologies for all you have suffered."

"Milord," Jane blushed. "There is no need for you to apologise."

"On the contrary. The treatment you've had to endure here was deplorable. I was remiss in not curbing my wife's... comportment towards you. Had I intervened earlier, much hardship could have been avoided."

He sighed heavily. "As you will have noticed, Lady Crawford isn't with us today. I'm afraid the recent strains have taken their toll, and she has left for a sanatorium in Switzerland to aid in her recovery."

Jane kept her expression neutral, but she rather suspected that the real strain was Lady Crawford's thirst for sherry.

"I'm certain the fresh mountain air will do wonders," Joe replied tactfully. "There's no finer climate for restoring one's constitution."

Lord Crawford gave a polite nod and took a sip of tea before continuing. "At any rate, my wife's absence has allowed me to reflect upon certain matters... and make what amends I can."

He turned his gaze to Jane. "I am in your debt for the safe return of my children, Miss Lee. You have my eternal gratitude."

With flushing cheeks, Jane shook her head. "I'm not certain if I'm worthy of such gratitude, milord. I failed most grievously in my duties as governess. Alistair and Penelope were snatched away while I should have been watching over them."

"But the villainy was none of your doing, Miss Lee. And let me assure you: I bear you no ill will whatsoever. I am thankful the children were unharmed, due in large part to your efforts."

Jane simply nodded, overcome with emotion.

Lord Crawford paused before adding gently, "In fact, I would be pleased if you would consider taking up your former position as governess again. The children are most fond of you."

Jane hesitated. As much as she adored Alistair and Penelope, too many unhappy memories lingered here in this house and in this city.

"You are too kind, milord. But I fear I must decline your offer. All things considered, I believe it is better for me to return to England."

"I understand," Lord Crawford said regretfully. "And I sincerely wish you all the best." Delicately, he cleared his throat. "Which brings me to the other purpose of our meeting today."

He took an envelope from his desk and extended it to Jane. "Please accept this token as a measure of my esteem, and as a compensation for your trials."

Bewildered, she accepted the envelope and opened it. There was a cheque inside and her eyes widened when she saw the extravagant sum written on it.

"My lord," she gasped. "This is far too generous. I can't possibly–"

"What my sister-in-law is trying to say," Joe quickly intervened, "is that she is overwhelmed by the enormity of your gesture, milord. But she is deeply grateful to you, and she will consider most carefully how to best apply your magnificent gift for worthy causes."

Joe gave Jane a discreet nod, making her see the wisdom of his words. This sort of money could help a lot of people in need. And with Joe's financial expertise, she knew it would last her a lifetime – probably even longer than that.

Placing a trembling hand on her chest, she replied, "As my brother-in-law so eloquently put it, I am humbled and grateful. Thank you, milord."

Lord Crawford inclined his head. "I count myself lucky to have had such a dedicated governess for my children, Miss Lee. And if you ever find yourself in need of my assistance in the future, do not hesitate to call upon me."

Jane tried to speak, but there was a lump in her throat. All she could manage was a grateful nod. Though her heart was heavy, Lord Crawford's compassion soothed her battered spirit.

"Before we leave," she said hoarsely, "might I bid farewell to the children, please?"

"But of course," Lord Crawford replied with a smile that reached up to his eyes. "I suspect they would be rather cross with me if they learned you had been here and I hadn't let you see them. You'll find them in the nursery."

He gave a polite open-handed gesture towards the door, inviting her to take her leave.

"Mr Thompson," he then said to Joe, "I understand you're an investor? Might I have a private word with you, while Miss Lee visits the children?"

"It would be my pleasure, milord," Joe replied while Jane rose quietly and left the study after a final curtsy.

With a bittersweet mix of sadness and excitement, she headed for the staircase. Why did it have to be so hard to say goodbye to the people we love, she sighed?

Chapter Thirty-Seven

"Miss Lee! You're back." Alistair jumped up from the board game he and his sister were playing, and came running over to Jane.

"We've missed you so much, Miss Lee," Penelope said as she too hurried over.

Laughing, Jane opened her arms and allowed the children to embrace her. When she was their governess, such physical displays of affection would have been considered unacceptable. But she was here as their friend now.

"I've missed you too, my precious darlings," she said, giving each of them a tender caress on the cheek.

They appeared to be recovering from their captivity just fine. Apparently, the kidnappers had treated them fairly well, Inspector Bouchard had told Jane the day after the rescue. And the doctors weren't expecting any lasting effects, either physically or mentally.

Stroking the children's hair, Jane smiled and admired the strength of their young spirits.

"Have you heard about Mama?" Alistair asked. "She's gone away to the Swiss Alps and there's no telling when she'll be back."

He sounded almost excited as he said it, Jane thought. As if he didn't mind his mother's absence too much. *And who could blame him?*

"Does that mean you'll be our governess again, Miss?" Penelope asked so sweetly it caused Jane's heart to bleed.

"I'm afraid I have to disappoint you there, my angel. I'm going back to England, and I wanted to say goodbye to you both before I left."

"Must you go?" Alistair asked with pleading eyes.

"I do, my dearest," Jane sighed. "It hasn't been an easy decision, and I shall miss you both frightfully. But it's for the best really."

Their small faces fell and they clung to her skirts, desperate to squeeze the most out of this final moment together.

Jane knelt down to look them both in the eyes. "You must promise to be good. To always be kind. And to take care of each other."

The children nodded, struggling to fight back their tears. Giving them a fond smile, she added, "And no more using the books in the library as building blocks for a castle, yes?"

That made them giggle, so Jane gave them a last hug before rising to her feet again. "I know you will grow up to become a pair of fine, upstanding young people," she declared proudly.

Disentangling herself from the embrace, she strode to the door, hoping she would be able to keep herself from crying.

"We won't ever forget you, Miss Lee," Penelope called after Jane.

"Neither will I, my sweet ones," she replied, choking back her tears. "I'll cherish our time together for the rest of my life."

She hadn't realised, until that very moment, that you could walk away from someone or somewhere, and yet leave half your heart behind.

Swiping at her eyes, Jane forced herself away from the nursery and down the stairs. She had one last important goodbye to say before she left this place forever.

Petit Jean was one of the precious few friends she had gained during her short time here. And she simply couldn't imagine leaving Paris without telling him.

Besides, she grinned as the most wonderful idea came to her, there was something else she wanted to give him apart from a handshake and a fond adieu.

Guessing he would probably be outside helping the gardener, Jane headed for the servants' entrance. But just as she passed by the kitchen, the door opened and she nearly collided with Marie.

"Well, well," the French maid sneered. "If it isn't the dull English girl. I heard you fancied yourself to be a police detective now." She laughed at her own joke and threw back her head.

"Hello, Marie," Jane replied, undaunted. "You must be so disappointed I didn't end up dead." She was calm, and determined not to let the spiteful maid get under her skin.

"I don't care about you one way or the other, little miss," Marie shrugged arrogantly. "So have you come to beg for your old job back?"

"No, I'm here because Lord Crawford invited me. He wanted to thank me for saving his children. And then *he* offered me to stay on as governess."

"Only because he felt guilty and took pity on you, of course."

"Or because he thought I was good at my job," Jane smiled. "At any rate, I refused. You'll be pleased to know I'm going back to England."

"Small loss."

A grin spread across Jane's face. "Oh, by the by, Lord Crawford also presented me with a substantial cheque. To compensate me for all the hardship I suffered at the hands of the likes of you and others."

She knew it was a vain comment to make, and not entirely right. But she couldn't resist inflicting that little jab. She watched with a sense of satisfaction as Marie's scowl deepened to a venomous glare.

"It really is a ridiculously large amount of money, you know," Jane continued with a beaming smile. "Much more than you can ever hope to make. Even if you were to work in that kitchen until you were 300 years old."

She turned and headed for the door with a light, dainty spring in her step. "*Au revoir, Marie.*"

Vindicated and glowing from that most gratifying exchange, Jane went outside where the sun on her face felt more glorious than ever. Taking slow and contended breaths, she followed the sound of clipping shears.

"Mademoiselle Jane," Petit Jean called out when he saw her approaching. "You have returned."

He jumped down from the step ladder he had been standing on while tending to the hedge, and came bounding over to her.

Jane smiled, her heart clenching. "I have come to say goodbye to you, my young friend." How she would miss his irrepressible spirit.

"You are not staying?"

"I'm afraid not." Jane perched on a stone bench, patting the spot beside her. The boy plopped down eagerly.

"My time here has ended," she explained. "I'm going back home to England. But I want you to know what a cherished friend you are to me."

Petit Jean nodded bravely, though his eyes glistened. "I will miss you, Mademoiselle. No one else is as kind to me as you have been."

Jane squeezed his small, calloused hand. "I have some good news as well though. Lord Crawford has just gifted me a great sum of money, to make up for the trouble I've been through."

"That's wonderful, Mademoiselle," the boy said brightly. "I'm happy for you."

"But there's one slight problem."

He looked at her in surprise.

"It's an awful lot of money, you see," she continued, trying hard to keep a straight face. "More than I could ever hope to spend alone. So I intend to share some with you, to start you on a path to an honest trade."

His eyes grew wide and his mouth fell open in astonishment. "Me? Mademoiselle, I don't know what to say..."

"Just say yes," she chuckled. "You're one of the most deserving young people I've ever met."

Overwhelmed, Petit Jean wrapped his arms around her side and pressed his face against her shoulder. "You are too generous, Mademoiselle."

"But not a single cent of it must go to your wastrel father," she said. "Is there anyone who could look after the money for you until you're old enough? Someone you trust?"

Petit Jean nodded. "My eldest brother Philippe. He's already married, so he doesn't live at my parents' house any more. He's very smart, and not like our father at all."

"Good. I'll ask my brother-in-law to set it all up for you. He's brilliant at this sort of thing."

Then she frowned. "Do you know what? I don't even know what your real name is. I've only ever called you Petit Jean."

"My name is Jean Baptiste," he said proudly. "But you may call me Petit Jean for as long as we both shall live, Mademoiselle."

"Jean Baptiste," she declared in a warm and earnest tone, "I'm honoured to have been your friend. And I believe you have a bright future ahead of you."

"I'm beginning to believe that as well now, Mademoiselle. Thanks to you."

They stood up and said their goodbyes. Then, Jane turned down the gravel path and slowly walked back to the house.

Nearly done, she thought. One last, and even more difficult farewell awaited her in Paris.

Once inside, she found Joe waiting for her in the grand hallway. "Ready to go back to the hotel?" he asked. "Abbie will have made all the arrangements for our departure tomorrow morning by now. So I thought the three of us could perhaps enjoy a little boat trip on the Seine?"

"Sounds lovely. But could we make a brief detour first, please?"

"Certainly. Anywhere in particular?"

Jane smiled. "Place Albertine."

Chapter Thirty-Eight

As their carriage rumbled through the busy city streets towards their destination, Jane caught herself becoming increasingly restless. She had only seen Georgie twice since the night they rescued the children, and their relationship still felt fragile.

They had reconciled, of course. But doubts plagued her about whether Georgie had truly forgiven her for her impetuous actions. Could it be that he still harboured some hurt or anger beneath the surface?

To settle her worries, she longed to see him one more time before departing for England. But apprehension gripped her too. After all they had endured, what if his feelings for her had changed? What if he realised he was better off without her, and that he could do without the trouble she had caused?

As the carriage turned onto Place Albertine, Jane's courage nearly failed her. But she had to know, one way or another, before she left Paris. Georgie meant everything to her, and she would pour out her heart if needed. She could only pray he would understand, and that their parting would not be one of bitterness.

"Patisserie Leblanc," the driver announced from atop his seat at the back while he pulled his horse to a gentle stop. Gripping her skirts with trembling hands, Jane waited for Joe to pay their fare and then followed her brother-in-law out of the hansom cab.

"Looks delicious," Joe said, eyeing the cake displays in the window of the bakery shop. "Edible works of art are my favourite," he quipped.

Proffering his arm to her, he motioned towards the door. "Shall we?"

Taking a deep, steadying breath, Jane nodded and allowed Joe to escort her inside.

A small brass bell tinkled above the door as they entered. Within moments, the imposing figure of Maître Leblanc himself hurried over, his broad face wreathed in smiles.

"Monsieur Thompson! Mademoiselle Lee," he greeted them with an obsequious bow. "What an honour to have you in my humble patisserie."

Jane blinked in surprise. The last time she had seen the French pastry chef, he had rudely chased her from the premises. Back then, he had wanted nothing to do with her or the scandal surrounding the kidnapped Crawford children. Now he was fawning over them as if they were royalty.

"The honour is ours, Maître Leblanc," Joe replied smoothly. "My sister-in-law was eager to pay a visit before our departure to sample your excellent pastries. And I confess, I have heard much about them myself."

"You flatter me, Monsieur." Maître Leblanc's smile broadened. "Please, make yourselves comfortable." He ushered them to a table by the window. "I will send someone to fetch Monsieur Georges immediately. He will be overjoyed to see you both."

After the master baker had scurried off, Jane leaned in closer to Joe and whispered, "I've never seen him this polite before. He used to grumble and moan whenever Georgie asked for a bit of time off."

"It's the way of the world," Joe grinned. "One moment, people won't give you the light of day. And the next, they treat you as if you're the emperor of China. It works the other way around as well, of course. Money is usually what makes all the difference."

Before Jane could reply, Maître Leblanc returned with two of his waiters in tow. He took the silver tray from the first one and placed it on Joe and Jane's table with a graceful flourish.

"Gâteau Saint-Honoré," he said proudly. "Our finest. Please enjoy this small present from me to you, as a token of respect and friendship."

"Why thank you, my dear man," Joe replied, marvelling at the artful confection of puff pastry, profiteroles and cream.

"Monsieur Georges will join you shortly. I shall make sure you are not disturbed," Maître Leblanc said while the second waiter served the coffee.

Behind him, a familiar voice suddenly sounded. "You called for me, Maître?"

"Ah, Georges, my good boy," the pastry chef exclaimed as he spun round on his heels and threw his hands in the air. "Look who has come to see you." Stepping aside, he gestured at his two esteemed guests.

"Jane," Georgie said, his eyebrows shooting up. "What a lovely surprise." Then he remembered where he was and shot an awkward glance at Maître Leblanc, blushing deeply.

But the Frenchman wrapped an arm around Georgie's shoulder and huffed up his chest. "I shall not hide from you, Monsieur Thompson, that your Georges is my finest pupil. The best I've had in years. Years, I tell you."

"That's wonderful to hear, Monsieur," Joe smiled.

"And now, I shall leave you all to enjoy the food and each other's company. Please take as much time as you like." With a parting bow, Maître Leblanc withdrew.

"What a remarkable change," Jane said once the Frenchman was out of earshot.

"He's become as sweet as a lamb," Georgie chuckled. "Apparently, several of the customers made comments while I was gone. They said the quality of the cakes was suffering from my absence. So the Maître was more than eager to take me back."

Jane smiled. "I always said you were good."

"Speaking of sweet lambs and all that," Joe interrupted. "Why don't you two lovebirds find a table to yourselves? I'm sure you might have one or two things to discuss."

With a broad grin he unfolded his napkin. "In the meantime, I'll do my best to work my way through the delicacies on this table."

Jane and Georgie laughed.

"Let's go sit outside," Georgie suggested. With a wink in Joe's direction, he added, "We're clearly not needed here."

Leaving Joe to his Saint-Honoré, Jane and Georgie made their way outside to one of the small tables underneath the striped awning of the bistro next door to the bakery.

"Have one of these," he said as he presented her with the plate of pastries he had brought along. "I made them myself this morning."

They were small cakes, sliced open and decorated to resemble butterflies fanning their wings.

"They're beautiful," Jane said. "Almost too beautiful to eat."

"Try one anyway," he smiled.

When Jane took a careful bite, the soft and delicately flavoured cake practically melted on her tongue. "It's divine, Georgie! Your baking skills are tremendous."

Pride lit up his face at her praise. "I'm glad you like them."

Jane continued eating her butterfly cake, relieved to have an excuse not to talk about more serious things just yet.

"Have you heard the news about Mr Dubois?" Georgie asked, filling the silence between them.

"Yes, Joe told me this morning."

The previous day, Mr Dubois had dismissed himself from the hospital, despite his bullet wound. He appeared to have vanished without a trace.

Probably, Joe had speculated, because the man was afraid the police might get wind of his involvement in the case and decide to pay him a visit at the hospital.

"Are you worried he might come back and cause you problems?" Georgie asked Jane.

"No, not really. I believe that, deep down, Mr Dubois is a good man. And I sincerely hope he will change his life for the better this time."

Georgie nodded and paused.

"So..." he said after a while. "I take it your decision is final then? You're leaving Paris?"

"Yes," she sighed. "I'm going back to England. Lord Crawford offered me to stay on as governess, incidentally. But I refused. In light of all that's happened..."

"I understand," he replied. But she could hear the touch of sadness in his voice.

"It's nothing to do with you of course," she hastened to add. "You're probably about the only reason why I'd want to remain in Paris. But it's just that–"

"Jane," he interrupted, giving her a warm smile. "It's fine, honestly. I understand."

"But do you really, Georgie? I wouldn't want you to think–" She threw down her hands in her lap. "Oh, I've been so awful to you."

"No, you haven't."

"Yes, I have. There were times when you must have hated me for my dreadful behaviour."

He shrugged. "I made some pretty poor choices as well, don't you remember? But I know now what matters most to me."

She gazed up at him.

"It's you, Jane. My love for you hasn't changed."

"Nor mine for you," she whispered.

"And that's why I've decided I'm coming back to England with you."

"No," she gasped. "Georgie, you mustn't. This apprenticeship in Paris means so much to you."

"You mean more to me, Jane."

"That's very sweet of you. But you should stay here." She covered his hand with hers. "You have a talent for baking. More than a talent: it's your passion. And I want you to take this opportunity to develop it fully. So you may achieve the success and respect you deserve."

Slowly he nodded, though she glimpsed the sheen of tears in his eyes.

"You're right, I suppose." He drew in a deep breath and met her gaze. "But that doesn't change how I feel about you, Jane. Will you wait for me?"

"Of course I'll wait for you."

"As soon as I return to England, let's get married."

Impulsively, Georgie snatched another of the butterfly cakes from the platter. "I don't have a proper ring. But will you accept this, as a symbol of my promise?"

Joy flooded Jane's heart. She laughed and blinked back tears as she accepted the little cake. "Yes, I do. You mad and silly darling, you. Yes, I'll be your wife."

Overcome with emotion, Jane embraced Georgie, heedless of the curious glances from the other patrons and passersby. In that moment, nothing else existed in the world but their love.

"I'll count the days until we're together again," she whispered.

Georgie cupped her face and kissed her tenderly. “As will I, my darling.”

Letting out a blissful sigh, she lost herself in his loving eyes, convinced that their future together would be sweeter than any cake he could ever make.

Epilogue

The golden rays of the late afternoon sun filtered in through the lace curtains of the cosy cake shop, casting everything in a warm glow. Jane hummed to herself as she wiped down the last of the tables, tidying up after another busy day.

Though the work was tiring, she felt nothing but deep contentment. After all her trials and tribulations, she had finally found her slice of happiness.

Once she had neatly rearranged all the chairs at the tables, Jane paused to gaze dreamily at the simple gold band adorning her left ring finger – a symbol of the new life she now shared with her beloved husband Georgie.

She let out a blissful sigh and smiled.

Thanks to the generous gift from Lord Crawford, she and Georgie had been able to open this charming cake and pastry shop together, making Georgie's baking talents available to the whole of London.

Closing her eyes, she did a little twirl, revelling in the sense of freedom and accomplishment that permeated her soul.

The weeks surrounding their grand opening had been hectic, but ultimately, extremely rewarding. Word of the exquisite confections crafted by 'Maître' Georges had spread quickly, and hardly a day went by that the little shop wasn't filled to bursting with delighted customers.

It gladdened Jane's heart to see their hard work paying off so sweetly.

Suddenly, the brass bell above the door chimed brightly as someone entered. Startled out of her daydream, Jane opened her eyes again and turned towards the door.

"I'm afraid we were just about to close," she started saying in the same friendly manner she reserved for all their customers.

But then she froze.

The man who stood in the doorway was one of the last people she had expected to see in her and Georgie's lovely shop. Why was *he* here? Had the past returned to haunt her?

"My apologies for the late hour," Mr Dubois spoke gently. "But perhaps you will make an exception for an old friend?"

He smiled warmly, creating amicable wrinkles at the corners of his eyes. This was not the cunning manipulator of before.

"*Bonjour,* Mademoiselle Jane," he exclaimed jovially. "Or should I say, Madame Thompson?"

Jane let out a breath she hadn't realised she was holding. "Monsieur Dubois! What a surprise to see you here."

He grinned. "A happy surprise, I hope?"

Jane smiled back, reassured. "But of course."

She noticed then the slender, dark-haired woman at his side. "And who is this lovely lady you have brought with you?"

His chest swelled with modest pride. "Please allow me to introduce you to my wife, Madeleine."

"*Enchantée,*" Madeleine said with a smile. She had an honesty and openness to her that caused Jane to take an instant liking to the woman.

"The pleasure is all mine, I'm certain," Jane replied. "If I may be so curious, Madame: are you French as well?"

"Heavens no," Madeleine giggled. "I'm British."

Jane raised an eyebrow at Mr Dubois. "I must say, Monsieur... I distinctly remember how you claimed to dislike the English. Yet now you seem to have married one of us."

Mr Dubois let out a booming laugh. "It seems I have mended my ways... more than you can imagine." A look passed between him and his wife, full of warmth and devotion.

Jane studied Madeleine curiously. She wondered just how much the woman knew of her husband's past and the shadowy dealings he had been involved in.

But Mr Dubois, perceptive as always, seemed to read her thoughts. "I know that look, Madame Thompson," he grinned. "You needn't worry. My wife knows everything about my former life. It was she who saved my soul."

Jane blinked in surprise, but recovered quickly. "Well, I am very happy for you both. What brings you to England?"

Before Mr Dubois could respond, Georgie emerged from the kitchen, flour dusting his apron. His eyes widened at the sight of their unexpected guest.

"Monsieur Dubois!" Georgie exclaimed. "What a wonderful surprise."

The two men shook hands firmly, the warmth genuine between them. Jane felt a rush of affection for her husband. The past was the past, and Georgie had clearly forgiven Mr Dubois for his role in those tumultuous events.

"Please, sit and tell us your story," Jane implored the happy couple, indicating a table by the window. "The last we heard about you was when you were in a hospital in Paris, recovering from a gunshot wound. But then you disappeared."

Mr Dubois gave an enigmatic little smile as he pulled out a chair for Madeleine before seating himself. "It is a long tale, but if you will permit me?"

At Jane and Georgie's eager nods, he continued. "I fled from the hospital to avoid any risk of being arrested for my crimes. For a while, I must admit, I felt lost."

He paused, until Madeleine placed a hand over his. "It's all right, Pierre," she encouraged him. "These people are your friends. They will understand."

"I wanted to change," he went on. "But the temptation to revert back to my old ways was... strong. Then I met Madeleine." He looked at his wife and beamed, "It was love at first sight."

"For Pierre anyway," Madeleine giggled mischievously.

"That is true," he conceded with a grin. "But I was besotted with you, and determined to win your heart as well as your hand."

"Eventually, I learned the truth about who he really was," Madeleine explained to Jane and Georgie. "So I issued him an ultimatum: change his ways or lose me forever."

"Luckily, you seem to have made the right choice," Jane said to Mr Dubois. "How wonderful." She knew not everyone could change so profoundly, but with the right person's love, anything was possible.

"You simply must stay for dinner," Georgie said. "We'll close up here, and then the four of us shall go out together. I want to hear all about your new life and how you met your lovely Madeleine."

"We would be delighted," Mr Dubois accepted gratefully.

Soon the shop was tidied up and locked for the evening. Jane tucked her arm in Georgie's as they strolled down the well-lit street with Monsieur and Madame Dubois.

Arriving at Jane's favourite restaurant, they were promptly given a table. Le Château d'Or was where Jane had first laid eyes on Georgie, years ago. The place was still run by the same ridiculous Englishman who liked to pretend he was French. But the cuisine was excellent.

Once the food arrived and the wine started flowing, Mr Dubois told Jane and Georgie about his adventures with Madeleine.

The dark days of lies and deceit were behind him, he assured them. His life now was filled with simple joys and honest work alongside the woman he adored.

Jane smiled to herself, watching the way Mr Dubois and Madeleine looked at each other. She recognised that look: it was the same way she gazed at her own dear husband.

"To new beginnings," Jane proclaimed, raising her glass in a toast. The crystal clinked in the intimate circle of friendship.

The past was nothing but a memory now, fading more with each new dawn. All that lay ahead was a future filled with possibility. And Jane intended to embrace it with a brave heart and an open mind.

The End

Continue reading...

You have just read Book 3 of The Victorian Orphans Trilogy. Other titles in this series include:

Book 1 ~ The Courtesan's Maid
Book 2 ~ The Ragged Slum Princess

And this series will continue!

Beginning with the story of how Madeleine and Mr Dubois fell in love...

For more details, updates,
and to claim your free book,
please visit Hope's website:

www.hopedawson.com

Printed in Great Britain
by Amazon